Was it Good For You Too?

by Naleighna Kai

D1526206

Macro Publishing Group
Chicago, Illinois

Was it Good For You Too? @ 2014 by Naleighna Kai

Digital ISBN: 9780982682982
Trade Paperback ISBN: 9780982682906

Cover designed by: J. L. Woodson www.jlwoodson.com
Interior design by: Lissa Woodson www.macrompg.com

Printed in the United States of America

Acknowledgements:

All praise is due to the Creator first and foremost. A special love and respect to my guardian angels, ancestors, teachers and guides.

To my spiritual mothers: Sandy Spears and Bettye Mason Odom; to my son, Jeremy "J. L." Woodson, who is the perfect example of determination and dedication. I love you more than words can ever say.

To the people who continuously inspire me: Renee Sesvalah Cobb-Dishman, Gretta Chamberlain, Debra Mitchell, Laverne "Missy" Brown, Ehryck F. Gilmore; the members of M-LAS: Joyce Brown (my "other" mother and my voice of reason), to Janice Pernell (Developmental Editor), Valarie Prince (Content/Copy Editor), and Katie Walsh (Content/Line Editor), Tanishia Pearson-Jones (Manuscript Evaluator), Martha Kennerson, Susan D. Peters, Candy Jackson, D. J. McLaurin, and Lorna L.A. Lewis.

To the book clubs and avid readers who support my work—I LOVE YOU!!! (there are too many of you to name!)

Pam Nelson, the woman behind the Soul Expressions Wal*Mart Tour that forever changed my life and put my literary career in orbit. Thank you for your vision, drive, and tenacity. You have the belief that books by all authors deserve a fighting chance--and we love your for it. You are the main reason I reached the national bestsellers list that year and you continue to be an inspiration and someone who I will always admire.

To the members of C.V.S. Class of 1984 who have supported my literary career and other endeavors (Quest anyone?)--Much love and respect.

To everyone I mentioned (and those that I may have forgotten to type), thank you for everything you are to me.

Wishing you all—peace and love, light and joy.
—Naleighna Kai

Dedication:

My mother, Jean Woodson
My grandmother, Mildred E. Williams
My brother, Eric Harold Spears
My niece, LaKecia Janise Woodson,
a rising star who left us much too soon

To Leslie Esdaile Banks (L.A. Banks),
one of the best storytellers the planet had to offer.

To Anthony "Green Eyes" Johnson,
the real life "Dallas" who taught me
what unconditional love was all about

to Derek V. Fields
and the C.V.S. graduating class of 1984
(full tribute is in the back of this novel)

"Here's the deal ... you can be married, but that doesn't necessarily mean you're ready to be someone's partner in life."

—Jada Pinkett Smith

"What never leaves is that friend love. And that's the commitment to ride or die with somebody through every step."

–Jada Pinkett Smith

Chapter 1

SOUL EXPRESS TOUR – DAY 1
MARRIOTT INDIANAPOLIS NORTH HOTEL

Tailan Song was juggling more balls than *The Best Little Whorehouse in Texas.* She had given an arm and a leg to put this Midwest book tour in play, but at the moment she'd throw in a foot and a couple of someone else's toes for just twenty minutes of sleep.

"Wake me when we get to the first stop," she said to her assistant.

"We'll wake you sooner than that if you start snoring," Terry shot back.

"I don't snore," Tailan mumbled, lowering into her seat at the back of the bus, hoping to catch a few winks before the luxury coach made it to Woodland.

Twenty-one authors were set to sign at twelve big-box stores in the Midwest over the next four days. That was the upside. The downside … she had promised several major publishing houses that she'd bring in record sales and she had to deliver or her career was over. Thanks to the four diva authors who were thrown into the mix, she was running on fumes. Oh, and her boss was on the tour bus to keep an eye on how everything played out. Great. Just great.

Unfortunately, her shut-eye was interrupted by her boss's voice. "Attention, everyone. We'd like to introduce you to a special guest celebrity who'll be joining us for the next four days. His new novel, *The Black House,* is a *New York Times* Bestseller," David crowed. "Give a warm Soul Express welcome to author and Oscar-winning actor Delvin Germaine."

Tailan's eyes flew open. She shot up from her lounging position as hearty applause rang out from the authors and the six members of the Nelson Entertainment staff. Everyone smiled as they took in the striking good looks of the man towering over David's stocky frame—everyone except Tailan. The last person she ever wanted or expected to see was Delvin Germaine.

"This cannot be happening," she whispered.

Sinking down in the seat, she tried to ignore the curly-haired author across the aisle who was giving her a suspicious look while mouthing the words, "Woman, what's wrong with you?"

"It'll be a pleasure to be with you on this tour," Delvin's rich baritone voice echoed throughout the length of the luxury coach.

Tailan stuck her head out.

"I'm sure it'll be …" Delvin's gaze narrowed.

Their eyes locked for a split second. Heads turned, following his line of sight. Tailan crouched lower and peeked around the edge of the seat in front of hers.

"Tai?" he asked.

"Damn!" she muttered. Tailan straightened in her seat, then leaned over into the aisle, noticing that his dark brown eyes were flashing with a glint of something she couldn't quite name. Shock? Maybe. Fear? Kind of. Well, he should be scared. He totally deserved a smack upside the head from the twelve-ounce can of whoop ass she carried in her back pocket.

"Tai?"

She snailed a nod, wishing she could deny the obvious. Given the vicious way they had parted, he should understand why she wasn't at all ready to do cheerleader splits just because he was in sniffing distance.

"It's good to see you," he said in that same seductive voice that had always melted women's hearts—and a few other parts. At the moment, Tailan wanted to kick herself because she was no exception.

"Methinks this trip just got a bit more interesting," David teased with a wink in Tailan's direction. She gave him the evil eye and a scowl, as nervous laughter and hushed whispers flared up around them.

Several of the "diva" authors, who had ignored Tailan since she had been forced to put them in check the moment they arrived in Indianapolis, now gave her the once-over, as though sizing up their competition.

"I'll see you all at the next stop," Delvin announced. He bestowed one last lingering look upon Tailan before he turned to exit the bus.

He didn't have one foot out the door before a sultry voice vibrated through the bus. "You're not riding with us?"

Like spectators at a tennis match, all heads snapped toward a golden beauty with shoulder length locs, who had pinned her hazel eyes on the movie star. Delvin did an about-face and looked at Nona, who wore a breast-baring outfit that would have every newborn in the area salivating. Got milk? Indeed!

"I was added to the tour at the last minute," Delvin countered, tightening his grip on the exit rail. "I have to check into the hotel and—"

"So whatcha tryin' ta say?" a brash voice across the aisle from Nona interrupted. Shannon's hands flapped around in a dramatic fashion. "You too good to ride with the rest of us squares?"

Tailan stifled a chuckle as Delvin's eyes narrowed to heated slits. She held her breath, half-expecting him to fall back on his stinging wit and mention that Shannon's weave had seen its best days in its former life on someone else's head.

"Could you say that in real English?" he quipped, causing a few people to laugh and Shannon's face to blush an angry red.

The driver cleared his throat loudly. He lifted his arm and tapped his watch, reminding them they had to roll if they wanted to stay on schedule.

Nona's head rocked as she snarled, "What she *said* was—"

"She's saying that maybe for once you can check your celebrity status at the door and get your behind on the bus with the rest of us," Tailan snapped.

David's glare was so intense, she almost regretted her sour words. The future of her career was riding on the success of this tour. And success was far from guaranteed—even the publishers thought it was a long shot. David's last minute publicity stunt would have her scrambling. It already had her beyond irritated.

Delvin's eyes tossed her a warning. "I think I liked it better when you kept your mouth shut."

Colorful, stunned dialogue moved like a wave through the bus.

"Whoa! Where the hell did that come from?" Lorna gasped, tendrils of red hair falling into her face.

"Ooooh, that was kinda cold," J. L., the youngest of the group, said with a grimace.

"Whew, better her than me, girl," Martha whispered to the woman sitting next to her.

Delvin glanced at David, who clamped his hand on Delvin's shoulder as though they were old buddies. "Actually people, he's had a long flight and …"

Tailan stood and crossed her arms over her full bosom, letting her stance speak volumes. Everyone was supposed to receive equal treatment across the board. Bottom line! This was not the right vibe to start the tour. Yet, as strong as the urge was to bark at the unfair preferential treatment, Tailan exhaled the moment Delvin turned to leave.

Then he did a complete one-eighty and locked eyes with her.

"On second thought," he said with a sly grin. "I can just as easily catch a few minutes of sleep on this bus as I could in my hotel room."

"You're coming with us?" David asked, a wide smile lifting the corners of his generous mouth.

Applause, hoots, and whistles followed Delvin as he headed down the aisle to take a seat.

Tailan dropped back into her seat and turned to her assistant, Terry. "Get him checked into the hotel pronto, and have them store his things in a secure location until we get back."

The blonde nodded, whipped out her cell, and went to work.

When Tailan noticed the team publicist eye hustling the actor, she snapped, "Hey, get your head back in the game, woman."

Elona cringed and turned impishly to Tailan.

"I want you on the phone like yesterday," Tailan directed. "Ask Ella Curry to put out a blast that Delvin Germaine's going to be at the Woodland in Indianapolis and to post the announcement on all major social media feeds."

Tailan studied Delvin's progress down the narrow aisle. A taloned hand landed on his upper thigh, halting his movements. She wasn't surprised that the owner of that obscenely expensive manicured hand was none other than Nona, the woman who had purred out the initial challenge.

Delvin looked down, assessing the proximity of Nona's hand to his family jewels. "A woman's hand should never be that close to the business end of a man unless she's washing or servicing. Since you're doing neither, I'd appreciate it if you'd allow him"—he gestured toward his groin—"to mind his own business."

Nona winked suggestively, stroked his thigh as though she was sizing him up for purchase, then pulled back and blew him a kiss. Hoots of laughter echoed around them.

These four divas—Nona, Shannon, Chanel, and Traci—were giving Tailan a special kind of headache—the kind that didn't go away with two aspirins and a call to the doctor in the morning. The foursome was forced on Tailan as a compromise—which now felt more like a punishment— for requesting that four *New York Times* bestselling authors be part of the tour. While the four she wanted, all mature women over fifty, were a literary event planner's dream, The Divas were more than a handful. They had missed their flights, missed the information briefing about the tour, insisted on costly upgrades at the hotel, and then somehow convinced the limo driver to cart them to a nightclub last night instead of straight to the hotel.

All of this forced Tailan out of bed at three in the morning to yank them out of the club, get them in the right rooms, and provide an hour-long briefing to cover the information they had missed earlier in the day. Operating on a mere two hours of sleep had Tailan ready to strangle all four of them. She gave each one a warning look before signaling to the driver to head out.

"There's plenty of room up here," said Traci, another scantily clad woman who was sitting next to one of the more outspoken divas on the bus.

Delvin ignored her and didn't stop until he reached Tailan. "Is this seat taken?"

"Yes." The novel Tailan pretended to be reading now commanded her complete attention. At least, that's how she hoped it appeared.

"Really?" he countered.

Tailan turned the page and gave him a haughty lift of her chin. "My imaginary friend is sitting there."

"Well, she won't mind if I sit on her lap," Delvin smirked.

Tailan turned another page. "She's a he."

"Makes no difference to me."

Tailan's right eyebrow winged up. She tilted her head and grinned. "So the rumors are true ... you do swing both ways."

"Watch it, Tai!" he said through his teeth.

She smacked her novel closed, grabbed her bag, and tried to angle past Delvin. Tailan was determined to vent her frustration where it belonged—on David.

Delvin blocked her escape with a firm grip around her wrist. "I'll follow you wherever you go."

"No you won't," she said through her teeth. "You'll get lost just like you did the last time."

Chapter 2

Delvin didn't have a quick comeback for Tailan. He could only take in the anger flashing in her soft brown eyes. She had creamy golden skin, a pert nose, almond-shaped eyes, and inviting lips—a beautiful, exotic combination thanks to her Black mother and Asian father. She looked absolutely sexy with a touch of magnificent thrown in to give him an erection that could plow through rush hour traffic.

Anger often made Delvin play dirty. He tossed over his shoulder to David, "I see I'm not the only star on this bus."

The warning look David flashed Tailan made her whisper to Delvin, "I'm going to put you over my knee and spank that ass." But she sat back down, scooting over to the window seat.

"Was that a promise or a threat?" he drawled.

She threw him a look that could melt the North Pole.

Delvin ignored her animosity and joined her. She kept her gaze firmly fixed outside the window, but he plucked the novel from her manicured fingers to get her attention and placed the book behind his back. "How've you been?"

Tailan's eyes nearly cut him in half as her head snapped in his direction. She dashed a quick glance to David, who continued to throw daggers her way. She took a deep breath and mumbled, "I was wonderful until you showed up." She gave a quick "I'll get to you later" nod in David's direction before turning her heated gaze again to Delvin. "You're playing with my livelihood, Delvin," she strained through a tight smile. "David is the Vice President of Nelson Entertainment Group. Because of you, he's watching me more closely during one of the most challenging events of my career."

"It's your own fault. All—"

"Shut it," Tailan commanded, snapping her fingers together like a duck's beak. "It's taken me months of fancy footwork and my best impression of James Brown's *baby, baby, baby pleeeeeeeassse*, to get the publishers *and* big-box retailers on board." Her eyelids dipped over her incredible eyes. Her lips pursed in a thin line, and Delvin realized he wanted to kiss them. She rubbed her temples as she continued. "Everyone expects this tour to fail. David has already warned—hell, more like flat-out threatened—that if this tour doesn't meet the projected numbers I guaranteed ..." Tailan shook her head and turned away.

Being in her presence was pleasure and pain. Delvin had loved this woman since the summer he had found her hiding in a classroom at school. She had no place to go and had eaten her last meal two days before. Even in her most vulnerable state, she was still the most courageous person he knew. He loved her to this day, and he knew that would never change. He had to make things right between them.

Tailan dug in her bag for another book. He confiscated that one too.

She looked over to David, who was now completely absorbed in his tablet, then back to Delvin.

Delvin waited. Tailan said nothing. Delvin waited some more. She still remained stubbornly silent.

He blew out a weary breath. "Talk to me." Delvin held out her coveted novel, and she placed it on her lap. "There's nothing to talk about."

"I've missed you."

Tailan waved her hand dismissively. "No doubt," she taunted. "Is your wife still serving it up to every Tom, Dick, and Harry, Sally, Sue, and Mary Jane?"

Delvin felt the volcanic rush of blood through him. "That was low, even for you, Tai."

"Really?" she asked with a toothy grin. "I learned from the best, so I'll take that as a compliment."

Delvin's surrogate-turned-last-minute wife had caused Tailan years of unnecessary tears and grief. Evidently that grief had turned into an anger so large it needed a zip code of its own.

After shooting three movies back to back, he had hoped this tour would afford him some quiet time to reflect on his next move in life, especially since Gabrielle's publicist recently leaked a "major alert" that they weren't divorcing—a blatant lie. His agent sold him on being part of the Woodland tour to promote his new novel. But Delvin saw the move for what it really was—a way to keep Delvin away from Gabrielle until this new issue was sorted out.

"You were engaged to me," Tailan attacked, effectively pulling him back from his trip down a memory lane that had more potholes than a Chicago street. "She lied to you and you married her instead. You made your choice."

"She was pregnant with my child—a child, may I remind you, that you told me to have with her!" he shot back. "Because you swore up and down you weren't having one."

Tailan sank deeper into her seat and studied him. The way her eyes traveled along every inch of his body triggered tremors of desire in him but also sparks of caution. He was right to be cautious, as she wasn't about to let him off the hook.

"Are you really that dense? That child isn't even yours," she countered. "If it is, that was the *loooooongest* pregnancy known to man. Ten-and-a half months, right? She was on a movie set those first two months. Last time I checked, numbers don't lie. The truth is plain. But then again, I didn't marry her, so that's not my business."

Delvin felt humiliation erode his normally stoic features.

"So, you still want to talk, sweetheart?" She flipped open her novel and looked down at the pages.

* * *

Twenty minutes out from the tour's first stop, Delvin finally had enough of Tailan ignoring him. Even in her finely practiced calmness, she was still the sexiest angry woman he had ever laid eyes on.

"Did I ever tell you just how grateful I was for how you were there for Jason, Tai?"

Tailan's sensually curved lips lifted at the corners as though she was struggling to keep her thoughts to herself. *Finally, a tiny crack in her resolve.* Her shoulders relaxed a bit, and for the first time since he stepped on the bus, Tailan was looking at him with something other than fire or ice in her eyes.

"How is he?" she asked.

He rewarded her with a warm smile. "Jason took being apart from you very hard."

Jason, Delvin's stepson, had bonded with Tailan in a way that defied reasoning. Her tender loving care and Delvin's had saved the boy from a life filled with the psychotropic drugs Gabrielle preferred to shovel into him so she could focus on her movie career and not have to deal with another child she never wanted in the first place.

If Jason was given his choice, he would have left his biological mother and lived with Tailan permanently. And if Gabrielle wasn't such a self-centered, cold-hearted shrew, she would have put the needs of her child ahead of her own. But then again, she never had been one to worry about what someone else wanted.

Delvin smiled as he added, "That boy still keeps your picture on his nightstand. Pisses Gabrielle off every time she lays eyes on it."

The instant Gabrielle's name cleared his vocal cords, Tailan's softening expression turned to stone.

"You want to talk about something," she snapped. "Let's talk about the fact that you changed the rules when you didn't stand up for what you wanted." Her eyes searched his for a moment. "And I thought you wanted … me."

"You think I *wanted* to give you up?" he asked in a low tone. "I had her sign that surrogate contract to make sure we were all on the same page. She changed the rules, not me." He reached over and stroked the delicate curves of her hand.

Tailan snatched away. "You got what you wanted. I'm done talking about this."

Delvin refused to shoulder all the blame for what had happened between them. Definitely time for a history lesson. "And let me remind you, there wouldn't have been a need for her in the first place," he challenged, "if *you* had been more open to having a child."

"What did you just say to me?" Tailan's tone would've given the Grimm Reaper the shivers.

"All I wanted was one child, Tai," he continued. "*One child.* Was that too much to ask?"

"You know what happened to me growing up," she retorted, folding her arms over her full breasts. "There was no way I was going to bring a child into this world."

"I would never leave you to fend for yourself, especially with my child."

"You wouldn't leave me to fend for myself?" she scoffed. "That's funny because that's exactly what you did when she laid a guilt trip on your door."

That mistake had left Delvin raw to the bone. He agreed wholeheartedly with Tailan's hostility towards Gabrielle. He had never loved that woman. He had only married her for one reason: she had flipped the script the moment her pregnancy was confirmed and penciled in her own agenda. The new agenda left Tailan Song, his fiancé, completely out of the picture.

Gabrielle's selfish act had cost Delvin seven years of happiness with Tailan. He had more than paid his dues. The reality of his choice was painfully clear. His sacrifice was based on a lie. Delvin had always shied away from the truth about his daughter. But at the time, he couldn't take the chance. Gabrielle was too lethal, too diabolical and would not have hesitated to terminate the life growing inside her. It was that one threat that forced him to yield.

He turned from his internal war to focus on Tailan. Her tense form was immersed in the book she was reading. A little smile lifted the corner of his features. He couldn't let a little thing like her desire to chop his balls off deter him. No sir!

Delvin noticed a tiny chip in her index fingernail. He reached out and stroked it lightly, causing her to tremble. Then she stiffened and tried to pull away. Delvin held firm. "Later, when we're done with all this tour stuff, we really need to talk."

She yanked her hand back, answering his gentle declaration with, "No."

"Do you still love me?" he asked. He stroked a fingertip across her cheekbone, eliciting another reaction.

Delvin saw it—the glimmer of desire and something he couldn't quite name. Faint, but it was there all the same. A spark of love? Something he could build on? Whatever it was, it gave him hope that he could get her to fall in love with him once again.

"Answer the question," he demanded, his gaze focused on her. "Do you still love me?"

She looked past him, and he followed her line of vision. Across the aisle from them, Valarie, an erotica author, tore her gaze from the laptop stationed on her fleshy thighs and looked their way.

Conversation amongst the Nelson staff behind them had halted. Shannon nudged Nona, who nodded to Chanel, and all three of them shifted in their seats to try and listen in.

"Don't you dare do this now," Tailan whispered, as the bus began to slow down as it neared its destination.

"Answer me," he demanded.

"No!" Tailan countered and pushed him back.

"You're lying." This time it was Delvin who crossed his arms over his chest.

She flinched, then her soft brown eyes shot him with bullet holes. That kind of anger could only come from one source—love. Anger and all, Delvin wanted to kiss her, do whatever it took to calm her.

"When you don't like the answer, you accuse me of lying?" She stood and tried to pass him. When he wouldn't let her by, she trembled with building rage as she stared down at him. "You know what? Why don't you take your tired ass to the front of the bus? There's a whole lot of women who'd like to get their hands on you."

Delvin yanked her back down. "I've never stopped loving you," he whispered.

Tailan shot to her feet the instant the bus came to a complete stop. She practically leapt over his long frame and darted to the front of the bus.

He watched her retreating form. The second the doors opened, he shouted, "Tailan!" Twenty-seven pairs of eyes ping-ponged between him and her.

Delvin rose and gave her his best smile. "I'm standing up for what I want. This is your only warning."

Chapter 3

SAME DAY, 8:03 P.M.
MARRIOTT INDIANAPOLIS NORTH HOTEL

"What do you mean she didn't sign the divorce papers?" Delvin paced the length of his hotel room, failing miserably at controlling his temper. The first round of signings had gone off almost smoothly, and he was "riding on ten" until he received this call from Maurice Blandin, his lawyer.

"Her attorney said that she wants to reverse the custody deal," Maurice replied.

Delvin needed to find an outlet for his rising fury. He snatched his suitcase off the floor and slammed it onto the bed, nearly yanking the zipper off. "She knows that full custody is the one thing I truly want. It's been the main reason that I've stuck in there so long. What kind of game is she playing?"

"The kind that gets played all the time," Maurice answered in a weary tone. "Too much in my line of work."

Delvin was sick of Gabrielle constantly pulling another fast one. For seven years, he found that Gabrielle was a stone-cold predator disguised in beguiling loveliness and with a lethal determination that turned him completely off. He endured Gabrielle's not-so-discreet affairs, the constant blow-back it had on his career, her dysfunctional family, and her embarrassing attempts at motherhood. "Let me guess, she wants more money."

"I don't think it has anything to do with it." The sound of papers being shuffled and the "click clack" of Maurice's keyboard echoed in the background. More than likely, he was looking for a clue to this latest setback. "You gave in to almost every one of her demands, even the ones I said you shouldn't. Are you sure you want full custody? Biologically, the children aren't even yours."

Delvin sucked in a huge gulp of air, trying to corral his anger and disappointment. "We've been over this, Maurice. Those children *are* mine, and I refuse to leave them with that woman." He wanted to be free of Gabrielle in the worst way but not at the expense of his children.

"Want to know what I think?" Maurice asked.

"That's what I pay you for," he grumbled, hanging his suits and slacks in the closet.

"That Paulo dude embarrassed her big time on worldwide television. Now she's trying to retaliate by not divorcing you."

"You'd better find her, put that pen in her hand, and make her sign," Delvin warned. "I need this noose off my neck."

"No worries. It'll happen."

"That's easy for you to say." Delvin walked over to his bed and collapsed on top. "I'm the one who's still married to her, and I'm not hearing anything on this call that's changing that fact."

"We'll have to go back to the judge with these new developments. You might get the divorce finalized automatically, without a signature, as long as we can prove that she's stalling even after the judge has ruled."

"Then get on it," Delvin demanded. "My accountant emailed me your latest invoices. *Earn my signature* on your check and get me unhitched from that hellion."

Delvin ended the call, snagged the keycard from the dresser and was out the door and in the lobby in a matter of minutes. He needed fresh air. His heart was heavy. For seven years he had been kicking himself for making the wrong decision. Gabrielle over Tailan.

A heated argument between him and Tailan years ago ended in an ugly ultimatum. "You want children," Tailan snapped, facing him in the center of their beach house, "you'll have to find another woman to have them because it certainly will *never* be me."

Yes, he had known how she felt about having children. Given her family's ugly history, her stance was totally understandable. However, he had always assumed that after years of watching him and his family interact lovingly and feeling their love herself, she would change her mind. He was dead wrong.

Delvin had taken Tailan's suggestion literally. He'd connected with a fledgling starlet and laid down an offer she couldn't refuse: he would pay for singing, acting, and dancing lessons if she would have his child. He thought he'd timed it flawlessly. His child would be born seven months after he and Tailan walked down the aisle.

Gabrielle DeLeon had seemed like the perfect candidate for what he had in mind. She was a classic beauty—café au lait skin, wide seductive eyes. She was healthy and more than willing to accommodate his wishes. He would have the best of both worlds—the woman he loved *and* the child he wanted.

Problem solved.

Well ... not quite.

Tailan went ballistic when Delvin's lawyer showed up with the surrogate contract. "I can't believe you actually went through with this! I made that statement out of frustration because you refused to accept that I'm not having children. My God," Tailan ranted. "This"—she picked up the contract—"says a lot about where your priorities lie." Tailan flung the papers at him, hitting him square in the chest. "Your desire to have children by any means necessary certainly outweighs any love you have for me." She wiped her tears from her eyes. "I can't marry you next month."

Delvin had to fight hard to ease his way back into Tailan's good graces. After weeks of wearing her down, Tailan finally calmed down. But it was a short-lived victory at best.

"I'd never ask if it wasn't extremely important," Gabrielle said one bright sunny Thursday in the living room of the home Delvin shared with Tailan.

"What's going on?" Delvin asked, alarmed that she had showed up unexpectedly—still not pregnant, but with something else equally as surprising.

Gabrielle rushed from the room and returned with a boy with honey brown skin and wide eyes.

"Who is this little guy?" Tailan had smiled, bending down to his eye level.

"His name is Jason." Gabrielle pushed him closer to Delvin, but the child instantly gravitated to Tailan. "I don't know how he found out that I'm his mother." She was wringing her hands nervously. "I put him up for adoption."

"For—" Tailan started.

"Adoption?" Delvin finished.

"One of my family members took him in. Now he wants to be part of my life," she said, and the sour tone told exactly how she felt about that prospect. "I tried to explain to him that my life is crazy—"

"Too crazy for your own flesh and blood?" Tailan challenged.

"It's not like that. I swear." Gabrielle lied with the best of them. "I just landed my first major movie role, and I have to leave town right away—like *right now*."

Delvin noticed how Jason stared up at Tailan. The child was completely taken with her. Tailan seemed to soften to the innocent affection. When Jason reached for Tailan's hand and she allowed it, Delvin noticed how comfortable the gesture was for her. He couldn't understand why she felt she wasn't mother material.

"Don't you have family that can help you with this?" Delvin asked.

Gabrielle shifted her gaze to Jason. There was a look there that gave Delvin pause.

"The family isn't happy with him right now," she replied, her expression sour. "When he found out about me, he created such a mess that one of them just dropped him on my doorstep and kept moving." She sighed. "They didn't even check to see if I was home! So inconsiderate!"

"Then he's got it honest," Tailan added with a pointed look at Gabrielle. She squeezed the little boy's hand. "Are you hungry, Jason?" He nodded and smiled up at her. "Well, I was about to fix breakfast. Would you like to help me?" Jason simply smiled harder. "Let's go to the kitchen."

Delvin watched them retreat into the kitchen before turning on Gabrielle. "Just this once."

Over the next two months, Delvin watched Tailan and Jason grow closer. Strangely enough, the youngster never talked about missing Gabrielle. From what Delvin could ascertain, Jason literally saw *Tailan* as his real mother.

The bond seemed to be going both ways.

"Delvin," Tailan said while they were enjoying a light lunch in the dining room with Jason, "I want you to cancel that *contract*."

His fork slipped through his fingers and clattered to the plate, which caused Jason to giggle. "Are you saying what I think you're saying?" Delvin asked with his heart in his throat and his lungs on pause.

Tailan's warm eyes moved to him then to Jason, who was watching them both with eager interest. She caressed the little boy's face and smiled. "Yes."

"Oh, baby." He stood and leaned over the table, kissing her gently and causing her to smile. "I love you so much." He turned to Jason and tweaked his nose. "And you're growing on me too."

Gabrielle returned from France and brought the couple two kinds of news. "Terminating the contract won't work for me. I'm actually pregnant," she said in a practiced silky voice.

Tailan answered that admission with, "Well, I'll just add my name to the contract and accept the responsibility of adopting and raising his child."

Gabrielle's lips lengthened into a bitter smile as she looked to

Delvin. "That won't work for me either. If you don't want me to abort this child," she placed her hand over her belly, "you'll have to leave her … and marry me."

Her ruthless plot to win at any cost forced Delvin to make a crippling sacrifice—Tailan's heart for the life of his unborn child. Delvin's choice unshackled all the despicable sides of Gabrielle's darker nature. She, her family, and even her *friends* sank their fangs into the new relationship and left nothing but torment in their wake.

Even his own home was invaded by her family, who moved in and literally took over. The situation was so out of pocket that Delvin built a three bedroom carriage house just to have a place to close his eyes in peace. Most days, he took the children to stay with him there.

Gabrielle didn't have a maternal bone anywhere in her body, and she was most certainly missing her moral compass.

Delvin was wiser now; too many years on the wrong side of love had taught him a hard lesson. That lesson—no longer would he live without the woman he truly loved, and no longer would his daughter and stepson suffer the consequences of his mistake.

He had a feeling that this book tour was going to be buck wild, but he was also hoping it would be the most enjoyable four days he'd had in ages. All that was needed now was Tailan Song. If he could sway her to give them another chance, life would be absolutely fantastic.

Somehow, he didn't think it would be easy, but he was certainly up for the challenge.

Chapter 4

Four days on the road with Delvin Germaine will be the death of me!

Tailan let her skin air dry as she sat at the desk in her hotel room wrapped in a plush towel. She wouldn't glance over at the bed ... too many steamy memories of the erotic dreams that visited her last night.

So much to do today. No time for a hedonistic trip down memory lane. Tailan flipped open her laptop and keyed in her password. The computer crept to life as she waited. Her laptop beeped, and Tailan quickly navigated to the blog that Nelson Entertainment Group had set up for the rookie authors. They would keep readers abreast of their personal journey on the tour. She had hoped that giving Pam and J. L. that edge would bring more book clubs and readers out to the stores to support the authors.

Tailan hesitated, her fingers hovering over the keyboard. She was almost afraid to peek in and see what Pam had said. She hoped Pam didn't write anything about the snide remarks The Divas threw Tailan's way because Delvin wouldn't leave her side.

Tension had escalated to an all-time high, and the fangs came out at lunch and dinner when Delvin maneuvered between the five mature women of the group he affectionately called "The Vets" to hold a seat for Tailan. The move made it abundantly clear he had no intention of sharing the space with either one of the trifling Divas who were jockeying for a position beside him.

Delvin was driving her crazy with his grandstanding. She prayed to the publishing god in the sky that Pam had the good sense not to mention the smoldering thirsty kiss Delvin planted on Tailan after dinner just before moseying down the hall to his suite.

Good Lord. He actually moseyed! Like an urban cowboy.

Then the man had the audacity to flash Pam a head nod as he passed by. Tailan looked on, breathless and horny—not exactly in that order.

Her fingers flew across the keys, taking her to Pam's blog.

Don't look at the bed. Don't look at the bed.

She looked. The dreams she'd had all stemmed from that kiss.

Delvin was all over her—holding her, kissing her, tasting her. Her fingers scrolled down Pam's blog as she fought her minds' efforts to conjure the last vestiges of that tumultuous dream.

Too late. The image slithered to the forefront—Delvin gliding up her trembling, aching body. His knee spreading her thighs, his back straining. His mouth swallowing hers as his hips slammed home in a raw passion that stung her eyes with joyous tears.

She tried to catch a breath as she read:

Day 1 - Well people, it's 5:52 a.m., and I'm up early because we board the bus at 8:30 to get to the Woodland in Fort Wayne today, then to Elkhart, South Bend, and Michigan City. But I have to fill you in on yesterday . . .

This Soul Express tour is total class, and the Nelson Entertainment people and Woodland employees treat us like royalty. This is a marriage made in literary heaven. And I'm down for the long program—with or without a prenup!

Tailan burst out laughing. "This is so like Pam."

The Woodland managers were amazed at the number of people

waiting for us to arrive. Some people admitted that they skipped work to be there. How cool is that? I sold every single copy of my book— Looking for D*ck in All the Wrong Places—then went on to promote some of my tablemates.

I'll tell you that two people on the tour didn't need any help at all: Brenda Jaxon and Beverly Jenkins. With more than one-hundred-fifty books penned between them, they sold out faster than a hooker can name her price and services. Christian fiction authors were racking up too. I have to tell you though, I read a few pages of that stuff, and if those are Christians they're writing about, then Satan never had truer followers. But hey, maybe that's just me.

The two street lit authors weren't short-stopping either. One fan wheeled in a buggy with two copies of everything they had in print— even the self-published versions. So to folks who say that street lit is only a passing fad, you'd better ask somebody.

The authors get along pretty well (well, most of us), and the sense of humor—one-liners and witty comebacks—on this trip is off the meter. (Hey, we are wordsmiths, right?) One diva on the bus (who shall remain nameless), has three new friends hanging with her. So she's clowning right about now. But I have a feeling that someone's going to turn her meter to "bitch" before this is over. Stay tuned, because then I'll start kicking ass and taking names.

Tailan could picture Pam and The Divas going head to head. Her money was on Pam. She scrolled down a little more.

By the way, J. L. gets teased because he's the youngest one on the bus. (Have your tweens and teens check out J. L.'s blog—it'll be the PG version of the story. I promise!)

"Good Job, Pam. Way to promote the little guy," Tailan cheered, then she frowned when she saw the next few sentences.

Since they've added Delvin Germaine to the tour, things have gotten a little interesting. Can you say mouth-watering, drop-dead gorgeous, and drop your drawers so you can sell 'em on Sunday? Hello!!! And I think he has a thing for one of the women on the bus. Will he act on it? Will she??? Hmmmmm. Stay tuned, people. It's getting hot with a capital H-O-T.

I have to go. Breakfast is calling. And this plus-sized diva is not one for missing a meal. Ciao!

Tailan chuckled. She was absolutely loving Pam's straight-from-the-hip style of writing. Pam was the epitome of the three H's—Honest, Heart, and Hustle. Tailan got a full blast of all three in a first meeting at a signing event hosted by Nelson a few years ago.

Pam worked the convention like nothing Tailan had ever seen. Even Fran Rae, a *New York Times* bestselling author, noticed. She leaned over to Tailan and whispered, "We could learn a thing or two from that woman."

Fran saw it just as Tailan had. Pam smiled at everyone, making a point to have a stack of books in one hand while she talked shop. The result was a fistful of cash in the other. "Marketing dynamo" did not come close to describing the magic the woman was making at the signing.

Tailan made her way to Pam's tiny area and said, "I can't do much for you right now, but if you ever get picked up by a major publishing house, I'll have your back."

To prove she was serious, Tailan bought several copies of Pam's book that day with an American Express Traveler's Cheque.

When Pam arrived at the Indiana hotel for the tour briefing yesterday, she had placed a copy of that seven-year-old check in Tailan's hand. "Thanks for keeping your promise to me by bringing me on the tour." She embraced Tailan in a heart-stopping hug that brought tears to Tailan's eyes.

Authors like Pam were why Tailan was inspired to buck a system that mostly catered to well-known authors instead of building the mid-list ones into national and *New York Times* bestsellers.

She closed her laptop and found the courage to walk to her bed and get dressed. Still leery of even sitting on it for fear that those graphic dreams would pay another visit, Tailan grabbed her shoes and rushed to the bathroom.

Just before she entered, her cell phone chirped. She ran back to the nightstand, glanced at the caller ID and cringed.

"What's cooking?" Tailan said with rehearsed enthusiasm.

David had conveniently disappeared at several points yesterday, making it impossible for her to grill him like she had planned.

"Nice to hear you so chipper this morning," he said blandly.

So, you were expecting me to rip you out a new one? That explains your ghost act yesterday.

"I'm chipper *every* morning," she shot back. "Especially since we're doing exactly what you and Margo swore up and down the company would never, ever, *ever* do—a tour with mostly debut authors."

"Tai, even a broken clock is right twice a day." His tone was pure annoyance.

David was still hot about Tailan going over his head and directly to the publishers and Woodland executives. She refused to apologize for her tactics. David's way of doing things always ended with the same results. "Next year." He had chanted that mantra for five whole years!

Now the odds were stacked against Tailan, and she had a point to prove. The point—great authors come in every color. Mid-tier authors are talented, and many can achieve the status of National and *New York Times* bestselling author if they are given the help and guidance they need to succeed.

"So, you're calling me this early in the morning because …?"

"First, I know you're upset about what I did."

"You think?" She took a seat on the edge of the bed and slipped on her shoes. "How could you do that to me?! You *know* I can't be distracted right now. Not with him. Not with anybody or anything."

"You needed something to snap you out of this … I don't even know what to call it." He let out an exaggerated sigh.

Tailan closed her eyes and tried to rein in her nerves and irritation. "You can't keep throwing me for a loop like this. I have everything riding on this tour," she snapped.

"So do I, dammit!" David gave it right back.

Tailan shot off the bed and began pacing the room. She sensed her boss was working overtime to calm down too.

David tried again with a softer tone. "I might not have said this before, but the way you drive yourself, the way you go headfirst into things, is dangerous. It's like you're trying to fill yourself up so you won't have time to think. I'm worried about you, Tailan. And I think if you can lay this Delvin Germaine issue to rest one way or another, you can be back to your old self again."

David had never sounded so sad. Tailan froze mid-step. "I didn't know you cared."

"Oh, I care, sweetheart," he said, his voice a scratchy whisper. "I learned a painful lesson with my daughter about the power of love. I lost her because I wouldn't listen. But even worse, because I refused to see." He paused before adding, "I forbade her to marry the man she loved and she ... she committed suicide."

Tailan gasped; her emotions were like a rickety staircase at the moment. She suspected something tragic about the sudden death of David's youngest daughter, but he had never shared the details with anyone. Tailan had never pressed the issue.

"You're doing the same thing, Tailan. Just much more slowly," he said. "It hurts to watch. And I'm not going to lose you without a fight."

"Why now, David? Why did you have to get Delvin?" She collected a tissue and dried her eyes.

"Because I know you weren't able to get the celebrities you wanted for this tour."

Truthfully, as hard of a time as she had with all those other A-list celebrities, she couldn't believe this good fortune. Another thought hit her, and she blurted, "Did you tell him that I'd be here?"

"Yes." David's voice rippled with a low throaty chuckle. "When he learned that coming here would help you, he took the first flight out to make it here on time. No appearance fee, no over-the-top demands."

Tailan closed her eyes to still the rush of emotion that washed over her. What David had done was sweet—then again, he was a hopeless romantic who had been married for like ... a kajillion years. But he didn't know that she had lost much more than Delvin ever had when he walked away. Now she had secrets of her own, and Delvin's presence was making those secrets even harder to manage.

Rather than dredge up too many intense emotions that centered on

Delvin, Tailan redirected, "I won't let this tour fail. Delvin Germaine is an added bonus, but my focus is on the breakout authors on this tour—Pam and all eleven members of M-LAS. I'll do my best to bring in the sales figures I predicted to Thomas."

"Well, I also called to inform you that Margo just added a ripple in the pond."

Margo, you are becoming the bane of my existence. "How?"

"She called the publishers and—thanks to her—they've changed the criteria they'll use to determine if this tour successful."

Tailan's lungs dropped into her stomach, taking every ounce of air with them.

"Now it's about more than just bringing in a certain number of sales," David continued. "Five of the unknown authors must hit the national bestsellers list."

"Seriously?" she shouted, then took a breath and lowered her tone. "I'll do my best."

"Oh, you'd better do more than that," he shot back, his voice devoid of his usual warmth. "Margo's little stunt now has *my* ass on the line too. While I'm pushing for you to get *her* job, she's trying to get her father to push you *and me* out the door. And if you don't succeed, we're both gone—no demotion, no second chances." He let that sink in a bit before adding, "After a termination like that, no other distributor, retailer, or publishing house will touch us."

Tailan's equilibrium shifted, and she noodled down on the bed. The walls weren't just closing in, they were doing a tango along the path to her demise.

"What have I done that always brings out the bitch in her?" Her eyes blinked as she realized the words slipped past the filter she normally used with him.

"It's what you *haven't* done for her," David countered smoothly. "And trust me, I don't blame you one bit."

They ended the call, and Tailan tossed the phone over her right shoulder.

Talk about jumping out of the frying pan and straight into Satan's swimming pool.

Chapter 5

Tailan would make this tour work if it killed her! Or if she had to kill The Divas and hide their bodies under the bus. Now *that* would be worth going to jail for.

When she turned the corner leading to the lobby, she crashed into the middle of a broad chest. A strong pair of hands reached out to hold her steady. She looked up and into dark brown eyes that were so intense, she instantly took a step back.

"Good morning, sweetheart." Delvin took the handle of her bag. "Here, let me help you."

She quickly snatched it from his grasp. "I've got it."

His lips stretched into a lazy smile, his gaze meeting hers fully. Delvin gripped the handle, forcing her to release her hold. "Tai, we're not going to play these games."

"No one's playing anything," she snapped, grabbing for the case again. "I can manage on my own—just like I've done for the past seven years."

"Damn," he said, shuddering in mock horror. "The woman's going for the nuts again."

The man didn't let her take another step. Delvin pinned her to the wall and scanned her face. A sensual softness flooded his features that caused her to melt. Focused, absorbed, and intense, he studied her like a priceless piece of artwork.

Delvin brushed a kiss across her cheeks in a caress so gentle, she couldn't pull back the sigh quick enough. His tongue cleverly joined the foreplay, lusciously exploring her, tasting her, teasing her to the point she instinctively curved into his long frame and wrapped her arms around his neck. He pressed her harder into the wall and devoured, not stopping even when her bag clattered to the floor.

When they finally pulled apart, the world swam in and out of focus.

Tailan didn't know if she should be angry with him for his boldness or with herself for allowing him liberties that were no longer his to take.

Delvin laced his hands in hers, holding her glassy stare. "I'm here for you in whatever way you need me to be," he whispered. "I messed up. I know that. I heard what I wanted to hear and not what you meant." Delvin planted a kiss on her temple. "But I'm here now. Forgive me enough to at least let me help you, Tai."

That was Delvin. Pushing straight to the heart of the matter and leaving her feeling like a complete ass for not letting bygones be bygones. "We can't go back and change the past," she said.

"But I can sow the seeds of forgiveness so we can shape our future." He kissed her nose.

"We have no future," she whispered. "There can be no *we*."

"Your words are saying one thing, but your body knows the truth." He leaned in and brushed his lips across hers.

"Stop," she whined, struggling to get her lust under control. "Cut it out!"

Delvin straightened to his full height and loomed over her. His eyes flared with a fire that made her visibly gasp. "I want you, Tai." He picked up her bag and moved forward. Over his shoulder he declared, "And I will fight like hell to reclaim what's mine."

Tailan sagged on the wall, trembling. She glanced at her appearance in the hallway mirror, adjusted her blouse, and blindly followed him without another word of protest. She couldn't fight him right now, especially since she was so vulnerable to him.

They reached the lobby. The authors were there, assembled in groups, chatting like old friends. They were all discussing the press coverage of their tour.

"Pam, you're quoted!" Joyce Brown, one of The Vets and a member of M-LAS, exclaimed.

Pam froze before letting out an elated squeal. She ran forward and took the newspaper that Joyce held out.

"Read it out loud," Beverly said, perching on the arm of a chair next to Brenda, her longtime friend.

Pam slipped into the space next to Joyce, bumped her shoulder as a thanks, then held the paper out and read, "The tour is an amazing way to meet readers, promote your work and have a lot of fun in the process."

Murmurs of agreement from the crowd made Pam nod. She held up her hand to quiet them. "The days of an author sitting behind a desk looking pretty are over, said Pam, who self-published her first two books before her latest, *Looking for D*ck in all The Wrong Places*, was picked up by Simon & Schuster and she hit the national bestsellers list."

Cheers went up from everyone in the lobby, then faded away so Pam could continue.

"Then she founded M-LAS, a support group of several authors who co-author published projects and cross-promote, with the goal of each member hitting the national bestsellers list."

The M-LAS members in question all raised both hands in a show of solidarity that made the other authors smile.

"Authors need to go out there and hustle," she continued. "Especially if you're a relatively unknown author, you have to encourage them to take a chance on your work. You need to tell them why they're going to like your book. This is a phenomenal tour. I'm so excited to be part of it. It really is a once-in-a-lifetime opportunity!"

A roar of excitement went up from the group and hearty applause followed.

Tailan and Delvin moved forward. He slid his hand around her waist. The action was snagged by The Divas. She wanted to slap him. Tailan could feel the anger and jealousy they were throwing her way.

Lord, where's some arsenic when you need it?

"People are watching," Tailan whispered, putting some pep in her step to distance herself from him.

He caught up with her in three long strides. "And?"

"Go somewhere and handle your business, and let me handle mine."

"You are my business."

Tailan froze, forcing him to turn back in her direction. She abruptly relieved him of her bag and started toward the restaurant to get something to eat.

Delvin's dark brown eyes flashed with anger. "Make no mistake, Ms. Song." He blocked her attempt to get around him. "Now that we'll be sharing the same space for the next few days, rest assured, I'll be taking full advantage of it."

Forget breakfast! Where's that damn bus?

Tailan sidestepped him and started for the hotel entrance where the bus was waiting.

"I was coming for you next week anyway."

That statement tripped her just a bit. Tailan rolled her shoulders, gathered her focus, and turned to him. "What's so special about next week?"

"I'll be a free man."

Tailan's lids dropped over her tired eyes, and she shook her head. Instead of being thrilled by the news, deep coursing resentment burst from her. "So you sacrificed it all for nothing," she sneered.

The expression that shadowed his chiseled face was sweet payback.

"Hate to break it to you, but I've moved on," she said. She lifted her chin in bold defiance and headed over toward the group that was camped out near the waterfall outside.

He fell into step with her. "Have you?"

"Oh yes," she proclaimed proudly. "I've done quite well without you. Unlike the rest of your adoring fans, for me, the sunrise doesn't depend on you taking your next breath. Now if you'll excuse me."

Delvin gripped her shoulders and held her in place. "Tai, I'm serious."

"So am I," she shot back. "You had your chance, Delvin. You chose a lie over our love. That choice was on you—not me. You won't get a lick of sympathy from me about how all this played out. You could have handled it better. You didn't."

"All I wanted was one child," he countered in a voice that made her tense up. "One child that we would've raised together, loved, protected."

"There's no protecting a child in this world," her voice radiated with raw pain. "I know that more than anyone."

Chapter 6

Tailan flashed Delvin an arctic blast with her eyes, and he released her. She increased the distance between them and felt his eyes track her every move, but he didn't follow. Breath seeped out of her mouth in steady bursts. She hated how adults so flippantly lied to themselves—to others. The terrified child in Tailan Song knew one unshakable truth: monsters were indeed real.

She had barely made it out of a turbulent childhood when her parents were killed before they were scheduled to testify at a drug lord's trial. A fourteen-year-old Tailan was forced to stay with her mother's brother and sister in an area of Chicago infamously known as The Bucket of Blood—a place filled with real blood, real danger, and real horrors.

During her short stint on the city's West Side, Tailan witnessed unspeakable acts of savagery and senseless violence. Some of the cruelty was outright sadistic. Even now, some of the things she had seen or heard of followed her like echoes of tortured ghosts.

There was the twelve-year-old girl who was gang raped by eight men in an alley half-way down the block. No one came to the girl's aid, even though people heard the screams for hours. Or the honor student who was gunned down simply because he dared to want more out of life than the people around him. Murders were a daily occurrence.

So much rage all around her made Tailan terrified to leave the house.

Then the tide turned, and being outside the house was a much safer place to be.

"She livin' here, we need to put her to good use," Uncle Lin's deep voice echoed through the old house one night.

The floors creaked under the weight of her aunt's heavy footsteps as she replied, "Now you know we can't do that. Them people's gonna give us good money to keep her here."

"Seven hunnert a month ain't enough," he growled.

"It's enough," Aunt Trish shot back. "She don't eat much. Picky little thing. She clean up real good. The house ain't *never* been this clean. With that money and she earning her keep, it's gonna hafta be enough. We the only family she got. She's our sister's child. And you know you did that girl wrong."

"It wasn't no damn rape," he protested. "She wanted that shit. Just like all them others." Then his voice took on a faraway tone. "But Lawd, she was a sweet li'l thing."

Tailan almost lost her dinner. Her uncle had raped her mother? His own sister? No wonder Mama never said much about her family.

"You ain't touchin' her child," Aunt Trish insisted. "That ain't right."

"But Trish, we could make a lot mo' money," he pleaded. "A lot mo. We'd have that seven hunnert and then some."

Now Tailan understood why she had always felt exposed and vulnerable around him. Pure instinct had compelled her to *never* be in a room alone with him no matter what. His leers and the fact that he was always trying to find ways to put his hands on her made her shiver with disgust.

"Uh-uh! I ain't doin' dat," Aunt Trish said, and for a moment Tailan felt a splinter of hope.

"She still a virgin, right?" his voice held a hint of something Tailan couldn't put a name to, but it made her tremble with dread.

"What's that got to do with the price of tea in China?"

"King say he'd pay a grand just to tap that chinky-eyed bitch."

Tailan's heart stopped, then jump-started at a thunderous pace.

"*How* much?"

Lin chuckled, "Yeah, and that's just for one time. He gonna pay somethin' every time."

Aunt Trish's feet shuffled along the hardwood floor. "Naw, Lin. We can't let him do dat. I heard he da one who kilt our sista. Be wrong to let him have her. She died protectin' dat girl."

The woman was more right than she could know. King wasn't just looking to sleep with Tailan, he wanted her dead. How he had found her on the West Side was cause for concern, but what she heard next would be her on notice.

"Baby, we can do whatever we want wit 'er," he said in a lower tone, and Tailan could image his watermelon-sized head nodding for effect. "You know I can break her in real good. Gentle like."

There was a scrape of chair against the floor, and it caused Tailan to jolt forward.

"She be good to go. He won't know the difference," he said. Then he added a statement so profane that Tailan was still trying to absorb the verbal blow before realizing that the conversation had moved on to him saying, "It'll just be me … and him, that's all."

Tailan cracked the door in time to see Lin stroke a hand across his sister's hips.

"You wanna keep me happy right?" Then he kissed her neck, and Tailan almost lost what was left of dinner. "I'll teach her, just like I taught you."

"Naw, Lin, it can't be him," she said in a soft voice. "And it can't be you either. We'd make more money from someone else … if she's still a virgin."

Tailan didn't wait to hear their final decision. She propped open her bedroom window and escaped that old wood-frame house with just the clothes on her back and a bookbag filled with a few personal items.

The night she left was one of the most terrifying nights of her life. At fourteen, she was homeless and literally on her own. Her father's people wanted absolutely nothing to do with her. Apparently he had brought his family *unforgivable shame*—by marrying outside his race. They considered her a *Bink*—which in Mandarin was slang for half Black, half Chinese or *Chink*. They wanted nothing to do with her tainted blood.

And the hospitality and shelter from her mother's people came at a grisly price—the same price that her mother had apparently paid. But for Tailan it would be worse—being raped repeatedly by her uncle, then sold to the man who murdered her parents and siblings, and who would eventually kill her too.

Too numb to even cry, Tailan had walked for hours until she reached downtown Chicago. Then by nightfall she headed up Jeffrey Boulevard for several miles until she made it to a place called Chicago Vocational School.

C.V.S., once an all boys' military academy turned co-ed vocational high school, stretched four blocks from east to west and three blocks from north to south. Surely amidst all that real-estate she could hide out until she figured out her next move.

Tailan broke a window in one of the classrooms in the aviation wing of the school. Once she crawled in, she did a quick perimeter check and settled on a small space in the corner facing the door as the ideal refuge. She inched the teacher's desk into the corner so no one could look in the classroom window and see her on the floor. Later that night, she took a shower in the girls' gym and washed her clothes, then made her way into the cafeteria and ate whatever she could get her hands on.

Two months later, she was startled awake when someone touched her shoulder. A scream leapt from her mouth as her lungs rushed to supply her with oxygen. The words of her uncle plagued her dreams. Terror seized her, and she lashed out at the blurry assailant.

"I won't hurt you," he said, holding out his hands to ward off the attack. "Calm down!"

Tailan inched away from the boy, trembling uncontrollably with fear. He simply looked at her, waiting for her to get it together. He remained completely still and silent.

Those precious few minutes allowed Tailan to focus, to find the courage to look at him. Vague recollection inched to the surface.

"Delvin Germaine?" she whispered.

He nodded.

"You're on the basketball team."

Delvin lifted his hands, palms up. "I won't hurt you," he repeated, his eyes caressing her with gentle concern. "You look cold. I'm going to take off my jacket and pass it to you. Will that be okay?"

She hesitated a few moments, then nodded as he reached up, pulled off the blue and gold varsity jacket, and held it out to her. When she didn't take it, he added, "It's all right—I promise." His smile practically melted her.

"Okay," she whispered. Tailan's limbs did not want to work. Fear still had a death-grip on her body. Obviously, Delvin had assessed the situation because he carefully stooped down and covered her with his jacket. His close proximity actually soothed her enough to say, "You were in my accounting class."

"And English," he added. "And band."

Delvin settled down on the floor next to her. He reached into a brown paper bag, pulled out a chicken salad sandwich, and offered it to her.

Tailan shook her head, even as her belly roared to life in blatant protest.

The sound reached Delvin's ears, and he smirked. "I think you need to eat something."

She hadn't in days. The cafeteria had been cleared for the summer, and almost everything was locked up and out of reach. What little she was able to gather up had been stretched out over that summer, lasting until two days ago.

"Here," he said, holding the sandwich even closer.

She looked at the tempting meal and suddenly gave in.

"I made it this morning," he said as she took a bite and tried to smother a grateful moan. "Shouldn't be too bad. I used Miracle Whip."

Trying not to inhale the sandwich, Tailan slowed down and tossed a smile to Delvin. "I like Miracle Whip."

He passed her a bag of chips, then reached inside again and pulled out a pack of orange Hostess cupcakes. "We're going to have to split these. They're my favorite."

Tailan took another bite of her sandwich, followed by a few chips. Still leery of his motives and cautious, she kept her gaze fixed on him.

He glanced up at her and winked, and before she knew it, she was returning a genuine grin.

"Practice started yesterday?" she asked around a mouthful of food.

"They had us come in early," he replied with a shrug. "They want us to go to State finals this time."

Delvin stayed silent as they ate their meal. Eventually his eyes shifted to a paint splattered throw cloth Tailan had schlepped over from art class. Her bed. Now that her stomach wasn't growling, embarrassment crept in.

"You can't stay here," he said. "You know that, right?"

She looked away, hating that he confirmed what she had felt earlier in the week. More sounds, more movement in the hallway. For the majority of the summer there had been none. Only her in the entire building. Safety. Pure safety.

"They're starting to prep the school for the new year," he warned. "People are going to be everywhere. Someone else is going to find you." He gestured to the door. "I just came in here for a break after practice and to eat my lunch. But there'll be janitors and teachers coming around soon."

Tailan looked out to the empty classroom seats and realized her peaceful time was going to come to an end. She felt her face fall. All summer, she had been reasonably all right. No threat of being attacked or raped by her depraved uncle. And no doubt he and her aunt were on the lookout for her. Dear God, what kind of sick family had her mother come from?

She personally never wanted to learn the answer to that question.

"I have no place to go," she admitted solemnly, keeping her eyes forward. "My parents died a few months ago. My father's people don't want me. My mother's family is ... they're ... I ... they ..."

Tailan flinched as Delvin's hand covered hers. Her eyes shot to his, to his hand over hers, then back to his face. She saw no lust in his deep dark eyes, only comfort as he said, "You can come home with me."

Her heart rate sped up, and she snatched her hand away. Tailan threw off his jacket and backed away from him.

The horror she witnessed in his startled expression shocked her.

"No, I'm not talking about that," Delvin promised. Again he threw up his hands, trying to explain. "I'll sleep on the floor, and you can have my bed. We'll have to sneak you in after my parents go to sleep, but they travel a lot."

Tailan blinked and blinked again as his offer took root in her brain. A soft bed instead of a hard floor? Food? *Real* food? Safety? Maybe. Oh, and a bathroom with real mirrors to see her reflection. Tailan had no delusions about her appearance. She accepted the fact that she must look a hot mess.

His offer was too good to be real. She could hardly wrap her mind around it. And yet, she was tired. So tired of always being afraid. Tailan wore her terror like a second skin, and that extra coating wouldn't allow her to hope. Even with him.

"I'll be all right," she insisted as she absently brushed her hair with her hand. "I can find my own way."

Delvin reached out to glide a finger across her cheek, and she froze. "You're going to have to trust somebody at some point."

Tailan pulled away from his touch. "Why should it be you?"

Delvin's eyebrow shot up. "'Cause I shared my cupcakes with you." He lifted his chin arrogantly. "And I don't share my orange cupcakes with just anybody. Chocolate maybe," he shrugged. "But orange …"

The haughty look on Delvin's face was too comical. A whimsical laugh found Tailan, and she gave in to it. After a few moments, a wave of embarrassment flamed her face. She looked down at their entwined fingers and the orange cupcake in her other hand. She could not remember how the second one ended up there.

"Taking the last cupcake, that's like being engaged or something." Delvin softened his words with a smile.

So many bad things had bulldozed over her life. To finally receive a little comfort was too much. The waterworks started, and she couldn't turn them off. Tears rained down her cheeks. Gasping groans of deep-seated agony consumed her. And for the first time, she accepted strength from another.

Delvin wrapped her in his arms, and she went to him, too depleted to do anything else. His warm body was just the pillow she needed. His cotton shirt, a welcomed tissue for her tears. His powerful, protective arms, her only shelter from the dark shadows.

Tailan relaxed in his arms as the tears receded. She wanted to trust him. She wanted to trust *someone*. But with what she had been through, she didn't know how.

Abruptly, Delvin stood and extended his hand. "Get up. You're coming with me."

She hesitated several moments before collecting her belongings and doing as he asked.

"I promise," he said softly as they made their way from the classroom, "you'll be all right. You'll always be all right."

Chapter 7

Delvin needed to regroup. Tailan's effect on him was more than he could handle. To be so intimately close to her and not be able to hold her, touch her, make love to her, was pure torture. But a wall was between them now—a wall he had built with his bad choices.

Well, if he built it, then he could tear it down.

Delvin tracked her steps to the bus and followed. As the pendulum of her full hips hypnotized him with every step, his mind returned to the first time he had boldly and publically declared his never-ending love for her—a declaration that was the beginning of the end of his fake marriage to Gabrielle.

Delvin was startled when Gabrielle slipped into the seat next to him at the Dolby Theatre. He had deliberately neglected to invite anyone to join him. So how his wife had managed to locate the ticket and finagle her way in was beyond comprehension.

"Why are you here?" he said through his teeth.

She waved off his concern with a dismissive hand. "People will think it's strange if your loving wife isn't by your side, won't they?" She gave him a sugary-sweet smile that told him she had planned this all along.

"Ladies and Gentlemen," the announcer started. Delvin shifted his focus toward the stage. *"Please welcome Natalie Portman."*

The applause was thunderous.

"Good evening," she started. *"Tonight I present five outstanding performances for best male actor in a leading role. And the nominees are ..."*

"Darling," Gabrielle whispered over to him. *"The whole world will know that you're the greatest, and that I'm the luckiest woman in the world to be married to you."*

Delvin slid her a baleful glance, still angered that she had stolen his *"plus one"* ticket from his carriage house and had come of her own accord. The seat next to him was supposed to remain vacant, a sign that only he and one other person would understand. *"The odds favor Matthew McConaughey,"* he reminded her.

"Your performance was soooo much better. Now, remember," she said, stroking his arm like a hissing snake, *"I left you a little note about your acceptance speech. Had it all written out for you."*

Delvin gave her a look that he hoped conveyed his annoyance. *"I will—"*

"And the Academy Award goes to..."—he shifted his focus back to the stage—*"Delvin Germaine!"*

The crowd exploded with applause. Gabrielle screamed and jumped from her seat. Delvin lowered his head and said a silent prayer of thanks. This win was nothing short of a miracle. Like most others, he had expected Matthew McConaughey to take the honor. He rose from his seat and greeted the audience with a wave before giving Gabrielle a timid hug.

Finally, the moment had come. He headed to the stage and over to the podium where Natalie presented him with the coveted trophy.

They exchanged congratulatory hugs and a kiss, and he turned to the audience.

"First, I want to thank God for giving me life and so many wonderful opportunities." He paused to let the applause fade away. *"I want to thank the academy and the other four nominees tonight. To be in a*

group of such distinguished gentlemen humbles me. There are so many people I want to thank. There are just too many to name but ..." Then he grimaced before saying, "All right ... my parents, Anna and Delvin Senior; my agent, Katie; and my lawyer, Maurice. They would not let me live it down if I didn't mention them."

The members of the audience laughed.

"But if you will allow me, I do want to take an extra moment to thank someone special." He looked directly into the camera and lifted the award. "To the one and only love of my life. Tai, I never thought I'd be accepting this without you by my side. I love you. I will always love you, and I will never stop loving you. This"—he lifted the Oscar higher—"is for you." He blew the camera a kiss. "Thank you." He left the stage with Natalie on his arm.

The screen near the off-stage area showed the cameras had panned to Gabrielle, who fumed with humiliation. The applause trickled down, and the whispers started. He smiled as he cleared the stage, already knowing what the world was thinking—who the hell was this "Tai" he was talking about?

Fueled by that memory, Delvin ate up the distance between them. Before Tailan approached the group, he grabbed her hand and pulled her to him. "I'm sorry." His thumb massaged the inside of her wrist. "So sorry for hurting you." He searched her sad eyes for a hint that he was reaching her.

"Do you know how much pressure I have on me right now?" Tailan seethed. "I don't have time for this."

Delvin squeezed her hand a little tighter. "I'll take your anger. I'll take your resentment, I'll take anything you throw at me." He pulled her deeper into his body, their breaths mingling as he said, "But I am not backing down."

He would've kissed her right then and there if a busload of eyes were not watching their every move with open interest.

Tailan's lids dipped and zeroed in on his mouth. He didn't move.

"Well it's about time." They looked over to Pam, and Delvin

shrugged at her knowing grin. Obviously she felt the smoldering heat rising between them and decided to dampen it. "I was about to put out an APB on you," she teased. "You know we're on tour right?"

Joyce peered over Pam's shoulder and added, "We could stop by the adult toy store and start y'all off right."

"Forget both of you," Tailan shot back with a chuckle and followed Pam onto the bus. "What do you know about adult toys?" she asked Joyce.

"Baby, I wasn't always sixty-five," she replied, patting her short-cropped hair. "This old girl's still got a lot of living to do." She leaned in and whispered. "And she's going to have a lot of fun doing it."

Tailan laughed as she made it to the top of the steps and faced the group.

Applause rang out from the crowd, causing Tailan to give them a mock bow before sashaying down the aisle to her normal spot near her team at the back of the bus.

Delvin took the seat beside her, then as an afterthought asked, "You don't mind if I sit here, right?"

"Yes, I do mind."

"Too late now." He stretched out his long legs. "I'm comfortable."

"It's hard to miss that with you plastered all over me," she quipped, frowning as Delvin curled into her lap, looked up at her, then released a playful, but happy sounding snore.

"You start doing that and I'm rolling you to the floor."

Delvin had missed her sassy ways. "Now you know I'm just playing."

"I haven't been with you enough to know that." Her eyes always spoke deeper than her words. Delvin saw hurt there. Hurt he had planted so long ago.

His smile vanished. "I'd like to change that."

"I'm trying to read," she said, cracking open a romance novel. "I'd be finished with Brenda's book by now if you hadn't come along."

Delvin cuddled into her breasts and looked up at her, letting her see all the love he had for her there.

Tailan gasped, cleared her throat, and quickly looked away.

Delvin knew this tour was make or break for Tailan. It was a bold move all across the board. Her fears and concerns about its success were justified. He knew her better than anyone. She would be devastated if this venture tanked. Tailan was a fighter, but Delvin could tell by the determined set of her face that she was overwhelmed at the moment and clearing her thoughts by plunging into the fictional world. He would have to find a way to lure her in and help her get this tour to the finish line.

He studied her profile while she was lost in Brenda's latest book. So much about Tailan was still the same, but Delvin couldn't ignore that she was also very different now. She was a grown woman for one. She was older, wiser, and stronger.

In their early years, Tailan shared the horrors of her family life. The cruel and sudden death of her parents and her brothers. The twisted sexual predator known as her Uncle Lin. The depravity of the rest of her mother's family. At the beginning, Delvin had tempered his attraction to her with tireless care. It was a habit he knew he would now have to practice again. Tailan wasn't going to just let him slide back in. She had too many scars buried beneath the exotic face she presented to the world.

Delvin let a bashful smile split his features. He adjusted a little more into Tailan's warm body. She ignored the movement and kept on reading. It was a ploy that gave him hope. Delvin was certain his woman was still in there. She had to be. She had survived so much before him.

With his head nestled in her breasts, Delvin could hear her heart thump harder, faster every time he stole a sultry glance her way.

He closed his eyes. Yes, his Tailan was still in there, and he was breaking her down.

Thirty minutes later, the luxury coach made a sharp turn, and Delvin's eyes popped open. He looked up at Tailan, who was studying something out of the window.

"Get up," she ordered.

Delvin sat up to let her pass.

Tailan was at the front of the bus before it came to a complete halt.

He rose as he glanced out the window to see Elona and Michelle, staff who had traveled by car to set up before the authors arrived. They were wearing solemn expressions that propelled Delvin to the front of the bus.

He looked on from the top of the stairs as Tailan hit the steps and made her way down. Something was very wrong. Delvin felt it down to his bone marrow. He watched Tailan stiffen as Michelle said, "We've got a serious problem."

Chapter 8

Tailan looked from one woman to the other and asked, "What kind of problem?"

They both remained eerily silent, forcing Tailan to whip through a set of scenarios in her mind that could pose an issue on a tour of this type. "The books didn't arrive?"

"No, that's not it," Michelle answered, giving Elona a quick glance as though hoping her co-worker would chime in and save her the trouble of sharing the unpleasant news.

Derek, the man in charge of making sure the authors had what they needed, and Karyn, her marketing guru, walked out of the store and straight to the bus. Their steps were brisk, almost a run.

"Telona Geans, spit it out!" Tailan demanded, using Elona's complete name instead of the nickname she'd taken on because people kept getting Tailan and Telona mixed up.

"Something's not right about this whole set up. You need to speak with the general manager," Elona said, running her hand through dark tresses that were already disheveled. Nodding to where Derek, Terry, and Karyn were helping the authors off the bus, she yelled out, "You might want to hold off on that."

"Where's the general manager?" Tailan asked.

"Right up front," Elona answered, with an uneasy glance at Michelle. "Trust me, you'll see him as soon as you walk in. The guy gave me The Willies," she said, shuddering.

"Ms. Tai, he won't tell us what's up," Michelle said. "Said he only wants to speak with you."

Tailan pivoted then hustled like lightning to the entrance of the store and was standing in front of the manager in thirty seconds flat.

The appearance of the man explained why Elona had caught The Willies. The bulky, balding, pale-faced human was as translucent as wax paper. The two buffoons flanking him were no better. All three men looked like undercooked aliens. She could practically see her reflection in them. They needed some sun—and fast!

The scowls marring their faces meant they weren't the most welcoming squad she'd seen all week. Maybe this motley crew wasn't feeling all the extra work involved.

Tailan extended her hand. "Good morning. I'm Tailan Song."

The general manager looked down at her hand as though it was contaminated with some type of disease.

That flipped her eyebrow clean into her hairline. "I was instructed to speak with you."

His beady eyes narrowed in on the line of authors swiftly taking their places at the grouping of tables stretched out in front of jewelry and children's wear. The icy vibes emanating from the men was enough to make Tailan shiver.

The manager's eyes cut back to her. "We don't want your kind here."

Tailan blinked and tilted her head. "Our kind? You mean authors? Highly intelligent people who write books?" she said, gesturing to the group who were conversing with members of the excited Woodland staff. "You know those things that your store sells more of than most book stores? *Those* kind of people?"

The two men behind the manager passed a look between them and folded their arms in unison.

"You mean the authors your corporate headquarters approved to do *this* tour at *this* spot at *this* very time?" she redirected since her previous approach garnered no response.

"They might've approved it," he countered, rocking on the balls of his stumpy feet. "But they don't know how we do things around here."

Tailan whipped out her cell, keyed in her password and clicked a couple of buttons.

The burly, beady-eyed worm got right in her face and trained his gaze on her. "You can call anybody you want," he challenged with a sly grin. "They can't do squat. We don't want your kind here. Now, I want y'all out." He thumbed in the direction of the entrance to make his point.

Tailan stared at him, disgusted. "I'm a little confused," she said, hitting a button on her cell. "So you need to make it plain for me. When you say you don't want *our* kind in your store, you don't mean authors. Because we have groups of them here all the time. So exactly what do you mean?"

"Them," he said, gesturing with a jiggly arm to the group of ladies who were smiling, chatting, and greeting the fans who were beginning to block the main entrance.

She eased the phone to her side. "I'm sorry, come again? I don't speak—" she mimicked his arm gesture. "You need to be a little more direct."

"Darkies. Nigras!"

The heaviest of the crew chuckled as Tailan's heart sank to her toes.

"Are you serious?! In *this* day and age?" she snapped. "You don't want them here because they're Black?"

"I can say one thing," the round man who looked the most like something from outer space said from behind the manager. "Nothing's wrong with her hearing."

Tailan had suffered the indignity that came along with being mixed raced most of her life. These loathsome creatures were nothing new to her, but it wasn't just about her. Besides the four males, she had a bus full of women, professional women—mostly professional anyway—to worry about.

She scanned the store and noticed some alarming issues. One—

there were a couple of men fiddling with shotguns like they intended to purchase them. But the weapons department was in the back of the store, not in the women's section where the men were casually standing. Two—the two snot rags standing behind the manager were wearing the store's security uniforms. They were in on this! From the looks of it, they were frothing at the mouth to start some mess.

Delvin came to her side, and the tension around her spiked to new levels. Delvin's presence propelled all three men to take a cautious step back. Time moved like molasses as she sensed Delvin doing the same thing she just had—sizing up the situation. Seconds later, his speaking glance let her know that he'd reached the same conclusion she had. "How can I help, Ms. Song?"

God bless him. The man could play it cold and direct like nobody's business. "Get the authors back on the bus," she said so only he could hear. "Now!"

Delvin pivoted, aiming in the direction of the autographing area. Tailan gripped his arm to hold him still for a moment. "But don't alarm them. Nice and easy—but *quick*."

He gave her hand a tight squeeze and seconds later, he was at Michelle's and Derek's side, relaying the information. Next, he told Karyn, Terry, and Elona, and soon everyone went into full retreat mode.

Tailan cut her eyes back to the men in front of her. They were celebrating their victory with handshakes and back slaps. She wanted to knee every one of them in the rubber parts. But that was only a temporary fix to her problem. This store alone brought in more book sales than five combined, and it was where they'd done their heaviest promotion. She sized them up, never revealing a single flicker of emotion on her face. Did they really think she was going to take this lying down?

Dummies!

"Fellas," Tailan drew their attention back to her with a perfect brilliant smile. "Now that I know how *y'all do things 'round here*," she lifted her phone, propped her hand on her hips and declared, "how about I return the favor and show *you* how we do things where I'm from."

Tailan snapped around and walked away. Over her shoulder she announced in her best southern drawl, "This ain't over boys."

She put the phone to her ear as though she was making a call. When she was out of range, she quickly saved the recording of her conversation with the manager and his posse and forwarded it. Next she flipped through her directory, found the number to the local radio station, and hit the send button.

Three minutes later she was connected directly to the host during the commercial break. "Damaris, I need you to get someone from your sister station—the television arm. Get them down to the Woodland in Fort Wayne right away. And if you have any pull with one of your competitors, get them in on it too. We've got a serious story brewing here, and I need all the coverage we can get."

"Cool," Damaris replied. "Robin's near that area, and I'm on my way. I'll call Ron Spoon. He's been trying to take me out to dinner since we left college. I'll owe him one, and you'll owe *me* one."

"Done! Make it happen, Captain!"

Fifteen minutes later, Tailan was back on the bus with the authors and her team. She needed to think fast and act even faster. These authors deserved a chance to shine, and she would give it to them.

The Vets took a long, hard look at Tailan, then one by one looked out to the men who had given Tailan a hard time and shook their heads. Several fans that were standing near the entrance were pointing in the bus' direction and were stunned speechless by the abrupt departure of the authors. Tailan was losing valuable time to turn this around.

Her mind was awhirl with thoughts. *Shotguns.* Media coverage would not be enough. She closed her eyes and stilled her mind, and an answer became clear. She whipped out her cell again. This time she dialed the police.

Tailan waved her hand to order the bus to quiet down as she said, "We have several celebrities on site, and the crowd's getting out of control," she told the dispatcher. "Can you send over some escorts right away?" She gave the location and ended the call, then turned to find Delvin standing right behind her.

"What's the plan, baby?" he said, sweeping a glance towards the angry men in front of the entrance. "I know you have one. Let me know what you need."

Her heart swelled at the vote of confidence. "Give me a minute. I'll need to clue everyone in at the same time."

Tailan snagged the attention of her key people by yelling, "Support team—to me, now!" Within ten seconds, her staff was huddled up in a semi-circle surrounding her at the front of the bus. "All of you have your iPads, right?"

"Right," they chorused.

"Download the credit card processing software." They whipped out their equipment and Tailan gave them the login and password to use, then slid an American Express card to Derek and a company Visa card to Elona. "I need you," she said, pointing to Derek and Michelle, "to go back to the Woodland on Wade Drive and buy every copy of our authors' books they have in stock."

"Done!" Derek said.

"You three," she said, gesturing to Elona, Terry, and Karyn. "hit the Woodland near Route 30 right off the expressway. If there's any problem, just tell them we'll restock everything by tomorrow."

"Cool," Karyn replied with a quick few keystrokes on the iPad. "We'll call the stores and have the books waiting for pickup at customer service so we don't have to wait."

Tailan grinned. "Good thinking."

Derek nodded, letting her know that he would do the same.

"I need you all back here in twenty minutes."

Derek looked at everyone and said, "Time to make it rain, people."

The five of them sprang into action. Michelle skirted around Tailan and was right on Derek's heels. Their cars peeled out in record time.

The second their cars cleared the parking lot, Tailan turned to the authors.

"Can I have your attention please?" She started and all eyes locked on her. "I want—"

"Why did we have to leave? What's going on?" The authors were jumpy, and a flurry of questions shot her way. Soon roars of excited voices volleyed back and forth, making it impossible for her to answer. All were in an uproar except The Vets, who were leaned into each other in a private conference.

Tailan held up her hand to silence them. Voices trickled to a halt.

"I apologize for the inconvenience," she said, making eye contact with as many authors as possible. "But things here weren't set up quite right."

"Bullshit!" Shannon shot back, causing a few murmurs of agreement from the other divas.

Nona rocked her neck. "The books were there."

"The tables were there," Chanel added, mimicking Nona's movements. "So what's really up, chick?"

"Yeah, what's really going on?" Shannon asked, slapping Nona some skin. "You throwing shade in the game?"

Brenda tugged Tailan's sleeve and said, "Tell them the truth, baby."

Tailan looked to Beverly, Brenda, and Joyce, then to Les and Fran. They saw it too—they understood.

She turned and stared into everyone's eyes. Once all attention was on her again, she revealed, "The manager doesn't want us here. He made it ugly clear that, in his words, 'our kind' aren't welcome in his store." Tailan moved up the aisle and stopped in the middle of the bus. "I didn't anticipate this on a tour in the heart of America. But that sicko manager out there was more than willing to remind me that right now we are 'red-neck' deep in Klan Country."

"Are you saying they didn't want us up in there 'cause we're Black?" Pam asked.

The gasps that followed that question were expected.

"Yes. I had to get you all out," Tailan replied. "Your safety will always be my first concern."

The silence was heartbreaking. Tailan looked out of the window. "All hope is not lost. I want everyone to look outside. See those people out there?"

All gazes focused on the right side of the bus.

"That crowd is here for you. People, mostly White people, came to buy your books, and we're not going to disappoint your new fans."

Soon everyone's attention was back on Tailan.

"But what choice do we have?" Lorna asked, her caramel face peppered with concern.

Tailan blew out a long, slow breath. "I say we take a page from the late great E. Lynn Harris and pop the trunk."

Understanding instantly dawned in The Vets' eyes.

A few smiles spread on the faces of M-LAS authors, who were familiar with the man's success and the way he had gone from self-published author to *New York Times* bestseller.

J. L., the youngest of the group, perked up, grinning from ear-to-ear. "So we're gonna sell the books right off the bus?"

"Damn straight," Tailan said, smiling at the fact that the youngster had peeped the plan too. She winked at him, and he practically beamed.

"Now, that's what I'm talking about," he said, giving Lorna, Susan, Tanishia, and Pam a high five before traveling up the aisle to do the same with The Vets, Candy, Valarie, Janice, Martha, D. J., and even the most quiet member of the tour, Malcolm.

Excited chatter and murmurs meant everyone was feeling Tailan's Plan B.

Well, *almost* everyone.

"I ain't selling my books like I'm some bootleg chick," Nona snapped.

Shannon scowled and added, "Naw, ain't happenin'."

"Nope," Chanel joined in, settling back into the seat and folding her arms across her bosom. Traci nodded and mimicked her friend's action.

"Then stay your raggedy butts on the bus," Tailan shot back. "Either way works for me."

Beverly Jenkins stood, faced Nona and her crew, pushed the glasses up on her nose, and said, "I wasn't going to say anything, but …"

Chapter 9

Delvin was jonesing for some popcorn right about now. This was about to get *gooood*. The Vets were all business. All had paid their dues with years of literary challenges and triumphs. He looked over to Tailan, whose grip on the edge of the seat meant she was bracing herself for what the spicy Vet would have to say.

His eyes darted to Beverly Jenkins and all he could think was, *uh oh.*

Delvin knew that look. His mother would give him one of those from time to time when he had the nerve to try her. Didn't work for him then, and it looked like The Divas were about to feel the wrath that lingered behind that look.

Beverly squared her shoulders, leveled a furious glare at Nona and went for the jugular. "This woman has been putting up with your bullshit for the past two days. And I, for one, am damn tired of it!"

The veteran authors all nodded. "That's right," and "Amen," followed from several others.

She wagged a finger at the four of them. "Now the time has come for you to be as hardcore as you're always bragging you are, and suddenly y'all acting like pampered punks."

Brenda stood beside her long-time friend. "You four need to think about the bigger picture, ladies."

"Sit y'all's old asses down!" Nona snapped, dismissing them with a wave of her taloned hand. "Nobody's talking to you."

Delvin nearly leapt from his seat to take the woman head-on for being so blatantly foul. But Malcolm, a street-lit author who hadn't had more than two words to say the entire trip, shot to his feet.

"Have you lost your mind?" he thundered at Nona. "That's mad disrespect! Coming at The Vets like that." His gaze shifted to the rest of the crew. "You broads better backtrack trying to come across as some hood rats. Y'all know better than that." He did a respectful bow to The Vets, then turned heated eyes back to Nona and her ignorant crew. "Cut all the madness and know what's what. It's 'cause of them that we're even on this bus. Before your head gets all swol' and your draws supersize ..." he pointed to the elder authors and finished with pride. "They paved the way for us. Y'all better recognize."

Delvin felt the swell of pride filter through to nearly everyone on the bus. Applause thundered. The Vets nodded in unison at the end of Malcolm's diatribe as if to say, "And that's that."

He hadn't put much stock in this dysfunctional circus of authors, but Delvin had to admit the brown-skinned, Kangol-wearing young man had said a mouthful in that one rhyme.

Tailan didn't waste another second taking it from there. She got directly in Nona's face. "He's right. It's because of gifted authors like these that *you* are able to write the kinds of books you want. They, along with several author pioneers, said no when publishers wanted them to change their characters to White. Now White people are reading the books they've written about women of color." Tailan scanned the bus for the other divas. "They kicked the door open, and you want to disrespect them?" She leaned forward, and Delvin held his breath. Tailan was going there. "Unacceptable," she sneered. "*You* won't be signing *any* books today."

Nona shot back with a response so profane, everyone gasped.

"Whoa," Delvin said, coming behind Tailan. "Dial that low-grade action back."

Nona sneered as she flicked her eyes his way. "You would stick up for her."

"Yeah, probably 'cause he's been sticking it in her all night," Shannon taunted.

The four divas cackled with laughter. A shocked silence fell over the bus.

Delvin did not miss Tailan's flinch or the frowns of displeasure on the faces of nearby authors. Beverly slowly gave her bosom a few warning pats, and he recognized the habit. There was no telling what that Vet kept up there.

Delvin readied to let Shannon and Nona have it, but Tailan got there first.

"*You two* are off the tour. Right now!" she said through her teeth. "I will not let you bring the rest of us down."

The bus became pin-drop quiet.

Delvin wanted to drag Tailan off the bus and ravage her. Just like that, she had shot his lust off the meter. He adored her. When she was pissed, sweet heavens, she was a force of nature—a swirling wind of unstoppable purpose. Pure passion.

"When my team returns, they'll put you on the first thing smoking, whether that's on wheels or four freaking legs." Tailan pinned Chanel and Traci with a vicious glare. "Would you ladies care to join them?"

Both looked at each other, then back to Tailan, then emphatically shook their heads.

"Riiiight," Tailan drawled with a lopsided grin at their lack of loyalty. "Love is love, blood is red, and money is green." Something in the way she slowly straightened to her full height let Delvin know that she wasn't done. With a quick shake of her head she blurted, "On second thought—no." Tailan stared at Traci and Chanel. "I've had enough of you too. Stick with your homegirls."

She glanced to Delvin then immediately gave her attention to the rest of the authors. "I appreciate you backing me up on this. The police are on their way. I told them we need escorts for our celebrities."

When everyone looked toward Delvin, Tailan added, "Not him."

The authors laughed.

"Well him too. But for *all* of you." She fanned her hand over the group. "You are literary superstars, and don't you forget it!"

A roar of approval went up on the bus, and Delvin nearly burst with pride. In the excited commotion he took her hand and gave it a quick peck, then held it up like the winner of a boxing match.

Joyce stood and faced the group and began to croon her take on an old gospel song. "I don't know what you come to do, but I come to sell some books."

"Some books!" the rest of The Vets chimed in, rocking in their seats.

"I come to sell some books."

"Some books," the rest of the authors chorused.

"I come to get sold out."

"Sold out!"

While Joyce and The Vets continued to bring the spirit in through song, and the four problem children huffed, a news van pulled up, and the camera crew piled out behind the reporter.

Tailan tossed back her head and laughed as she clasped her hand in his.

* * *

Time was a precious commodity for Tailan. For her plan to work, all the pieces had to fall into place without a hitch. *Showtime!*

Tailan nudged Delvin in his side. "Get out there and do your thing."

With a caress of her shoulder and a whisper of, "I've got this, baby," in her ear, he was down the steps and walking toward the female reporters.

Tailan moved to the driver. When he looked up she ordered, "Ray, move the bus near that crowd of people." She pointed over to the steadily growing group in front of the store's main entrance.

The driver pulled about one hundred feet forward and opened the door.

At that moment, The Nelson Entertainment Group team wheeled around the corner, tires squealing in protest as they stopped in front of the bus. Authors piled out and swiftly went to unload the books out of the cars.

"Teamwork makes the dream work," Tailan whispered. "Hallelujah!"

The authors' enthusiastic rushing about caught the attention of their fans. Stampede style, the excited book buyers hurried from the store and created a cul-de-sac around the bus. The authors were lined up, side by side with their books neatly stacked on the ground before them. Tailan wanted to kiss every single one of them.

Still no police. Their presence would ease her fears immensely. She turned to the four authors on punishment. "You'll have to wait until this signing's over to go back to the hotel. I need all of my team with me right now."

"What can we do to help?" Nona asked in the softest tone she had used—*ever*.

Tailan pursed her lips and absently massaged her temple. "Seriously?" she questioned. "Now you want to act like you've got some sense?"

"Yeah," Nona started. "I was being difficult—"

Tailan nearly choked on her response.

"Okay, a bitch, and I know it," Nona admitted. "Apologies for what I said to you and The Vets." She cleared her throat twice; apparently, the humble pie was lodged in it. "I didn't mean to disrespect them like that."

Decision time. Tailan blew out a frustrated breath. The crowd was building. She looked out the window to where her team was trying to direct traffic. Some people were scrambling out of their cars, others were craning their necks, probably trying to see the four hood stooges she had on lock down on the bus.

"Shoot," she muttered, then focused on the anxious four. "You need to make sure you say it to them," Tailan said, nodding toward The Vets stationed at the middle of the line.

Nona nodded. And so did the other three.

"And in front of *everyone* when we get back on board."

Silence ticked by for a few spells.

"Fine!" Shannon shouted.

"Watch your tone, Shannon!" Tailan was in no mood to play.

An involuntary tick started just above Shannon's eye. She took a moment. "Sorry." Her inflection was controlled and steady. "I will."

Traci said, "Okay."

"Yes Ma'am!" Chanel groaned.

Tailan had an epiphany. A little street cred on the ground out there with the others couldn't hurt if something jumped off. Two of them looked like they could throw down and be the last one standing when it was over. They needed to be on either side of The Vets, and they'd better live up to their hard core image.

But first ...

Nona moved barely an inch. Tailan took her nose-to-nose—eye to eye. "And the next time you feel like putting my bizness in da street, I'ma whup yo' ass. You ain't the only one wit' a li'l street in 'em. Southside—Chi-town, baby. Jeffrey Manor—ride or die. Remember dat."

Nona blinked, flinched, then gasped at Tailan's slip into hood-speak.

Tailan pointed to the front of the bus. "Now get out there and sell some damn books."

She didn't have to say it twice. They almost carried her with them as they ran out.

The moment Tailan stepped onto the pavement, the general manager came running over, his burly entourage in tow. "You can't be here!" he screeched. "Get that bus off the lot! Get those people back on the bus!"

Tailan ignored him and went to Delvin's side. She extended her hand to the wavy-haired newswoman with the angular face and wide smile. "This is"—Tailan looked at the badge clipped onto the pair of his baggy jeans—"Bill. He's the general manager of this store." Tailan clapped a hand on the man's back and pulled him in close like they were old buddies. "And I'd like *him* to tell you the reason the authors are signing *outside* in the parking lot rather than *inside* at the tables that Woodland has all set for them." Tailan blinked her eyes innocently and relished the fire flashing in Bill's baby blues. "Bill, the floor's all yours," she said with a flourish of her hand. "Tell them what you told me."

"Well ... well, they didn't tell us so many would be coming," he whined, his cronies nodding to support the lie.

Delvin whipped out the advertisements that were made for the tour.

He passed one to Bill, then to both reporters, who scanned the paper, then looked at Bill for answers. All of the authors, all of the books being promoted, were listed clearly on the flyers.

Shoppers were leaving the store and wandering over to see what the ruckus was about. Most were vying for spots near the cameras. People were lined up in front of the authors, patiently waiting for their autographs, while Tailan's team collected monies for the sales.

Two Woodland employees exited the store carrying a table and chairs. They were followed by several other employees who all carried tables, book stands, and chairs, which they hurried to set up outside the bus. The store's staff nodded to Tailan and completely ignored the general manager's glare.

"You stop this right now," Bill bellowed as two of the henchmen rushed to get in front of the employees to halt their movements.

Five squad cars pulled up, they stopped close to the crowd, and the officers hurried out of their cruisers. They approached Bill. "We heard there's a problem."

"Yes, get these nig—"

The first officer's eyebrow shot up to his hairline.

"—people out of here!" Bill boomed, gesturing to the authors and their fans. "This bus can't be here. It's taking up too much space in the park—"

"Officer, I made the call," Tailan said, passing him a flyer. "There's a book signing here today. And the manager seems to think we shouldn't be inside *his* store, so I found a way to make it happen out here. But the crowd …" She gestured to the hundreds of people spreading out around them. "The crowd is a lot bigger than I thought it would be. Plus, with the media coverage here …" She pointed to the table of authors where the reporter was interviewing The Vets. "We thought you all could make sure the celebrities are safe."

"How many are there?"

"Twenty-one." Tailan sighed and placed a dramatic hand over her chest. "I thought it would be too much for us. And definitely too much for the store's security team."

Tailan drew the attention of the officer over to the men holding the shotguns. "At least I *think* they're security. They don't have badges. And—wow! The price tags are still hanging off the guns."

The officer's gaze narrowed at the group of men. "Are they supposed to have those outside of the store?" he asked Bill, his tone cold and lethal.

Bill's eyes bulged, his flabby jaw unveiling his shock. "They just bought 'em."

"Really?" Tailan crossed her arms over her chest and countered, "Do they have a *receipt* for them?"

Bill flushed beet red.

"You know officer"—her eyes snagged his name plate—"Hinton." Then her eyes lifted to the face of her uniformed guardian angel. "Not having a receipt and being *outside* of the store with merchandise ..." She scratched her head and frowned. "That's called stealing where I'm from."

"Well, they ... I ... We ..." Bill sputtered, waving his boys back toward the store.

Officer Hinton grinned, signaling to his fellow officers to make tracks in their direction. "If they don't have a receipt for those, take them into custody."

Bill came at Tailan. "You have no right to sell those here," he growled, gesturing to the area where the impromptu signing was taking place. "Those aren't even our books!"

"You're damn straight," she said in a low tone that only Bill could hear. Then she added with a louder tone, "Satan will sell ice cream in hell before I'll let you make one dime off *our kind.*"

"So it's like that, huh?" A tall brown-skinned officer glared down at Bill, whose self-preservation instincts prompted him to take a few steps back.

"Ma'am," Officer Hinton said to Tailan. "I've got a better idea of what's going on now." He tipped his hat to her. "We'll take it from here." He pointed to two other officers. "Spread out and corral the crowd in an orderly fashion. Also, have cars thirteen and four move over to the street and redirect and manage the traffic flow."

The officers nodded and got on the job.

Bill was in Tailan's face with his godawful breath as he growled, "You won't hear the end of this."

Delvin came to her side, and the warmth of him was comforting. She looked first to Bill then to the officers and Delvin, then smiled.

"I won't hear the end of this? Well, neither will you." She flipped out her phone and played back their recorded conversation for the whole group to hear. All of the remaining officers—Black and White— soon pinned angry gazes at the general manager. She relished Bill's shocked expression. "I've already sent this to corporate. The next time we come back, *you* won't be here."

Bill glared at her, spun on his heels, and stormed away.

"Hey Bubba," she said to one of Bill's pudgy cronies who was being placed in the back seat of a police cruiser. "You're right. There's nothing wrong with my hearing." She winked. "And there's nothing wrong with my brain either."

Tailan turned from the defused situation to see David exiting his limo, which was parked near the bus. He rushed toward her with a smile wider than the Mississippi. "The team called me in to get a truck of books out this way," he said. "I swear I couldn't have handled that better myself."

"I'm going to head back over to the signing table," Delvin announced. He gave her a quick peck on the cheek. She nodded and turned her attention back to David.

"I put in a call to Dan while I watched you handle the problem," David continued. "He's putting out a nationwide blast to all Woodland Stores about the authors."

Tailan yelped for joy and jumped into his arms. "Do you know what that means?"

"Yes!" David said, embracing her. "If Margo wants to deal from the bottom of the deck, she'd better come with a better set of playing cards. Because right now, my dear, you've got the winning hand." He waved to the team then jetted over to his waiting limo.

Tailan returned to Officer Hinton and said, "What kind of books does your wife read?"

He grinned down at her. "Romance novels—the fluffy stuff. But I like something with a little bite to it."

Tailan looked at Pam and took the officer's arm, guiding him to the marketing queen. "Then I have just the books for you."

Chapter 10

Delvin couldn't believe the burst of envy that bubbled up in him as Tailan and "Officer Friendly" made it over to the signing table. The officer was hanging on Tailan's every word. She introduced him to Pam, then gave a brief pitch for the woman's book. The camera crews had split their attention between the men being arrested and carted away and the lively crowd that was surrounding the authors.

Soon a few other officers, who were giving Tailan an appreciative once-over made their way to her. Delvin rose and rounded the table. His approach to Tailan pulled the camera guy's attention. He pushed his way between the officer and Tailan and said, "Ms. Song, on behalf of all the authors here today, I wanted to personally thank you for your quick thinking and ingenuity." That was the only warning he offered. Then he whispered in her ear, "Remind me never to get on your bad side."

Her smile was all blushes, but her comment was not. "You *are* on my bad side."

"Not for long." Delvin captured her mouth in a kiss so steamy that anyone observing it would assume they were the most "in love" couple in the world. The media camera and countless cell phone cameras caught it all.

He pulled away and finished with a wink. Delvin returned to his seat, but not before noticing how the officer's lips spread into a knowing smile.

* * *

"I come to get sold out!" Delvin cheered several hours later as he stepped onto the bus and danced his way up the aisle. The others laughed, cheering with him as their new mantra started again.

"Lord, have mercy," Susan piped in. "I can't believe we pulled it off!"

"Gotta admit, Delvin," Lutishia said. "Your idea was pure cross-promoting genius."

Delvin shook his head, aiming to deflect the attention from himself.

"Oh no, Delvin!" Brenda exclaimed, gripping his arm to hold him in place. "Lutishia's right. When you put out the word that they could *only* get an autographed copy from you if they also bought at least two books from the rest of the author panel, that put us over the top!"

"And it worked!" Beverly laughed. "My God, those people were picking up books left and right and flying over to the registers. God bless you, baby!"

Delvin gave a fist pump, and the whole bus roared with laughter. Then he took a bow before dropping into his seat. He appreciated all the adoration, but it all concealed his ulterior motive—doing his best to help Tailan *win*. He was determined to help Tailan turn this lemon of a day into grape juice and let the world wonder how she did it.

He glanced over to Tailan, who was still giving the colorful gang high fives. She turned and mouthed, *thank you.* But her eyes held the real reward. Tailan's exotic deep pools reflected the only thing he wanted—all of her love. Finally, she let him see it.

Delvin returned the smile with a wink.

The only time the signing had gotten a little tense was when they dipped very low on book stock. All of the available books in a five mile radius—except, of course, those from the store in front of which they were sitting—were now on the lot and going fast. As much as Delvin wanted this to remain *The Tailan Song Show*, he knew her too well to avoid the issue any longer.

"Tai," Delvin said while taking a quick break to assess the situation, "I know you're upset with the general manager, but you can't leave these people hanging either." He gestured to fans who had been waiting for nearly an hour. "They're going to fire him." He stroked a hand across her cheek. "They're not going to put up with folks who let personal issues get between them and making a profit. Trust me on that. Sell the store's books, Tai, and quit being so bullheaded." He kissed her again and walked back to his place. She gave him the evil eye for a few moments but eventually complied.

No sooner did he have Tailan ushering out all the book stock from inside the Woodland store before another annoyance reared its head.

A tall, blonde Amazonian charged out of a limo and zeroed in on Tailan. Delvin observed the hostile stance of the woman and made quick steps to Tailan's side.

"Delvin Germaine," Tailan said, "Meet Margo Nelson. She's the daughter of the man who owns NEG."

Everything about Margo put Delvin on edge. But what really held his attention was the tension the woman ignited in Tailan, who studied the blonde as though she was connecting several dots. "I knew something wasn't quite right," Tailan proclaimed.

Margo's green-eyed gaze swept the area, her frown was every shade of ugly. "So you managed to make it work."

"Absolutely," Tailan replied, a smile lifting the corners of her sensually curved lips. "Your father's counting on it."

"My father has nothing to do with it," she countered with a sly smile that annoyed Delvin. "I'm the one managing this fiasco."

"This book event will sell out, Ms. Nelson," Delvin fired back before he could catch himself. "If that's your definition of a fiasco, then this tour is the most successful fiasco in history." He turned to Tailan just in time to see a sly grin streak across her features.

Margo looked past Tailan, scanning the store's entrances as though searching for someone in particular.

Delvin's hands clenched into fists as Tailan blurted, "So you're the one who called Bill and told him to put us out?"

Margo feigned outrage better than any actress Delvin had ever worked with. "I did no such thing," she gasped, taking a step back.

Liar.

"Your father's going to be real happy about what went down today," Tailan said.

Margo waved her off, and Delvin took deep offense to the gesture. *Nobody dismisses my woman!*

"He won't know a thing about it," Margo promised.

You really don't know Tailan, do you Margo? Boy, are you slow on the uptake.

Tailan mimicked Margo's nonchalant pose and placed a hand on her hip. "If Bill and Bubba go down," Tailan batted her eyes innocently before giving Margo a cold, lethal stare, "trust me, those morons *will* take you with them."

Margo's arrogant smile disappeared.

* * *

The cheers on the bus pulled Delvin from his private thoughts.

"We did it! We did it!" Tailan screamed and shimmied up the aisle.

Delvin had never been so proud of her in his life.

When her little dance was over, she stopped in front of Nona and gave her a hard look.

Nona was on her feet in a jiffy. "Everybody, I've got something to say."

The boom of Nona's voice attracted the attention of everyone on the bus. With a few gulps and a deep breath, she said, "I'm sorry for what I said. Beverly and Brenda, I was outta pocket for that. I'm truly sorry."

A few murmurs and quite a few shocked expressions followed that statement.

Apologies then echoed from the other three, extended to everyone on the bus.

Beverly stood and swept a look across The Divas, before moving to Nona's side. "It's okay, baby."

"When you know better, you do better," Brenda said, giving Beverly an almost imperceptible nod. Beverly put a few reassuring pats on Nona's back and finished, "But the next time you come at us like that," she cleared her throat and patted the upper edge of her bra, "I'ma havta cut ya."

I knew it! She's packing a weapon. That's old school right there.

Nona's eyes bulged and her mouth dropped as she sized up Brenda and Beverly. "Y'all ol' heads from the hood too?" Her shock was authentic. She plopped down, too stunned to speak.

"Detroit, baby." Beverly flipped her a steely gaze. "Like Malcolm said, you better recognize."

Delvin's laughter was contagious. Soon everyone except The Divas was rolling in their seats.

He had tears in his eyes as it went even further.

"No, no, baby doll," Beverly commanded, pulling Nona out of her seat. "You sit up here with me." She ushered the sputtering woman to the front of the bus. "I plan to enjoy the rest of this tour. Which means," she directed Nona to the window seat beside hers, "you and your posse will remain separate for the rest of the tour. Just like we did the *children* in church back in the day."

Brenda snapped her finger and pointed to Shannon, "You,"—she crooked her finger—"to me."

The whole bus choked back hysterical smirks of laughter as Shannon crept forward with her belongings and slumped into the window seat next to Brenda. "Y'all get into too much trouble sitting together," Brenda finished as she sat down.

Delvin was howling as Joyce and Les got in on the fun.

"Traci," Joyce announced, "this window seat has your name on it, sugar."

"Chanel, darling," Les opened his arms invitingly, "that leaves you with me."

Traci and Chanel huffed, puffed, and whined all the way to their final destinations.

Once everyone was settled in, and the comedy act was over, Delvin rose and moved to the back of the bus to his favorite spot next to Tailan.

The tension, strain, and turmoil of the day had taken its toll. She looked tired but no less beautiful. Delvin nearly moaned as she absently fell into an old habit he had always loved. Tailan's head dipped and settled on his shoulder. She closed her eyes and mumbled, "Thank you for having my back today."

The sweet joy of that quiet moment was promptly altered as Malcolm stood and asked Tailan, "Ms. Tai, how come you didn't tell them news people the truth?"

Delvin looked down at Tailan's resting head and felt her entire body lock with tension. Slowly her lids lifted, and he gripped her hand for support as she stood to address the entire bus, whose attention was now focused her way. "I couldn't tell them what really happened," she sighed. "I never want to give Woodland or any big-box retailer a reason not to carry your books or host future book signings."

Tailan stepped into the aisle. Delvin could not allow her to face this obstacle alone. Boldly he reached for her hand and squeezed and hoped she would not let go.

She kept their hands clasped as she continued to address the group. "I've put everything on the line for this tour—for you. Some of your own publishing houses weren't all that sure it would work." Tailan took a moment before adding, "Even Nelson's been dragging their feet because it's all about numbers. Our genre—*Black* books—represent only one percent of Nelson's sales."

Murmurs of realization echoed from everyone.

"NEG puts its resources for marketing and promotions to the other ninety-nine percent. This tour can change all of that. My goal—*our* goal," she amended, sweeping a gaze across everyone, "is to make them notice the cold hard facts. And the fact that they can't ignore is that book sales—no matter the race of the author—equal cold hard cash."

A chorus of *Amens* ensued.

Tailan scanned the bus. "So, we all agree. The real story stays between us. Corporate knows what happened here, so we'll let them handle it without blasting it to the media."

"Yes," the whole bus chorused—even The Divas.

Tailan turned to Delvin and smiled. That smile filled him with so much longing, he felt like his heart was bursting. She gave his hand another squeeze, then he lifted it to his lips.

As he did, Delvin peered into the row to their right. Michelle wore a horrified expression that did not seem to fit in with the jovial atmosphere of the bus.

He pulled Tailan down to earshot and whispered, "Check that out."

Tailan turned as Michelle hurriedly put her phone away, ignoring a call that had just come in. Tailan moved over to Michelle's seat and stooped. "Man troubles?" she asked.

Elona shrugged and addressed Michelle, "You might as well tell her."

Michelle passed the phone. Tailan scrolled through the call log. Her mouth sagged.

"Tai," Delvin said, noticing the abrupt change in her demeanor. "Everything all right?"

"It will be," she tossed to him, then turned her attention to Michelle. "What's going on? Margo's called you forty-three times."

Michelle slumped down in the seat. "I'm going to lose my job because I won't spy for her."

Tailan's eyebrow shot up. "Give it to me quick and dirty."

"Since you haven't been following the original schedule, she wants to know every single thing you're doing on the tour. Where you're going next. Any drama. Hell, the woman practically wants me to sneak in your room every night and learn what toothpaste you use." Michelle shook her head. "I couldn't do it. I've been letting the calls bounce to voicemail. Now she's calling me on every number I have—she even left a few messages on my home phone."

Delvin felt a mischievous smile forming on his lips. Tailan's profile was one he remembered. His little firecracker was thinking. Her "give-away"—she was tapping Michelle's phone against her chin. Suddenly Tailan handed Michelle the phone. "Misdirect her."

"Come again?" Michelle said, frowning.

"If she wants to play games, then let's change the rules," Tailan replied. "She's not aware that we're onto her. So, answer the next time she calls."

"I don't want to talk to her," Michelle huffed, her voice edged with anxiety. "I might slip up."

"No, you won't." Tailan smiled, the wheels of cat and mouse playing in her head. "We're on the road. We're on a tour bus—horrible reception, no cell phone towers. As soon as we land back at the hotel, you call *her*. Tell her your phone died, there was no signal anywhere for hours. And you won't lose your job."

"But what about all the Intel she wants me to gather?" Michelle asked, her thin lips pulled into a frown.

"Easy fix." Tailan smiled and caressed the girl's trembling hand. "Going forward, you give her what she asked for—Intel on the places we're going, but only after we've already left. That way, she'll be behind us instead of ahead."

Michelle gulped her concern. "She plans to have you fired when the tour ends."

"With the numbers we brought in?" Tailan gave the woman's hand a reassuring pat. "Margo's selling wolf-tickets. Her father speaks one language—money. If it doesn't make dollars, then it doesn't make sense. And baby, we cashed out today!"

Chapter 11

They were on the bus following a successful beginning on the third day of the tour. Two stores, all sold out, and the authors were getting along famously. Especially since The Vets were keeping The Divas in check. The last store took longer because they had to wait for more stock to arrive.

"And this puts us way behind schedule," Tailan said to her staff with another weary sigh and a quick look at her watch. "We're supposed to stop at Benihana's for lunch on the way to the Marriott reception. Now we don't have time."

"How about pizza?" J. L. piped in.

"Quit eavesdropping."

"Ear hustling," he corrected.

"Whatever," she shot back, giving him the "stink eye." "I can't serve them pizza."

"Why not?" Beverly said, rubbing her flat abdomen. "Our stomachs aren't too ritzy that we can't enjoy some good ol' Italian pie."

"You can say that again," Lutishia chimed in.

Tailan shook her head. "This tour has been classy and I'm going to keep it that way."

"Then put the pizza on some China and keep it moving," J. L. countered. Then before she could rein him in, he stood and yelled out, "Hey peeps!"

Everyone turned to the youngster.

"We're low on minutes. How about some pizza?"

"Pizza sounds great!"

"Sausage and cheese please," several called out.

"Make mine pepperoni."

"Anything but anchovies," J. L. said, wrinkling his nose in disgust. Almost everyone grumbled their consent to that one.

Tailan playfully ruffled the young man's unruly waves as he grinned. "See? Told ya. Italian Fiesta Pizza is the bomb. If it's good enough for Obama, it's good enough for us too."

And then it happened. The age-old arguments about Chicago pizza versus New York pizza started.

Tai shook her head and leaned over to Renee. "Call it in and we'll pick it up on the way to the hotel and eat lunch there. My credit card's on file."

"Eat pizza much?" Delvin teased and she snickered.

Delvin tried to focus on Joyce's book, *Getting Away With Everything*, and realized that he was not "getting away" with putting Tailan's presence out of his mind.

"What did David say to get you here?" she asked him in a voice just above a whisper.

"That you hadn't been the same since our break-up and you needed help," he replied.

"He had no right to tell you that," she said through her teeth, her body tensing again.

Delvin turned her around and locked eyes with hers. "He had *every* right."

Tailan's eyes dropped to his mouth. He could feel her emotions battling for ownership of her actions—give in to her passion or put up her dukes and punch him.

Fight it out apparently had the stronger hold as she blurted, "Since you want to talk, let's talk about the fact that you're under the misguided notion that I *owe* you a second chance."

Delvin froze at her harsh tone, but said, "I was wrong—completely—I'm not ashamed to admit it. I should've believed you and I thought I could change you."

He fought the urge not to traipse into the past, but his mind wouldn't let him hide from the blatant warnings he chose to ignore.

* * *

When they had arrived home on Sunday after their prom night, Delvin's parents knew without them even opening their mouths.

"So, it finally happened," Anna Germaine had said, sounding a little relieved as if she had been expecting it to happen long before now.

Tailan's face turned red. Delvin was quick to announce, "We kept our promise," as he took Tailan's hand. "And honored rule number one—never in the house."

"You are using protection?" Delvin Senior questioned.

"I'm keeping up with that," Tailan piped up instantly. "I don't want children. Ever."

The conviction of her tone gave the small group pause. Especially Delvin.

No children? No little angels conceived and born from our love?

Delvin's mom looked to him, then cast her eyes over to Tailan and said, "Let's hope you'll feel differently once the two of you finish college and get married—in that order of course."

Tailan shook her head and lifted her determined chin. Delvin saw the first hint of her unwavering stubbornness. "After what I've seen, I'd never bring a child into this world. There's too much ugly in people."

"But that's not what you've learned from us—from Delvin," Anna

countered, her concern etched into her classically beautiful features.

"You all are the exception to the rule," she said softly.

"No, Tai," Delvin chimed in. "Your aunt and uncle are the exception. Don't let their warped sense of family taint your interpretation of what a loving family is." He brought her hand to his lips.

His mom sighed and rose to take Tailan into her arms. She pulled back and shared, "Delvin's right and so are you. But," she caressed Tailan's face, a gesture Delvin knew was meant to soothe. "There's real beauty in the world. Maybe if you talk to someone about—"

Tailan pulled away from Anna. She looked to Delvin then again to his mom. "I trust you enough to tell you, and that's only because you insisted, but I never wanted to dirty another person's soul with what I know."

She shook her head and an eerie feeling slithered up his spine.

"I appreciate what you're saying. But my mind is made up. I will never, ever have children."

Delvin felt Anna's eyes on him and turned. They mirrored his. In his mother's deep brown pools he saw only one thing ... heartbreak.

* * *

The brisk walk around the hotel had simmered Delvin's spiked emotions. Tailan was within reach. She was in his world again and he was determined to keep her there.

He headed for the elevator and came up short at the screech of a familiar voice. "You're cheating!"

Delvin edged a little closer to the commotion, making sure not to be seen. "You don't know how to play," Les snapped back. "It's Joker, Joker, Ace, King, and then on down the line. I don't know where you get that mess that the deuce is supposed to kick in before the Ace."

"That's the way it's done," Shannon snapped, shifting in the café chair.

"I don't know where you learned to play cards," Les said to the opposing team. "But in Philly, we don't make up the rules as we go along."

"Amen," Susan agreed.

"You weren't paying attention," Nona said, dealing the next hand.

Les let out a chuckle. "You're just pissed that you got your ass whipped."

Sitting on the sidelines, Brenda, Beverly, Fran, and Joyce—mature women he had termed "the Vets"—all shook their heads before they burst into laughter.

The bawdy laughter from the rest of the group near the table prompted Nona to sass, "It's too much estrogen up in this camp. Where's a man when you need one?"

The Vets' attention snapped to Delvin and all five of them gestured for him to hang back.

"Yeah," Delvin mumbled. "That's my cue. I'm out of here."

And before the Divas could spot him, Delvin gave the Vets an appreciative nod and quickly sidestepped that little show. He dashed inside the elevators just as the doors were closing.

Once inside he could not hold back a little chuckle. This book tour had more surprises and twists than he could keep up with.

Chapter 12

Tailan inched across the lobby as waves of nausea overtook her. She struggled just to stay standing. The trip from Indiana to Chicago after the last two stops of the day was the longest that she could remember in a while. And it wasn't the distance that was the issue.

She slipped over to a quiet corner of the lobby of the Marriott Magnificent Mile and leaned against the wall to get her bearings. Tailan took several long breaths and prayed that whatever was going on with her would pass. She couldn't afford to be sick. There was one more day left on the tour. Just one more day.

Tailan slumped against the wall.

Good Lord! What's wrong with me?

Tailan's gaze locked on Pam, who came to a sudden halt several feet away. Pam scanned the area—first left, then right—before hurrying past, wheeling her travel bag across the green marbles tiles. Then she ran toward the front entrance leading toward the taxi stand.

"Pam, where are you going?" Tailan called out.

Startled, Pam's head snapped to the corner wall of the lobby where Tailan was barely holding ground. Her shoulders slumped in defeat. She grimaced before changing directions and coming to stand in front of Tailan.

"I'm going home," she whispered.

Alarmed that something had transpired that had not been brought to her attention, Tailan moved a few inches from the wall. "Why? What happened?"

Pam shifted her brown-eyed gaze to the entrance. "I live in Chicago. It doesn't make sense for me to stay here."

"What are you worried about? The cost? It doesn't matter; your publisher's paying for it," Tailan shot back.

Pam pursed her lips, then quickly looked out toward the line of taxis stretched out on Rush Street.

Tailan touched Pam's arm, focusing the woman's attention where it should be. "Your publisher *did* pay for your hotel, right?"

Pam was silent for a few moments, her bright white teeth holding her bottom lip prisoner.

"Pam?"

"They only paid airfare to Indiana for me to get to the start of the tour. Ground and hotel have to come out of my own pocket."

"Those cheap mother—" she sighed, catching herself before she let the rest slip out. "Why didn't you tell me?"

Pam shrugged. "You've done enough already."

The NEG team walked into the lobby and acknowledged Pam and Tailan with waves and head nods as they made their way to store some items with the bellman.

"I don't want you separated from the group," Tailan said.

"It's all right," Pam replied, putting a tighter grip on her suitcase handle. "I'll be at the first store on time tomorrow."

Tailan didn't doubt it. But she was angry that a major publisher would require Pam to cover some of her own expenses when another imprint of the same house paid the whole nine yards for one of the other authors. Tailan knew that Pam was already suffering from the loss of her mother and a financial setback as well. She didn't need this.

"Michelle," Tailan said, beckoning the blonde over. "See, if they have another king room available and put Pam in it."

"You don't have to—"

Tailan glanced at Pam, who promptly clamped down on her protest.

Michelle looked from Tailan to Pam and back to Tailan. "Actually, they're booked solid. That's why I had such a hard time getting all of us here. She can have my room."

"I can't let you do that," Pam protested, her round face panicked at the thought.

Michelle waved her off. "I want to go home to my husband for a hot minute anyway. I could use a little … tender loving care. " She handed the key card to Pam and lifted her eyebrows, "Well, maybe not so tender," then went back to the bell desk and grabbed her things. "Hey, I think Margo's figured it out though," she said to Tailan. "The woman hasn't called me at all today." She gave a two-finger salute and was out the door and in a taxi before anyone could say another word.

Tailan reached out and embraced Pam. "We'll reimburse you those ground and hotel costs too."

Pam choked up, then gave Tailan a brief account of all the wonderful things that the people on the tour had done for her. When she was finished she said, "Mama's looking out for me from up there."

"Yes she is," Tailan whispered and at the moment, she felt a pang of sadness because she missed her own mother. "And she'd be so proud of you." She gripped the woman's shoulders and gave her a playful shake. "Now enough of this!" Tailan teased, drying Pam's tears with the sleeve of her aqua silk blouse. "Go on upstairs and get some rest. I expect you to be on your best hustle tomorrow."

"No worries," Pam said, giving her a mock salute. Then her gaze narrowed on Tailan. She placed a hand on her face. "Hey, you don't look so hot."

"I think it was something I ate." Tailan's hand splayed across her belly as the telltale signs of another problem became evident. "I'll be okay," she lied. "Now get going."

"Are you sure?"

Tailan shooed her away.

Pam trudged toward the elevators but looked back at Tailan, who gave her a smile and a thumbs up to keep her moving.

* * *

Delvin snatched open his hotel room door and froze when he saw Nona's barely dressed form on the other side.

"I thought you'd like to have a drink," she purred, holding up a bottle of Tanqueray—something she probably believed he drank by the bucketful since he was their latest spokesperson. He rarely touched the stuff. When he did indulge, it was only for the cameras. He was very careful of the things he put in his body.

Nona stroked her talons across his chest. "And I thought I could properly ... *apologize* for what I said about you the other day."

Giggles echoed down the hall. He would bet dollars to donuts that the doors to several rooms were cracked open, their occupants listening in.

"You just don't get it, do you?" he asked. He plucked her claws from his chest and tossed them to the side. "I stopped dating your kind in high school."

Nona took a step back. "My kind?"

"Sleeps with anything wearing pants and shoe laces," he shot back. "*No* taste whatsoever."

She scowled but slid her eyes all over him. "But I want you. That means I have pretty good taste."

"I'm just a fallback option because I'm convenient," he answered, then leaned on the door jamb. "Question. How many men—besides your husband, that is—have you slept with in the past three months?"

Nona blinked, opened her mouth, then clamped it shut. *She's actually trying to come up with an answer!*

"See?" he said, grinning. "If you have to think about it, it's not a number worth knowing. Have a good night." Before the door closed all the way, he said, "Try Derek."

"He's married to Elona's daughter," she said sourly.

"Oh so you *do* have morals! Then try J. L.," he teased. "He looks like he could use a little schoolin'."

"He turned me down," slipped out before she could cover her mouth and keep it in. The shocked gasps from the adjoining rooms were unmistakable. *Checkmate!*

"Goodnight, Nona," he said, bawling with laughter as he closed the door on her mortified face.

Delvin's cell rang, and he laughed all the way to the bed, silently cheering the youngster for his intelligence. "What's up, Katie?

"Forgive me for chewing in your ear," his agent said. "I didn't think you were going to pick up. How's the tour going, my man?"

Delvin popped open his suitcase and slid out two pairs of slacks. "I didn't realize that books were such a hot commodity."

"Well, put your name on it, and it's going to sell like crazy," Katie said. "Did you get the script that I overnighted to you? That one's going to land you another Oscar."

Delvin glanced at the UPS package on the bed. "I'll check it out in a few."

"I'm getting calls from Gabby's publicity team. They want to do damage control."

"I'm not the one who's damaged," Delvin protested, placing his outfit for the next day in the front of the closet. "I don't want her love life crap to splash on me. Keep me busy until the divorce is done."

"Deal," she replied. There was a lengthy pause before she said, "So come on man, spill it. We could've made a mint on that tour, but as soon as you heard Tailan's name, you went all Black Knight—ready to charge in and save the day."

Delvin laughed, settled in a chair next to the window, then propped his legs up on the suede ottoman. "The minute this divorce is final, I'm doing what I should've done in the first place. I'm currently trying to rebuild the bridge I burned and lay a firm foundation."

"And here I thought you'd be trying to lay something else right about now," she zipped back, and he could imagine her wiggling her penciled eyebrows for comedic effect.

"You know I don't go in for it like that," he replied. "I like long term, stable relationships."

"Come on, Delvin. You have a rep to keep."

He could only shake his head. "Please. Sell that to somebody who doesn't know better. We both know my current reputation was fabricated by your agency."

About a month before he joined the tour, a myriad of billboards were plastered around major cities with him wearing nothing more than a Movado on his wrist, a smile, and some carefully placed shadows to obscure his nether region. They caused such a stir in some metropolitan areas that they were causing traffic accidents and had to be taken down.

"You make more money when women believe you're readily available."

"If only they knew the truth," he said, reaching out to scoop up her package. "I only sleep with women who mean something to me."

"Well, that group definitely doesn't include your wife."

"Soon-to-be-ex wife," Delvin shot back.

"I'll drink to that."

"You'll drink to anything," Delvin chuckled as he flipped to the first page of the script.

"True," Katie admitted. "Which reminds me, I'm out of here. I'm meeting a new client at Solstice for a little libation."

He scanned the page for the description of the lead part. "Anyone I know?"

"You will when I'm done with her," she said proudly. "I put you on the map, didn't I?"

"And oh, the mileage you've racked up." He ended the call and tossed the phone on the bed.

Delvin was glancing over the last part of the intro section of the script when there was a brisk tap at his door. *Tailan?* His heart shot up to his throat. He sprinted to the door and snatched it open. His smile dipped. Pam.

Optimism sank to his toes as he realized this visit could only mean one thing. "Aw, come on, Pam. Not you too!"

"Hold ya nuts, dude," she snapped, frowning up at him. "I don't want 'em."

Delvin didn't know whether to be pleased or insulted. His "nuts" were normally in high demand, as evidenced by the fact that every single one of The Divas and the freakiest member of M-LAS had all made their way down to his door over the past three nights.

He gestured for her to come inside.

"I came to give you a heads up," she said, sweeping a look around the room. "Something's going on with your girl. She wasn't looking so hot."

Delvin swept past her and was down the hall in a matter of seconds.

* * *

Tailan braced herself against the railing as the elevator car pulled upward. She doubled over with pain.

The minute she opened the door to her suite, she made that infamous fifty-yard-dash to the bathroom door. Dinner was making an untimely comeback—in both directions. She hadn't been this sick since the first time she'd laid eyes on the man who had slithered into her life and changed it forever. Her mother, a fierce advocate for police presence within the community to stem the tide of drugs and crime, had finally met her match in a drug lord who had made it his mission to snare a member of the Song family in his web just to prove a point.

"You can't come over here disrespecting my house," Lana Song had snapped when King showed up at their house demanding payment for drugs that Tailan's older brother had taken. "You come here calling us all kinds of MF's and what not." She gestured to the anxious ones behind her. "My children are in here," she said, shaking a fist at the burly man. "Your issue is with him. You're not supposed to be selling that stuff anyway," she warned. "And he's not supposed to be taking it. So don't bring that mess over here anymore. If you gave an addict drugs on credit, that's your fault. You take it up with him—and not with some foolishness that you're going to have my daughter to settle his debt."

King stiffened with anger. "That's his sister," he said, eyeing Tailan as she froze under his lust-filled gaze. His thick lips spread into a sly smile. "I'ma be nice this time, but next time he serves her up, I'm coming to collect, and I'm tapping that ass. I don't give a damn what you say."

Two days later, Tai and Lana Song hurried to enroll their daughter into an out-of-state summer camp for gifted children. Then Lana called in the police to arrest King so that the family would be safe. The boys in blue had failed miserably, dragging their feet before taking her as seriously as they should. By the time the complaint was heard and her parents were set to testify at King's indictment, Tailan's addict brother was found floating in the Chicago River. Her mother, Lana, was raped, tortured, then killed. Her father was shot by one of King's minions when he had tried to protect his wife from the men's brutality. Her brothers, San and Lang were killed in their beds while they slept.

Tailan had left for the camp with a nearly perfect family life behind her. She came home to mayhem, and the abandonment by her father's family had left her practically alone.

Worst of all, King was still searching for Tailan because she also could testify against him. When his people finally located Tailan on the west side at her new home with Uncle Lin and Aunt Trish, instead of protecting her, Uncle Lin entertained a horrible request causing the two men to form an unholy alliance that extended far beyond just the initial demand for Uncle Lin to turn Tailan over to King.

Tailan had barely escaped the fate of her family, but then what had happened in that house was nearly a fate worse than death.

* * *

A few minutes later, as Tailan tried to wash her hands and face, and rinse her mouth with a stinging antiseptic, a relentless banging came from her door.

"Go away!" she screamed

"Let me in, Tai!" Delvin yelled, banging once again.

"Go away!" Tailan shrieked, with a sudden need to grip her midriff.

"Woman, if you don't open this door right now, I'll break it down!"

Tailan staggered toward the door. She gripped the handle, feeling overheated and clammy. The smooth metal almost slipped from her hand when she tried to use it to brace herself. "Delvin, now is not a good time."

He ignored her and pushed his way in. Her stomach churned as they faced off.

Between their heated glares he said, "Pam said you're not feeling well."

"Pam needs to mind her own business." She looked over his shoulder to give the woman in question the evil eye, who had the nerve to give it right back.

Delvin's gaze swept over her, and he frowned when she doubled over. He balanced her weak frame with his own, saying to Pam, "I've got this. Close the door."

Pam didn't need to be asked twice.

"I don't need you here," Tailan whispered. "I can take care of myself." As if to prove her point, she made a dash to the bathroom and actually made it in time.

Delvin opened the door several minutes later.

"Please leave," she begged him.

"Not when you're like this," he whispered.

"You want to help me out?" she asked, connecting with his gaze in the mirror. "Get me some ginger ale and crackers. And some Lysol while you're at it."

Delvin grinned at her reflection. "I'm not leaving you. I can call room service for that."

"This time of night? That'll take forever," Tailan countered.

"7-Eleven's right across the street. Get moving!"

Delvin hesitated for a second longer. "Where's the key?"

"I'll let you in."

"Then we'll wait on room service."

She glared at him. He glared right back.

"On top of the television," she finally conceded and sank against the bathroom wall.

Chapter 13

Delvin moved with purpose to the convenience store. In short order, he had all of the items Tailan needed and was standing at the check-out when his eyes snagged on a familiar treat that made him smile.

"Will that be all, sir?" the cashier asked.

"I'll take two of these," Delvin replied, placing the items on the counter.

Delvin weaved his body through oncoming traffic to return to the hotel. Memories of Tailan's first days at his home came to mind—days when he had done everything in his power to make her feel safe from whatever it was that haunted her dreams. He never took for granted that she would be there in the morning.

Each day he would ask her to stay until the next day, and it pleased him when she trusted him a little more—and soon he didn't have to say anything.

* * *

Germaine Residence - November 17

Delvin was on a makeshift pallet spread out on the carpet in his bedroom. Tailan was stretched out in his bed. They had talked for hours until she had finally fallen off to sleep. The nightmares were less frequent, but she still slept better if he was in the room. Deep inside, that made him feel good. She was beginning to trust him even more, and that was no small thing. A sudden noise down the hall made him jump up. His parents were back. They weren't supposed to arrive until tomorrow!

"Delvin, sweetheart …" Anna Germaine's voice had trailed off as she froze at the threshold and stared openly at the young girl in his bed. Soon his father, Delvin Senior, was by her side. He too, frowned.

"What's going on here?" his father bellowed.

Tailan jerked up, pulled the blanket to her chin, and cast a frightened look at Delvin.

"I had a friend stay overnight," Delvin said in a low voice. "That's all."

His mother's gaze narrowed on Tailan, who quickly looked at Delvin for reassurance.

"Who is she?" Anna demanded. Her creamy skin flushed a bright red as she moved further into his room, her nostrils flaring as she tried to subtly sniff out a lie.

"A classmate."

Anna's eagle-eyed gaze swept the room and landed on his pallet. She let out a visible sigh of relief. "We need to call her parents."

Panic rolled off of Tailan in waves. He held out his hand to keep her in place. "She doesn't have any parents."

"Rubbish," Anna snapped, her slender hand dismissing that notion with a flourish. "Everyone has parents."

"My parents were killed."

Only then did his mother become contrite; her eyes softened, and her hands lowered to her side as she leaned against his desk. "Oh, I'm sorry to hear that. So who were you staying with?" An arched eyebrow shot up. "I mean, before you came here."

"My aunt and uncle."

"Then you'll need to go back to them," she said simply, gesturing to the clothes that were folded on Delvin's chair. "Get dressed, and we'll take you."

Tailan scrambled off the bed and hurried to gather up her things. "I'm not going back there. I'm *never* going back there," she said as she locked a steely gaze with his mother. Then she crammed her meager belongings into one of his duffle bags. "I'll leave."

Her voice softened as she looked at him and said, "I'm sorry, Delvin. Thank you for everything. Really. Thank you so much."

Delvin's heart melted at her gratitude. She never took anything for granted—not the meals they prepared together, not the clothes he gave her to wear. She appreciated every kind gesture. This was the Tailan he knew—vulnerable but strong.

Anna stepped closer to Tailan. "We can't drop you out on the streets by yourself. We'll call DCFS, and they'll find you a place to live."

"Right," Tailan said sourly. "A group or foster home where the same thing can happen."

"Same thing?" Anna turned to Delvin for some sort of explanation.

"My uncle and aunt wanted me to pay for my living," Tailan offered. When Anna's expression showed she didn't understand how that was a bad thing, Tailan added, "On my back." She ignored Anna's shocked gasp and continued packing. "That's all right. I'll be fine."

Delvin Senior's eyes narrowed on the items in her hand. "How long have you been here? Really?"

"Three months," Delvin replied. He didn't lie to his parents, and he wouldn't start now.

"My God!" Anna splayed her hand over her bosom. "How could we not have known?"

"Because we were careful," Delvin answered, facing them head on. "She needed a place to live. Something to eat. I made sure she was all right."

Anna's bottom jaw dropped. "Three whole months in this bedroom together? Did you—"

"Oh, no. Never," Tailan immediately chimed in. "Delvin hasn't touched me. He's been the nicest person I've ever met." She timidly moved in front of Anna. "Please don't punish him for helping me."

The various emotions Delvin was feeling battled for supremacy within him. His parents' silent condemnation tugged at his mind. But his promise to protect Tailan was gaining traction. So many others had let her down. He couldn't do the same.

He grabbed some clothes and stuffed them into a bag he yanked from the closet.

"What are you doing?" Anna asked, moving closer to him.

"Mom, I can't let Tai go out there alone. If she's leaving, I am too," he said. "I brought her here to keep her safe. I'm not going to stop protecting her just because you say she can't stay here."

"Delvin, you can't go with me." Tailan reached out a hand and stilled his movements. "You have parents who love you." She glanced over to the Germaines, then lowered her voice. "The love they have for you is evident everywhere in this house." Tears surfaced, and she blinked them back. "It's in the photos over the fireplace. It's in the artwork on the walls. Every room in this house makes people want to stay. There are people who would kill to be in this kind of family." She shook her head. "Don't leave that. Don't give that up for me." She stepped back and placed a few t-shirts inside. "Besides, I was doing fine before you came along."

"You were starving," he snapped. Then he turned to his parents. "I found her sleeping on the floor in one of the classrooms at school."

"It won't be like that again," she whispered, keeping her back to them to try to hide the flush in her cheeks.

Delvin turned from his parents, took her by the shoulders, and shifted her so they were face to face. "Where will you go? Tell me that."

Tailan tried to pull away. His grip tightened. "I don't know. But I'll see you in school every day," she said, nodding. "Trust me. I'm getting my education. Then I won't be anybody's problem anymore."

Delvin pulled her into an embrace. No matter what she said, he couldn't let her walk away. He stepped back and again turned to his parents, facing them like the man they had raised. "If she leaves, I'm with her." He took Tailan's hand in his. "We'll make it on our own."

His parents' expressions changed from shock to concern to raw fear. Anna dropped down on the bed, her hands folded into her lap. Delvin Senior joined her. They mumbled and sighed and mumbled some more.

After a rapid-fire debate between them, Anna said, "The two of you have given me a major headache."

Delvin squeezed Tailan's hand. He wanted to smile. If Mom had a headache, things were looking up.

"Tai, we will allow you to stay. But Delvin's father and I will lay down all the ground rules going forward. Is that clear?"

"Yes, Ma'am," Tailan whispered, with a gentle squeeze from Delvin's hand.

"We have three for right now, then we'll discuss more as the need arises."

"Yes, Ma'am."

"Rule number one—no sex in this house. Ever," Anna ordered with a pointed look at Tailan and Delvin.

They both nodded.

"Rule number two," Delvin Senior added, "Tai you will now reside in the guest bedroom. Gather up your things from Delvin's room."

Delvin opened his mouth to protest, knowing that Tailan couldn't sleep well without him nearby. She squeezed his hand, signaling him into silence.

They again nodded.

"You will have chores, homework, and such going forward, and we expect to see your grades from school."

"Yes, Ma'am." Tailan cried. Delvin gave her a hug to settle her nerves. His parents shared a speaking glance, but he smiled at them, letting them know that they wouldn't have reason to worry.

Anna Germaine was at Tailan's side, placing a gentle hand on her shoulder as she asked, "Are you all right?"

Tailan tried, but failed at a smile. "No, but I will be." She scanned the older woman's face and said, "I swear to you we never did anything like that. It's the only reason I feel safe here."

Their gazes locked for what seemed an eternity, and there was some unspoken message between his mother and Tailan that Delvin couldn't decipher.

Anna whispered, "I'm glad to know that I raised that kind of son."

To which Tailan nodded emphatically.

"Finally," Delvin Senior said once she stopped crying. "We'll still have to deal with the legal issues involving your family regarding your custody. But we'll handle that when the time comes."

"I promise I won't be any trouble," Tailan said, with a look to both of the adults.

And for a while Tailan Song became part of the Germaine family.

Safe, but only for a little while. Because trouble found them.

* * *

Tailan was still in the bathroom when Delvin returned from the convenience store. She looked worse, which caused him to flip through his memory banks to try to figure out what was going on. "What are you allergic to?"

She moaned and shook her head. "Nothing that I ate tonight."

Delvin helped her out of the bathroom and over to the bed. "What *did* you eat?"

Tailan rattled off her menu selections, and Delvin did a mental rundown of the ingredients he knew would be used in those meals. "And you're sure you're not allergic to any of that?"

"Positive," she moaned. "Oh, my head."

Delvin dialed the restaurant and spoke with the manager, who, in turn, spoke to the chef. After a brief investigation, they discovered that an "ambitious" new student added one other ingredient to the meal—tasso.

Delvin covered the mouthpiece with his hand. "Tai, you still stay away from pork, right?"

"Never touch it. I told the restaurant that, and also that Nona and Les were allergic to shellfish."

"There's the culprit," he mumbled. "Sir," he said to the manager, "the woman who had the private party tonight is having a serious problem since she doesn't eat pork. And that was something she told you all ahead of time."

"We're so sorry about that," the manager said quickly. "We'll reimburse her for her dinner."

"They'd better do better than that!" she shrieked when Delvin repeated the man's words. "I'm practically dying up here."

Delvin grinned at her dramatics. "You might want to reconsider. She's been out of commission for the past hour."

Tai shouted, "Three!"

Delvin's head snapped to her. "Three?! Baby, you need to go to the hospital," he said, suddenly realizing that all the color had drained from her face.

"We'll wipe out the entire party's bill," the manager added. "And send her a certificate for a romantic dinner on us."

Delvin repeated it to Tailan, who said, "Well that's more like it."

He ended the call, removed his tie and jacket, then took a seat on the sofa.

Tailan glared at him, then spread-eagle on the bed as though she was fallen timber. She lay there silently while he warred with the urge to take her into his arms. Good thing he hesitated. A few minutes later she made a beeline for the bathroom again.

"I'm taking you to the hospital," he said from the other side of the door.

"No!" she cried. "I can't go to the hospital. I have a book tour to run."

When things were silent too long, Delvin invited himself in. He found Tailan clutching the towel racks for balance as she attempted to reach the taps on the other side of the tub.

"Aw, baby."

"What are you doing?" Tailan gasped when he stepped through the door.

"The obvious. Trying to get so fresh and so clean."

She frowned first, then a cute giggle bubbled forth at his reference to the Outkast song.

Delvin reached into the tub to lend assistance. "I don't see how you can laugh at a time like this," he said.

"Sometimes laughter's all a woman has to hold onto."

Tailan's tone brought him up short. Delvin put his arms around her waist and tried to lift her from the tub. "Let me get you out of there."

She shook her head. "I need a shower, Delvin," she pleaded. "But I can't keep my balance."

"Baby, it's okay really."

"I feel ... soiled ... please," she whispered.

He had heard those few words uttered often enough when she had first arrived at his parents' home. At one point his father made a teasing reference to the amount of water that Tailan used on a daily basis. Never lazy, Tailan went out and got a job the very next day. While at the dinner table two weeks later, she slid her first paycheck to Delvin's dad and announced proudly, "This is for my portion of the water bill."

His father never mentioned showers, baths, or water bills ever again.

Delvin planted an understanding kiss on her head. He rose and made quick history of his clothes. When he got to his boxers, Tailan gasped, "What the hell are you doing?!"

He stepped in behind her and used his body as her anchor. "I'm helping you, my love. Let me."

"I didn't mean for you to get in here with me," she grumbled.

"There was no way to do this without getting wet," he said, pressing his body close to hers. "Trust me, I won't touch anything that doesn't need touching."

She looked up at him as he held her close.

"I promise," he reassured her.

Delvin lathered her body, relishing the feel of her against him. The moment he lowered his hand to her belly, she relaxed. She allowed him to take care of her the way he had so long ago when touches were gentle, warm, and welcoming—introducing her to the softness that a man had to offer. Delvin became immersed in the soothing comfort of the moment.

He kissed her shoulder, then turned off the water, wrapped a thick thirsty towel around his hips and eased her out of the shower. In a quick, practiced, efficient manner, Delvin had Tailan dried, her body oiled and scented, then covered in a nightshirt in less than twenty minutes.

Delvin settled Tailan on the bed and presented the ginger ale and the saltines. He handed her a book and put up his hand in warning. "Before you try to throw your weight around and act all tough and toss me out, let me make a few things clear to you."

The saltines slipped from her hand as she stared up at him.

"One, I'm not leaving you alone tonight. That's the reason I handed you a book. That should keep you occupied so you can ignore me. Two, you really should let your team run the tour tomorrow—"

Tailan parted her lips to protest, but he held up a hand.

"But I know you'd die before you'd let that happen." Then he leveled an intense gaze her way. "But if I see any signs that you're going down for the count, I'm pulling your ass out and taking you to the hospital."

She opened her mouth, but he held up a finger and she clamped down.

"Three, Pam told me not to wear you out making love to you all night, so I'll take a rain check for another time."

Tailan gasped at his gall and tossed a pillow at him to show exactly how she felt.

He caught it, then tucked her in before planting a kiss on her forehead.

"Delvin?"

He paused, looking down on her.

"Thank you."

"It's my pleasure," he whispered, draping the blanket over her. "Go to sleep, baby."

Chapter 14

MARRIOTT MAGNIFICENT MILE—TAILAN'S SUITE
11:03 P.M.

Tailan couldn't sleep. So much had unraveled her day. On the other hand, so much was so very right. The tour's momentum. Delvin's steady, unshakable support. The worrisome Divas finally acting like they had some sense and getting in the game instead of constantly bitching about it.

Whew. Delvin Germaine was back in her life. Could she handle it? Growing up together, they had always made an unstoppable team. And even though right now he was an enigma to her, he still understood her, understood exactly what she was going for without even knowing the whole game plan.

They were always in sync with one another. It had started way back when they were still in high school. Tailan was good at English and history. Delvin was great in math and science. They helped each other, encouraged each other to succeed. So it was no surprise that C.V.S. made an exception, allowing them to be co-valedictorians because their GPAs had only one one-hundredth of a point between them.

Tailan shivered as she realized that accomplishment would've been a pipe dream if she had remained with her Aunt Trish and Uncle Lin. She pulled the covers up to her chin when her mind conjured up that outrageous confrontation that occurred when her living arrangement with the Germaines was challenged by her aunt and uncle.

* * *

An intercom crackled to life while Tailan was attending Mr. Richardson's English class. She was to report to the principal's office right away. When she walked into the anteroom leading to the main office, she discovered that Aunt Trish and Uncle Lin had charged into C.V.S. and demanded that she be turned over to them. Fear slammed into her. Knowing that she had been staying with the Germaines, the principal called them in. Seeing that he might need help controlling Uncle Lin, he also called the police.

But the paperwork her newfound guardians carried didn't silence Uncle Lin and Aunt Trish. "You belong with your family, girl. I don't care what papers these uppity folks say they got," Aunt Trish threatened.

"I'll never go back home with you and him," Tailan said, trying to rein in her anger.

"Officer," Mrs. Germaine chimed in, "we have legal papers granting us temporary guardianship of Tailan."

The muscular police officer reviewed the documents carefully.

"As you can see," Mrs. Germaine continued, "everything's in order."

"It also says that there's a court hearing on this matter next week," the officer said, scanning the page.

Mrs. Germaine and Tailan nodded.

The officer turned to Aunt Trish and Uncle Lin. "She's right. All of their paperwork is in order. I suggest you take this up in court and not here at the school." He gestured to the door. "I'll escort you off the premises."

Uncle Lin pierced Tailan and the Germaines with an ugly glare. He snatched Trish by the arm and said just before storming off, "We'll be there. Y'all ain't gonna get away wit' kidnappin' our family."

During the hearing the following week, Uncle Lin and Aunt Trish spread lie after lie after lie about Tailan. She was ungrateful. She was lazy. She never listened and was nothing but trouble.

"Your honor," Aunt Trish squeaked, "I've tried to do my best by the girl. She's a real handful, sir."

"Then it shouldn't be an issue that she doesn't live with you anymore," Anna Germaine said. Her husband nudged her into silence.

Tailan didn't care what her aunt was saying. She kept her eyes glued to the judge. His honor looked bored out of his mind, but Tailan's life was on the line, and if this man held her future in the balance, she had to put the real story before him.

Tailan trembled as she stood.

"Your honor, they're not telling the truth." Tailan's voice echoed loudly in the courtroom, causing her aunt and uncle to finally fall silent and glare at her. She stared boldly at her kin folks, then narrowed a gaze at her aunt. "Tell the judge why it was safer for me to sleep on the streets than to stay in your house." When Trish remained silent, Tailan continued. "I can't live in a house where my aunt was going to allow my uncle—her own brother—to rape me."

Gasps and murmurs of dissent rippled through the courtroom.

Aunt Trish's eyes bucked wide when the entire courtroom—bailiffs, clerks, attorneys—focused intently on the two people standing before the judge.

"I wasn't gonna let him do nothin' to her." Trish looked at the judge timidly, then lowered her gaze to the carpet.

When the judge didn't respond, "She's a liar!" Aunt Trish screeched, under the scrutiny of every member of the court personnel. "She'll say anything just so she can live with those uppity ass—"

Tailan's laughter stopped Trish cold. "Then let me refresh your memory," Tailan shot back. "The night I escaped, you and Uncle Lin were talking in the kitchen. I. Heard. Everything."

Uncle Lin and Aunt Trish flinched, sharing an anxious gaze between them.

The chorus of voices grew louder, causing the judge to bang his gavel for silence.

"Mr. and Mrs. Germaine, Ms. Song, I'd like to have a word with you in my chambers."

Delvin's eyes had closed for a moment, but his hand snaked out to grasp Tailan's, providing a silent bit of courage that was sorely needed.

"He should come too," Tailan said and the judge beckoned for Delvin to come along.

Once inside, the judge gestured to the chairs in front of his desk and took a seat across from them. "Those are very dangerous accusations, young lady," the judge warned, his bushy eyebrow shooting up to his thin hairline.

"But it's true," Tailan said, then related the entire events which transpired that night.

The judge's jaw went slack as Tailan continued. "And my aunt was no better. When she heard what King would pay to have sex with me, she told Uncle Lin that they could get even more money from someone else if I was still a virgin."

"Holy Mother of God," Anna Germaine gasped, mirroring the sounds from the majority of the courtroom earlier.

"Strangers have shown me more kindness than my own family." So many emotions were bubbling up in Tailan, she was afraid she was going to break down. But she wouldn't allow them to win. Like her mother, she would be brave enough to bring these monsters into the light for all to see.

"Your honor," she said over to the judge, never taking her hands from Delvin's. "My uncle gets off on preying on little girls ..." her voice broke on the next set of words she needed to say. "Really gets off on them being blood kin." She tamped down on her nausea when her mother's beautiful face swam into her mind. "He's already gone to jail once for raping my mother. My mother was a little girl the first time he touched her, and I'm sure my aunt out there was underage the first time too." She gripped Delvin's hand tightly. "Unlike my aunt, my mother spoke up. She wasn't afraid to tell the truth about that monster. And now, neither am I. Aunt Trish has lived with him all her life. And now there are children in that house. And those children have had children," she said, swallowing her fear and revulsion at the ugly truth she was trying to convey. "They aren't safe either."

Anna came to Tailan's side and said, "Your honor, are you going to look into these allegations? A conversation with the children and DNA will provide the court with all the evidence that's needed."

* * *

They returned to the courtroom and Tailan slid a disgusted glance at Uncle Lin's frozen features. He could spin a tale until his lips fell off, but once the court had the truth …

Trish yanked free of the security guard's hold and charged Tailan, bringing her fist up to punch her.

Anna Germaine caught Trish's strike midway. "Oh no you don't, you pathetic human being!" She pushed Trish back into the bailiff's grasp. "We *uppity* people don't do that. We consider it and your kind of trash uncivilized." Anna gave Trish such a look of disgust that Tailan felt it all the way to her soul. "This is what happens when women put a man before the children they're supposed to protect."

"But they his," Trish protested, not realizing the ramifications of those words. "He took care of all of 'em. They got food. They got clothes. They got a roof!!"

"And you let them pay the cost with their bodies," Anna snarled. "How disgusting!"

"Lady, you don't even know me," Trish yelled.

"Oh yes, I most certainly do," Anna Germaine shot back, stepping toward her. "I was raised by a woman like you," she spat, crossing those few feet between them. "So don't tell me I don't know you. *You* don't know yourself. You didn't have to do that to your children. You didn't have to do this to yourself!"

"You believe her?!" she said, a hand grasping her heart.

"Her nightmares tell the story. The fact that she doesn't trust anyone—" She flickered a gaze to Delvin, and added, "Well, *almost* anyone, speaks to a child who has seen more than any child has a right to see."

The judge motioned for a raven-haired woman to approach the bench. "Get someone over to that house right away. I want a child psychologist assigned to every minor child, along with a reliable social worker to interview them separately. Then set each of them up for DNA tests."

"But what about her," Anna Germaine said, gesturing to Trish, whose tears streamed freely down her face.

The judge grimaced and gave her a sad look. "From the sounds of things, Mrs. Germaine, she's also a victim. There are procedures we have to follow. For now, we'll need to protect all of them—her included— from him. I'm doing that by taking him into custody just on everyone's unsubstantiated statements, and setting a high bail. And that's stretching what I'm truly able to do."

The judge called for a recess.

"Why didn't you tell us?" Anna asked as she joined Tailan on the bench.

"Ms. Anna," Tailan turned tearful eyes to her. "I was too afraid. I'm such a coward."

"What?"

Tailan turned a tear-filled gaze to Anna. "Those children didn't have a voice. I ran away to save myself, and I abandoned them. I was only there a week, but I knew something was wrong. I didn't see it, but I could feel their pain and sadness. They were always terrified when he came near them." She balled her hands into fists. "The night I heard my uncle and aunt talking, it clicked. And I left them in that house with those animals. I could've gone to the police. I could've done more, but I was so scared they would find me." She held a trembling hand to her breast. "I was only thinking of myself. I didn't want to think about what they'd done." She dropped her head into her hands and finally cried for those children—her own cousins, her mother—and the sexual abuse they had suffered at the hands of one man.

Anna wiped the tears with her thumb.

"They couldn't speak," Tailan whispered. "Today I had to be their voice. I should've done something sooner so someone could protect them. I feel so bad."

Delvin stepped forward, but his mother shooed him away.

Tailan froze, suddenly ashamed by the comfort she didn't deserve. "I don't need your pity."

"And you won't get it," Anna countered. "Starting today, I'm going to treat you like the daughter you've become."

"But I wasn't raped," she whined.

"That doesn't mean that the trauma wasn't just as real," Anna said, cupping Tailan's face in her hands. "Instinct propelled you out the door that night. You've been dealing with the emotional fall-out of that decision ever since you came to us."

She wrapped her arms around Tailan, who visibly stiffened at first. Moments later, Tailan laid her head on the swell of Anna's bosom and nearly passed out with relief.

"I'm still so scared sometimes."

"They'll never get anywhere near you. If it makes you feel better, we'll put you in a self-defense class."

Tailan took the tissue Anna offered. "Yes ma'am. I'd like that."

When Anna pulled away, Delvin quickly stepped in and brought her into his arms and held her. "I won't let anything happen to you."

Chapter 15

Tailan shivered at the memories of what had happened in that house.

"Delvin, are you still up?" she whispered, gripping the edge of the hotel blanket, trying to keep her sadness at bay.

"Yep," he answered. She could hear the weariness in his tone. "What's wrong, baby?"

"I can't sleep."

He sat up, looking in her direction. "You want me to get you something?"

"No, but I ... I just need—"

Delvin moved from the sofa and was in the bed in a matter of seconds, pulling the covers around them as he held her in his arms. "Is that better?"

"Yes, thank you."

She held onto him, shivering from a chill that went all the way down to her soul.

"Are you cold, baby?"

"A little," she lied, reluctant to tell him that shadows of guilt surrounding what Uncle Lin had done to punish those who turned on him were more prevalent than ever. King bailed Uncle Lin out of jail after the court session where the judge put in the order for an investigation into abuse and neglect of Aunt Trish's children and grandchildren. The two of them waited until late that night, barricaded the doors and windows, then set fire to the house on the west side that contained all of his damning secrets. That night Aunt Trish, his children, and the children he spawned from them, perished in that fire in his attempt to leave no evidence of what he had done.

The day that Tailan found out about her relatives' fates, she packed to leave the Germaine's. Her uncle was going to come for her next, and she didn't want the family who loved her to feel his wrath.

"What are you doing? "Anna Germaine asked from the threshold of Tailan's bedroom.

"I'm not putting Delvin's family in jeopardy," she replied, stuffing a few pieces of clothes in a suitcase.

"*Your* family."

Tailan's head whipped to Anna. "What?!"

"*Your* family. You said *Delvin's* family," Anna replied gently, but her eyes were intense. "We're your family too. And it's time you stopped making decisions as an individual and realized that we're on your side."

"But I—"

"But nothing, young lady!" she said, snatching the suitcase from Tailan's hand and tossing it aside. "We're a unit! We. And don't you forget it."

Tailan stared at her for several moments. "Yes ma'am."

"Now it's time that you stop acting like you're in this alone."

Tailan sank to the edge of the bed and mumbled, "Yes ma'am."

Anna took the space next to her and pulled her into an embrace.

Only a few days later did the search through the rubble of that house turn up Uncle Lin's body. He was unable to escape the blaze himself, as he stood nearby to lay sight to his handiwork. King was arrested as the culprit and was serving time in jail for the murders of all the people who were inside that burning building.

* * *

"I'm proud of what you've done on this tour," Delvin said, lacing his hands in her hair.

"Really?" She looked up at him.

"I don't think many people could've outsmarted those men the way you did."

She smiled, and her focus shifted from unsavory memories to the moonlit sky and the calmness in his voice. "We sold more books at that one store than the other eleven combined. Those authors had some serious backbone. I couldn't have done it without them."

"And what did you say to the weave sisters?" Delvin gave her a comforting squeeze.

Tailan laughed. "They're not all wearing weaves. One of them has locs."

"Even those are a little suspect," he said dryly.

"Delvin!" She swatted his chest.

He chuckled at her playful punch. "When they came off the bus, it was like they were totally different women."

"That's who they really are," she said in their defense. "All the rest of it is an act. They probably feel they can't represent the genre if they're not coming out all hard, like they're ride-or-die chicks. Rappers do it all the time. Then they get busted when their fans find out it's all a big lie."

"But The Divas met their match when they came up against The Vets."

Tailan couldn't help but chuckle.

"I still can see them slinking to their new seats," he said. "That right there was priceless. I don't think I've laughed so hard in my life. The Vets shut them all the way down. Hey," he said, peering down at her, "do you think Beverly really had a switchblade up there?"

"Yep," Tailan answered. "Brenda? No. But Beverly—I think she might also be packing a .22 special."

Delvin busted up laughing.

"And Les? She's straight Philly, so it's all fists and a verbal takedown. Joyce carries a mini-taser."

"Seriously?"

Tailan grinned at his expression. "It's why we couldn't fly her in. Mama don't take no mess." She shifted so she was nestled into his body like a second skin. "Delvin, how did you end up here? I mean as an author."

"I had an idea for a book, and my agent pitched it to a publisher," he replied, stroking a hand over the swell of her buttocks. "They put me with two of the best writers in the industry—a husband and wife team who were both national bestselling authors. And I'm hoping that a studio will want to make it into a movie."

"So you can star in it?"

"I definitely want to be involved in some way." His hand lowered to rest on her thighs. "I saw the book as just another vehicle to keep me on the screen, but to the authors on this tour, writing books is so much more. They live to write." His hands stroked across the roundness of her bottom, causing a small shiver of pleasure to run through her. "Why did you go into this line of work?" Delvin continued.

"When the first job I wanted was taken by someone else ..." she began dryly.

"Tai, you were smart," he countered, his hands pausing on their way down her thighs. "Way more intelligent than you gave yourself credit for."

"All I wanted was to be with you. *That's* what would've made me happy."

Delvin angled her body so that they were eye to eye. "Being a housewife would've bored you to tears."

"Is that what made Gabrielle so appealing?" she asked, unable to keep the bitterness from her voice. "She had dreams and I didn't?"

"You know it had nothing to do with that." For a moment he was silent, and she knew he was weighing his next words carefully. "I wanted you to trust me, Tai. Trust me enough to believe in what we—*we*—would have accomplished together. A family." He sighed, as though trying to rein in his own frustrations. "I did what I had to do to keep you safe. I kept my promise, Tai. Why couldn't you believe in me … in *us*?"

Tailan was silent behind that admission. The pain of his voice ripped through her heart. Even now, trust was so hard for her, and it was impacting almost every relationship in her life.

"That summer I spent hiding out at school, I spent most of my time in the library," she redirected. "I read about new worlds and people. Books were my friends." She looked up, giving him a small smile. "Until you showed up. You know, I still love orange cupcakes."

"I actually found some across the street," he confessed. "Planned to eat them for breakfast. I bought you some too."

"You did?" A gleeful smile split her face before she could pull it back.

"I figured you'd feel better this morning."

She nodded. "When I see them, it brings it all back. The good things." Tailan splayed a hand across his chest. "I'm sorry, Delvin. You were right. I should have trusted you, and I'm so very sorry."

Delvin kissed her then—a warm, tender kiss that exploded into a world of need and passion that had been long muted.

She forced herself to pull away. "Sometimes I wonder what would've happened if you hadn't come into the classroom that day."

"Let's be grateful you never had to find out."

Chapter 16

Delvin was no one's fool. More than anyone, he knew Tailan was vulnerable at the moment. She was a lousy sick person and cranky to a fault when she didn't feel well. But they needed to clear the air between them—needed to deal with the elephant in the room.

Having her in his arms resting peacefully would only stave off the inevitable. Tailan could play possum like nobody's business, but he knew she'd been awake for a while. He'd spent too many warm nights with her cradled in his arms. No way he could miss the change in her breathing and the gentle rise and fall of her breasts that signaled that she was awake.

Delvin feigned slumber as she covertly slipped out of bed. He listened to her morning ritual in the bathroom. The luxurious shower and dry-off. The breakneck pace of her slipping into something professional and stylish. Delvin glanced over to the alarm clock on the nightstand. Right about now Tailan was sprinkling her beautiful face with a hint of make-up and lip coloring.

Right on cue, she opened the bathroom door and hurried to the dresser mirror to put on her earrings.

Delvin slid from the bed and embraced her from behind. "Good morning, love."

She shrugged him off and replied, "Morning."

His eyes narrowed on her. "Baby?"

Tailan didn't look up as she slipped on a necklace. "Yes."

"We need to talk."

She paused for a moment, then snapped a bracelet onto her wrist. "'The Talk' will have to wait," Tailan responded. "I don't have the time. My life—this tour—"

"Make time," Delvin fired back.

Tailan turned from their reflection and stared coldly at him. "I won't be dictated to, Delvin."

He crossed his arms over his chest, giving that ugly eye better than she ever had. "Answer one question for me."

Her stance was pure defiance.

"Do you forgive me?"

Tailan's lids dipped so low that her eyes almost appeared closed. She fumbled with her watch—a nervous habit that gave Delvin hope.

"Most definitely," she answered.

"And do you still love me?"

Her head tilted. "That's two questions." Tailan moved past him, but he caught her by the arms.

"Answer it."

"Yes!" she shouted and broke away from him. Tailan straightened her clothes—another sign Delvin recognized. She was buying time to think. "But I can't act on that love right now."

Her answer made him somewhat relieved. "Now we're getting somewhere."

Delvin walked to the sofa and gathered up his clothes. He could feel her watching his every move, and it stirred a heated wave inside him. If he didn't act now, there might not be a later. "If I don't push you to talk to me ..."

"You mean any more than you already have?" Tailan countered.

He chuckled and approached her. "I just feel that if I don't, I could lose you again."

She moved out of his reach, causing him no small amount of frustration.

"We're going to deal with this right now," he snapped. "I don't care if you respond or not but you sure as hell are going to listen, *Tailan Song*."

The use of her full name did the trick. Her entire body went into battle mode.

"I worked my ass off for us!" he said. "Everything I did was for *you* and me."

The tension and anger was coming off her in blasts. He stepped closer, letting his size crowd her. "None of it mattered without you—not the fame, the money. The victories felt hollow, unfinished, without you there."

After a few spells, her shoulders relaxed. "Gabrielle was never with you on all of those red carpets," she whispered.

"Why would she be?" he bit out. "She hadn't earned the right to be there—*you* did."

Tailan turned from him, and Delvin seized on the weakness. His voice softened. "*We* were together every night, sharing our dreams. When this acting thing landed in my lap and I was hesitant, it was you who encouraged me to go for it—not her—never her. She wasn't even part of the equation."

His lips caressed the curve of her ear, and Tailan trembled at the contact.

"If it wasn't going to be you by my side, then it wasn't going to be anyone."

Her minuscule nod filled Delvin with optimism. She eased away from him and over to the window. He joined her as they took in the

Chicago skyline and traffic rushing along Michigan Avenue.

"I'm so confused right now," she whispered.

"Then talk to me, Tai." Delvin had to push her to the breaking point. He saw no other way to get her to open up and let him in. When she didn't say anything right away, he said, "All right, let's go there."

"You know I wasn't serious when I said have a child by someone else," she snapped, her chest heaving with indignation.

That's right, baby, get it out!

"I know that now," he admitted as he tried—unsuccessfully—to pull her closer. "But you could've been a little clearer."

"By the time we revisited the issue, Gabrielle was already pregnant!" She inched further away from him. "She knew the deal."

"And unfortunately, so did her grimy family," Delvin growled.

Tailan paced before him, then moved from the window. "What are you talking about?"

"Here's the quick and dirty," Delvin started. "Gabrielle's mother learned of the arrangement and put in her two cents. Soon the whole family had added a dime, a nickel, quarter, and a fifty cent piece. Suddenly their *precious starlet* felt *duped* about entering into the contract when we both know she signed it faster than a New York minute because she wanted the money to advance her career."

Gabrielle became unhinged after she drilled her claws into Delvin's influence, money, and notoriety. She went over the cliff with her ridiculous demands, her drama queen antics, and outrageous publicity stunts.

Her family had burrowed in deep as well. Gabrielle's mother literally ran shotgun over Delvin's entire household. By the time his daughter, Ariel, was born, the only place of peace was in the carriage house he'd had built where he spent his time alone or with Jason and Ariel.

Only five months ago did Delvin finally see a splash of sunlight in his otherwise dreary existence. Gabrielle fell in love with Paulo, a Brazilian artist. Their torrid affair was a blessing from above and the perfect vehicle to escape his farce of a marriage. He didn't have all the details, but he knew this much: Paulo demanded he and Gabrielle marry, but wanted no part of all of her excess baggage—i.e. two kids and a thirsty extended family. The minute it became convenient for Gabrielle not to have a husband or children in tow, Delvin was on the horn with his attorney, his publicist, and his agent. Their assignment was to get him divorced, get him permanent custody of his children, and spread the word of the amicable split.

Delvin saw the end of his long-suffering turn on its head until Paulo flipped the script again. Somewhere along the way, Paulo, unlike Delvin, had figured out that Gabrielle and her dysfunctional kinfolk were matching bookends. The man dumped her in a live interview on international television.

"I understand why you got hitched," Tailan reasoned, snatching him away from the unpleasant memories. "What I don't get is why you stayed after your daughter was born."

Delvin massaged his temples and took a seat on the arm of the sofa. He felt Tailan follow. "Ariel had medical issues soon after she was born. Before her first birthday, she had a tumor removed from her brain. The surgery went well, but there was a major complication."

Tailan's cell rang, but she let the call go to voicemail, she leaned against the wall, waiting.

"When Ariel came out of her coma ..." he whispered, the images of that day floating in his mind. "When she opened her eyes, the only person she recognized ... was me."

Delvin smiled, and Tai's expression softened.

"I couldn't leave my little girl," he said. "Blood tie or no, I couldn't leave her because she needed me. And I sure as hell wasn't about to leave her to Gabrielle's maternal care."

Tailan cringed.

"I told Gabrielle that I'd take custody of both children so she could focus on her career."

"She must've felt like she'd hit the trifecta after that announcement," Tailan cracked.

Delvin shook his head. "On the contrary. Once again she played lowdown and dirty. Gabrielle bragged quite often that making me as miserable as possible was her new career. And if I tried to leave her, she'd make it so I never saw the baby again."

Tailan gasped, "That skank!"

"Yep, and a whole lot of other adjectives I could use," he agreed.

"After all you did for her, for her son?"

"Tai, you don't know the half of it when it comes to Jason. If not for me and my love for that kid, Jason would most likely be in a mental ward."

"What?!" she screeched.

Delvin nodded. "I learned how Jason found out about his mother. He was under the care of a family member who let it slip who his real mother was. He found Gabrielle that day she showed up with him at our house." Delvin paced the area in front of the sofa. "I later learned that Gabrielle had paid a doctor to misdiagnosis Jason with a mental illness. She kept the boy pumped full of drugs. I snapped. It was the only time that Gabrielle got a real taste of exactly how I felt about her. She backed off and literally left the boy and our daughter in my care. She didn't give a damn about either one of them." Delvin watched Tailan's reaction intensely. His next words would hurt. "I couldn't leave my kids, Tai. Not for you—not for anyone."

She turned from him then, concealing the tears rising in her eyes.

"That's why keeping Ariel and Jason with me became my first priority," he confessed. "Your words always echoed in my head." Her head snapped his way. "Monsters are real, you used to always say. That truth compelled me to keep my children with me as much as possible. I accepted parts in movies that took me across the country or the globe, but they were always with me. My stomach would twist into knots at the idea of ever leaving them with strangers for too long."

"What about Gabrielle?" Tailan asked. "Didn't she want to pimp them for publicity?"

"I put my foot down about that," he replied, his anger fueling him. "Over time she cared less and less, so long as the rest of our lives remained the same."

"Why didn't you just keep them overseas?"

Delvin stretched out his hand and waited. After a moment she accepted it, and he slid down the arm of the sofa beside her. "Jason's not my biological son. At first, Gabrielle refused to let me legally adopt him—another way to ensure I remained miserable. Then when Paulo laid down his demands, she couldn't get rid of me and the kids fast enough. She agreed, in front of the judge, that I could have full custody. But now that he's dumped her …"

"I so despise that woman," Tailan mumbled.

"Get in line." Delvin brought his arm around her shoulders and pulled her closer. "I love my children, Tai. Jason is as much mine as Ariel."

"I understand," she whispered.

He followed her gaze to the clock on the nightstand.

"We can't be late," she said. "Get showered and dressed. We have to get moving. The tour waits for no one."

Tailan stood from the sofa, and Delvin grabbed her hand. "Tai?"

"Yes."

"I'm not giving up this time."

She gave him a small, bitter smile that didn't sit too well with him. "You didn't have to marry her."

"You know what Gabrielle threatened to do," he said finally. "You have said for years that people are ugly. So, would you have wanted the death of my child on our hands?"

Tailan was silent for a long while until finally she whispered, "No."

He stared at her. The tears threatened to spill down her cheeks, and he realized that her pain ran deeper than anything he could fix in four days.

Delvin went to her, held her for as long as he dared, then gathered his things in his hands. He aimed in the direction of the door but headed back to place that package of orange cupcakes in her hands before leaving her to ponder all he had said.

Chapter 17

SOUL EXPRESS TOUR – DAY 4
WOODLAND IN EVERGREEN PARK

Tailan stood at the front of the tour bus, smiling as David stepped out of the limo and climbed on. "Everything's squared away on my end," he said. "I've been watching the news. Woman, you've been, as Pam says in her blog, kicking ass and taking names."

"The authors are putting in the work, but ..." Tailan's focus shifted to the woman with ivory skin, dark curly hair, and owl-rimmed glasses who stepped onto the bus directly behind David. She gave Tailan a wide smile

"I'm Sabrina Adrian, and I'll be joining the tour for the last day," she said to Tailan. "They want me to do a write-up in *Publishers Weekly*."

At the mention of the premiere literary magazine, all of the occupants on the bus became pin-drop quiet; just dropped-the-pregnancy-bomb quiet.

Tailan lifted an eyebrow as she pinned a steely gaze on David.

He pointed a finger upward, signaling that this idea came from up top.

"We're thrilled to have you," Tailan proclaimed, extending her hand. *Margo, I'm going to snatch you bald-headed the next time I see you.*

"Why don't you have a seat back there with the staff?" she continued, while thinking *away from my problem children.*

The petite woman moved forward, giving a few smiles along the way. Sabrina stopped like a child playing one-two-three-red light when her gaze snagged on Les. "That vampire article I did on you got so many responses."

"Thank you," Les said, giving the woman a warm smile that disappeared the second Sabrina moved on.

She continued along, practically beaming as she spotted a familiar red-haired, cinnamon-skinned woman. "And Brenda, the release of your 100th book was the talk of the staff."

"Glad to hear it," Brenda coyly answered, her Southern manners coming through.

"If you don't mind," Sabrina said, gushing at the leery Vets. "I'll sit up here with them."

After four days with The Vets, Tailan could practically read their thoughts. The Vets' expressions were nothing short of *strained* tolerance.

Tailan made a circling motion with her index finger, signaling the driver to get moving. Once the bus pulled into traffic, she sat in the back and whispered to her staff, "Man, talk about having to be on your best behavior in front of mixed company."

"Mixed company?" Terry asked, confusion painting her delicate features. "But we're white, too," she said, gesturing to herself and Tailan's boss.

"Yes," David acknowledged. "But we're considered honorary Black folks. We *earned* our hood cards years ago."

Terry's pink tinted lips pulled into a frown as she scratched her head. "I don't think I know how to take that."

"It's a compliment," J. L. chimed in, tearing his gaze away from his iPad. He looked at Terry. "You're considered family. That chick," he nodded toward their new guest, "is not."

"Do we have a problem?" Terry echoed the whole team's internal thoughts.

"Yep," J. L. answered with a pointed look at Tailan. Then he nodded toward The Divas. "Especially since those four were tipping the bottle at breakfast like eighty-proof was oatmeal. All of 'em are juiced off that top shelf. No telling what they might say—in *mixed company*." A shadow of sadness lit in his eyes as he added, "My father's an alcoholic. Trust me, anytime brown liquor is on the table like that velvet purple bag, 'Cardi Black or Remi and José , even the best of people act real stupid. Ask me how I know …"

The sadness in his voice touched Tailan's heart, and she reached out to place a hand on his shoulder. His wan smile was tinged with a pain she knew all too well. He nodded toward The Divas as if to say, "Thanks, but handle your business."

Tailan was out of her seat and hovering over The Vets in two seconds. She placed a hand on Beverly's shoulder. The minute Sabrina's focus fell on the notepad in her hand, Tailan's eyes ping ponged to each Vet, to The Divas, then back to The Vets. Each Vet gave a wink or slight nod, conveying that they understood their new mission.

She wanted to kiss each of them because they would be working double duty—keeping Sabrina moderately entertained while covertly keeping The Divas under firm control.

On her way back to sit next to Delvin, J. L. gave her a thumbs up and said, "You know, I could use a summer job at Nelson, since I'm practically a member of the team already."

Tailan's eyebrow floated up to her forehead. "Isn't it past your bedtime?"

"Not that again," he grumbled and slumped down in the seat.

Everyone around them broke into laughter.

* * *

Tailan had to call upon every angel and ancestor she had in her spiritual rolodex not to explode when she followed the general manager to the back of the Woodland's store where the authors had been stashed.

Stashed being the operative word.

"Seriously?" she snapped. "Is this the program we're on right now?"

She whipped around to Pinky, the sleek-haired manager. "The lawn and garden section?!"

Pinky didn't bother to hide her embarrassment. "It's the best we can do."

Tailan scanned the solemn faces of the authors and boiled.

Brenda was nestled between the fertilizer and shovels. Beverly pushed a heavy palm tree leaf out of her face, only to have it spring back and nearly take her eye out.

Her people were being treated like afterthoughts. This setup had Margo's fingerprints all over it.

"Nobody's going to know we're back here!" Tailan snapped. "We're supposed to be up front, right where customers walk in."

Pinky shrugged and said, "I'm sorry, but you're going to have to deal with it." Then she zipped up the aisle, putting as much distance between Tailan's anger and herself as possible.

Sabrina stood by, alternating between scribbling on her notepad and looking at Tailan as Nona scrambled from behind the table with her crew following fast on her heels.

"So what's the move, boss lady?" Nona asked in a surprisingly businesslike manner. "What are we gonna do?"

The fact that the woman said, "we" and not "you" was telling. Evidently the liquor hadn't dulled her senses, and she was still in the teamwork frame of mind.

"No Ma'am," Shannon said. "This one's on us. Come on, y'all, let's roll out." Shannon squared her shoulders, puffed up her chest, and moved with laser intent. Like a battle cry only The Divas heard, Nona followed suit, with Traci and Channel bringing up the rear. They were at the front of the store and out the door before Tailan realized that she should try to catch them.

She feared those four would not be returning until the problem was handled properly. It was their definition of "properly" that had her the most worried. *Like eighty-proof was oatmeal.*

A headache was kicking its way up the side of Tailan's head, and she desperately needed it to go sit down somewhere.

Sabrina gave Tailan a rueful smile, then took off in the direction of the four divas.

Delvin edged over to her, watching the foursome's retreating backs. "Another glitch?"

"You could say that," she mumbled, keeping her focus on the entrance to the store.

"Are you mad at me or something?" he asked.

"No, not mad … just busy."

"So what are you saying?" he asked in a low tone.

Tailan looked over to him. This was not the time—not the place. She had so much riding on this tour that spared feelings were a luxury she couldn't afford. She kept her eyes glued to the store entrance but eased away from the majority of the group.

"Delvin, it's clear you want me back. But I'm not available. I'm with someone. And it's serious. I've tried to be understanding, but you won't listen."

He had her pinned to the end display in less than a second. "Evidently, he's not handling his business, or you're not handling yours. Tell me honestly that you didn't want to make love last night."

"No," she squeaked.

"Woman, don't play games with me!" he ground out.

Nona saved her from Delvin's interrogation when she suddenly appeared with her friends in tow. Tailan broke free from Delvin and looked down the aisle to the crowd steadily growing behind The Divas.

Even Sabrina was sprinting.

"Good Lord, what have they done?" Tailan whispered.

"The store people said y'all had left," a woman panted, out of breath as she tried to keep up with Nona.

"They told us y'all didn't make it," another woman added as she halted at the table. "I was almost out of the parking lot."

A growing crowd spread out in front of the tables, and the sales were on!

"We set 'em straight," Nona said, with a proud lift of her chin and a glare at Pinky. "Everything's cool."

Well spank my ass and call me Sally. By George, The Divas are growing up!

Pinky's face had flushed angry red. Her eyes were even worse, glazed over with shock. Tailan was too afraid to ask what the foursome had said to the woman.

Instead, she looked at Nona and said, "Thank you, ladies. Let's get to work."

"Tai, we're not done," Delvin said as she tried to walk away.

"Oh, yes we are. Very done!"

Shannon whipped around right before making it to her spot. She was at Tailan's side in a Chicago second, her expression both hopeful and predatory. "You're putting his fine self back on the market?"

"I never took him off," Tailan answered, retrieving the novel one of Delvin's adoring fans held out and thrusting it into his hands. She could feel his angry glare heating up her back as she hurried toward Pinky and Sabrina to do some damage control.

* * *

Delvin was a tight ball of anxiety. The hairs on the back of his neck rose as the signing event concluded and Tailan was nowhere to be found.

It was customary for her to always call the group together to congratulate them on another job well done. Not this time. She had hugged and whispered something to each member of the tour while they were inside the store. All except him. Now her staff was conducting the exit meeting and giving each of the authors a parting gift from NEG.

Something was all the way off.

Delvin shot over to Terry. "Where is she?" he barked.

She jumped without taking her eyes from the itinerary she held. "Where is who?"

"Tai. Where is she?"

Terry shrugged guiltily. "She went to check on some things."

Delvin waited a moment and noticed something. Not a single member of the staff would look his way. "When is she coming back?" he demanded.

Several ticks of time passed before Elona finally confessed, "She's not. She went home."

"Come again?" Delvin asked. "Home?"

The limo driver cleared his throat, which caused Delvin's attention to snap to him. He was waiting patiently next to the Black SUV, ready to whisk Delvin off to the airport. Delvin had planned to make a detour with Tailan to see his folks. It had been years since they had laid eyes on her.

He pinned his gaze squarely on David while addressing Tailan's staff. "I understand."

David exhaled a long, slow breath, then clicked the keys on his cell. Instantly, Delvin's phone vibrated. He looked down, then up at David.

"Tai's home address," David confessed to the shocked gasps of the rest of the Nelson team.

Delvin broke for his limo driver. The man read the address and replied, "That's about twenty minutes from here."

"Good. Then let's step on it."

The driver hurried to open the back door. "But I thought you had a plane to catch."

"My man, I've got a *woman* to catch."

Chapter 18

Tailan opened the front door to her North Pullman row house and used the remote to disengage the alarm, then froze when she saw a lone figure lounging on the sofa.

The man was holding the wedding ring she had taken off and tossed at him before she left for the book tour. She had ignored his calls all week. Tailan had told him they needed a break and she didn't want to see him for at least two weeks. So his presence here could represent one of two things—neither one of them pleasant.

She wheeled her suitcase and positioned it in front of a chair near the door.

"Why are you here?" she demanded.

"Delvin Germaine," Amir bit out. His caustic tone gave Tailan pause.

"What about him?" she asked, wondering how the name of the man who had driven her into Amir's arms in the first place was now dripping from his lips.

He stared openly at her. He was silent, but his light brown eyes spoke volumes. He was handsome, his olive complexion and thick, dark hair was Bollywood perfect—so perfect, in fact, that many East Indian woman were insulted that he would choose her over women from his own culture.

"He was on the tour," she said, using her foot to close the door behind her.

"And you knew this and did not tell me?"

"I didn't know anything about it," she replied. "My boss brought him on board." Inwardly, she was ticked. Tailan had demanded a temporary seperation from Amir because of the things his family put her through. But they'd mistreated her for the last time. She had endured it for years had finally had enough. She'd given him an ultimatum, but he hadn't been man enough to balance the scales. So she gave him a wake-up call. And now he was grilling her about something that wasn't within her control.

"Did you sleep with him?"

Images of lying in Delvin's arms flashed in her mind, but thankfully she'd had enough self-control to not fall for him again—at least not totally. Not in body. But her heart and mind …

"No." She took a seat on the edge of the sofa and faced him. "But that's something I want to talk with you about."

Amir tore his gaze from the ring he held and looked over at her, his shoulders tense with the anticipation of bad news.

"I would like to take Delvin on as my lover."

Amir was on his feet and in her face in seconds. "I forbid you to sleep with him," he said through his teeth. He was shaking with rage.

She stood so she was toe-to-toe with him.

"Forbid?" she echoed, her hands slowly riding up on her hip. "I'm a grown woman. And I didn't *forbid* you to be with Laura, Sheila, Joan, or Willow."

"But they," he said, waggling a finger at her, "were within the terms of our agreement. We agreed that we would only develop intimate relationships with married people."

"He *is* married," she shot back.

"Ah, but he is not in the polyamorous community, and you know it!" he shouted. "Stop playing games."

"Wait a minute!" she said, circling him. "You only said that our lovers had to be *married*. You didn't say they had to practice polyamory as we do. *That* I have in writing."

"It was implied," Amir snapped, his eyes practically shooting daggers in her directions.

"Peddle that bull somewhere else," Tailan snapped back and got in his face. "*Implications* are not *stipulations*."

Amir ran his fingers through his silky hair. He stormed the length of the living room and into the dining room, then braced himself on the kitchen cabinet for several moments before inching back to the living room and standing directly in front of Tailan. "He will take you from me."

Strong odds on that one, slipped into her mind before she could rein it in.

Delvin had made his intentions crystal clear from day one. And when he was set on something, nothing short of the Apocalypse would keep him from it. Because of that, she knew she had to sneak away while he was still engaged with his fans.

Amir walked away again, as though he took her silence for assent. This time he made it as far as the dining room before he turned back around to her. "He did not deserve you. He never deserved your tears," Amir reminded her. "You were so heartbroken. Where. Was. He?" His voice broke on those three words. "I was the one to make it all better."

"You did," she said. She did not finish that sentence with what was in her head—*for a time*. "And that's why I agreed to the new terms of our marriage in the first place. Terms you have put into practice numerous times, while I never have." She didn't take her eyes off him as she admitted, "This is my time."

"I did not want them," he confessed. "I wanted you. All of you! I wanted you to take notice that I needed you!" He implored, thumping a hand to his chest. "I wanted you to finally let go of him and love me," he whispered, "the same way that I love you." He took her hand in his. "Even you admit that you weren't all there for me."

"I was honest with you from the beginning," she said, causing Amir to pull away. "That's why I agreed that you could take lovers. I always hoped that you would find a woman to love you the way you needed to be loved."

"You refused to let anyone with any true feelings come in," he protested, his normally sultry voice at a slightly higher pitch. "Where was he when you were so low that you … you could have died. Where. Was. He? Where—"

Tailan stopped him with an icy glare, but he was not cowed.

"Now you want to go back to the same man who threw you away because you wouldn't give him what he wanted?"

Tailan tried to formulate a response, but Amir was ripping a Band-Aid off a wound that had never quite healed. And he was right, but she had played a part in things too. Delvin had expertly brought that point home during the tour.

"I accepted the limited amount of love you have for me," Amir said, lacing his fingers in her hair. "It has not been enough, but I am still here because I know what unconditional love is."

Tailan buried her head in the wall of his chest. His arms went around her, and he held her close. "I love you, Tailan. One day you will heal from his hurt so you can see that." After a while, Amir cupped her face in his hands. "Only then will you finally be the wife that I need."

"Amir, we're not even addressing the real issues with our marriage."

He grimaced, then lowered his hands to his sides.

"Once again, I made the mistake of choosing a man who puts the need for family over me. So if we're calling it square—I'll never be enough for you either."

Chapter 19

Delvin stood outside Tailan's door. His hand hung in the air, halted on its path to the dark green door. He was in shock.

Poly—what?

Had he heard that right? Not only was Tailan with someone else, she was *married* to that someone else. And the man had taken other lovers *with her permission*?!

Surging with anger he was trying hard to contain, Delvin tapped his knuckles against the door. From what he had just heard, their marriage was in a precarious state, and he was going to exploit the hell out of that.

Moments later, the door was yanked open by a tawny man with a muscular build, thick dark hair, and tawny, but rugged features. His eyes burned a hole through Delvin.

"Ah, the real source of our marital problems has arrived," the man spat, but it wasn't hard to place the thickly accented English as Middle Eastern or East Indian. "Followed you home like a stray dog."

"What kind of bullshit marriage are you in?" Delvin roared at Tailan as he swept past her husband into the living room. "You're committed to him, but he gets to sleep with whoever he wants?

"How do you know that?"

"How the hell do you think I know?!" he snapped. "Your door is paper thin. And it's not like y'all were whispering—I listened and heard every-damn-thing."

Amir closed the door and pressed his back against it.

The rising color in Tailan's cheeks advertised an overwhelming embarrassment. She cleared her throat and said, "Only married women." Her hand shot up to keep Amir from coming closer and she continued, "He can only sleep with married women."

"Whatever," Delvin barked, circling a finger to encompass her and the husband. "Is this your life? Really? A man who doesn't put you first?"

"We are in a polyamorous marriage. It's allowed," Tailan clarified.

Delvin let the words shift like puzzle pieces in his head. "Polyamorous? Isn't that just a five-dollar word for swingers?"

"Polyamorous people are married couples who have multiple *long-term relationships* with others," she said, giving him a pointed look. "Swingers are just about sex. Different vibe. Different purpose. But either way, everything's done with permission. Our kind of marriage keeps the primary family together, while allowing the adults to be fulfilled in other ways. But there are boundaries and rules."

Delvin scratched his head. "So this is why you wouldn't let—"

"Delvin, please don't make things worse for me."

He purposely ignored her plea and turned to her husband. "This is going to take a minute. You don't mind if I have a seat, do you?" Without waiting for Amir to answer, Delvin planted himself on the sofa and rested his elbows on his knees. He surveyed the space and was disheartened by what he saw.

The place was tidy and organized, but the furniture was simple, almost sparse. A modest dining set with four multi-colored chairs in the small dining room took up almost the entire room.

Delvin's heart did a flying leap out of his chest and to the carpet. He had been living in the lap of luxury while Tailan was evidently living from paycheck to paycheck. The staircase led upward to what he could only assume was a dollhouse-sized bedroom. Outside, there was just enough grass to roll around twice before hitting the wrought iron fence. That should have been his first tip-off to Tailan's station in life. She loved gardens and lots of space—so this home was totally out of character. Evidently, hubby wasn't bringing home enough bacon to make a single layer sandwich.

"Why is he here?" Amir thundered.

"Isn't it obvious?" Delvin answered in Tailan's stead. "She's allowed to be with other men."

Tailan gasped, and her eyes bulged as that statement confirmed that yes—he *had* heard everything.

Delvin winked to Tailan before turning his conversation back to the husband. "*Married men* to be more precise." He flashed his award-winning smile. "Since you're being all *open* and honest about everything, I'll just tell you straight up ..." his smile widened at the Indian man, who looked like he was ready to jump down his throat. "I. Want. Your. Wife."

If silence was a percussion blast, then everyone's ears would've been bleeding.

"Out of the question!" Amir growled.

Tailan locked an intense gaze on Delvin as she asked her husband, "Why? I've never asked to be with anyone. Not once!"

"Yes, I know," Amir conceded. His eyes became glazed and predatory. "But I sense you want this man only because you have already slept with him. And that is most definitely against our agreement."

"I have not—"

"I saw you!" Amir bellowed.

"Excuse me?" Delvin jumped in.

"It was all over the television!" Amir shouted, shaking a fist at Delvin. "My brother called me, told me to turn it on. They played it more than once." His gaze shifted to Tailan. "You were kissing him in public, shaming me in front of my family."

"Correction," Delvin said grinning. "She didn't kiss me; I kissed her."

"Semantics!" Amir snapped. "She had lips. You had lips. And they were both in the same place at the same time." Amir trained his gaze on Tailan. "Did. You. Sleep. With. Him?!"

Delvin just couldn't resist. "She sure did!" he offered. "All night long. And it was off the freaking meter." He slid a sly wink to Tailan before saying to her husband, "Our girl snores a little. Did you know that?"

"Delvin!" Tailan shrieked, and he faked like he was buttoning his lips. Her frantic gaze snapped over to her husband. "I did not sleep with him in the biblical sense."

Amir stiffened with anger. "What the hell is *that* supposed to mean?"

Delvin leaned back in the sofa, yawned, and gave Amir a sly smile that spoke volumes.

"We didn't make love, have sex, or have *any* physical relations. Does that spell it out for you?" Tailan pulled in a deep breath, trying to regain her composure. She added, "I came home to discuss this with you first because our agreement stipulates that we inform the other party when we intend to bring another partner in." She went to her husband, placed a manicured hand on his chest. "I want this man in my life. I want a relationship with him. I want your blessing, just as I've given you mine. All. Four. Times."

"Damn, player," Delvin smirked. "You've been getting it in." He sat up and added with a taunting shimmie, "Turnabout is fair play. So let's all play together."

The vein at Amir's temple throbbed. "Anyone but him."

"You don't get to choose," Tailan quickly reminded.

Her phone rang, and she jammed her hand into her pocket. Glancing down, she said, "I have to take this."

"But we're not done!' Amir growled.

For once, Delvin agreed with her husband.

"It's my boss. You know, the person who signs the checks that help us keep a roof over our heads since your family still has you in the penalty box."

Oh, that's cold.

She slipped the earpiece in and said, "Hey, David. Now's not a good time. And why the hell did you give Delvin my address?" Tailan faced the two men in her living room. "He showed up at my house, David. My husband was home."

"Yes," she barked. "I'm married."

Delvin could just imagine the look on David's face.

"You know I'm very private. My marriage is not ... the usual kind, so I don't mention it."

Delvin let out a low, throaty chuckle that snatched Tailan's attention from her call. Again he buttoned his lips.

"Yes, I heard you the first time," she groaned, giving Delvin a hostile glance. "Does the word polyamorous mean anything to you? Then Google it."

You know, that's not a bad idea.

Delvin whipped out his cell and hit the internet to do a little more research on their marriage—and to give himself a lot more ammunition.

"Once you look it up, you'll have a better understanding why I don't talk about it," she said. "People get the wrong idea and see me as untrustworthy because they think I'm on the hunt."

Delvin lifted his head from his phone and caught Tailan's attention. He showed her his phone and mouthed, *Great idea.*

She gave him a squinted evil eye that should've stopped his heart. His ears picked up the tail end of her conversation with David. "Now I have both my husband and my ex squaring off in my living room, and it's all your fault."

Tailan rubbed her temples. "What did you call me for anyway?" Her entire body snapped to attention. "Retiring? Oh, so *nooooow* that you've wreaked havoc in my personal life, you're out the door?" She listened for a moment, then said sourly, "I have to go." Tailan ended the call and to no one in particular said, "David is leaving Nelson. I've been promoted to his position."

"That's awesome," Delvin said, getting up to congratulate her with a hug. "I've seen you in action, baby. You're great at what you do."

Amir stepped into the fray. "Tailan, if you love me, you will respect my wishes."

She moved away from Delvin and faced her husband. "Amir, if you love me as much as you proclaim, you'll allow me this experience."

Delvin spooned his chest to her back, signaling to Amir he was not going away.

All parties remained silent when Tailan calmly added, "You were the one who suggested we have this fluid marriage. Now you want to put restrictions on it because I want to take advantage of what it has to offer. That's beneath you, and you know it!" Her head tilted. "That's not the real issue, is it?" she whispered. "We both know what's tearing us apart."

"I want you to leave our home," Amir directed at Delvin. "We no longer require your presence. I need to speak with my wife. Alone."

Delvin looked to Tailan. "Tai?"

"For me, Delvin, please leave," she pleaded softly. "Amir and I need to clear the air. I'll call you later."

"Promise?" He nuzzled her ear. Amir's eyes shot daggers in Delvin's direction.

Tailan released a long, slow breath, her shoulders finally relaxing as she whispered, "I promise."

Delvin walked to the door, snatched it open and was nearly run over by a pint-sized, golden-skinned child barreling into the house with an olive-skinned child right behind her. "Mama! Papa!" they screamed. The girls ran towards Tailan and Amir as a horn tooted three times, signaling a goodbye from whoever dropped them off.

Everything stopped for Delvin—his lungs, his heart, his brain, and the blood flowing in his veins.

Delvin snapped around and bellowed, "You wouldn't give *me* children, yet you had them for *him*?!"

One child froze a few feet away from Tailan and slowly turned back to Delvin as if noticing for the first time that there was a stranger in the house. She looked up at him, seemingly frightened by the outburst. But then her lips split into a smile so wide that his heart did a little backflip.

Terror streaked across Tailan's face. She rushed to collect the girl, but it was too late.

"Daddy?" the child said in an ecstatic whisper. "You finally came for me! You came!"

In a split second, Delvin's gaze swept across the child, assessing the features that were a perfect blend of his and Tailan's. His nose, her almond-shaped eyes, his lips, Tailan's dark silky hair and honey cream coloring.

This breathtaking little being was *his* daughter—*his*!

The other little girl was now in Amir's arms, watching Delvin intently. The resemblance between those two was obvious.

Delvin's eyes widened as his daughter inched toward him as though in a trance. He lowered to his haunches so they were at eye level. He stroked a finger across her smooth skin before taking her into his arms. The emotions tearing through him collided. Anger, rage, shock, wonder, and the one gaining ground on all the others—pure love.

Minutes passed before Delvin looked over his shoulder at a scowling Amir and a panic-stricken Tailan.

Offering a deceptive calmness that he in no way felt, he looked at his child as he gently said to the grownups, "That leaving thing? That's *definitely* off the table now." He smiled, but it in no way mirrored what he truly felt. "Looks like I'm not going anywhere anytime soon."

Chapter 20

Delvin held his little girl like he would never see her again. He cast a condemning glare at Tailan. His heart was pounding in his ears. This wonderful little angel was his, and he never even knew she existed.

"You hated me so much that you'd keep my child from me?" he asked.

"Neena, Devi, go upstairs for a moment," Tailan directed to the children.

"Mommy," Devi whined, wrapping her arms tighter about Delvin's neck.

He returned the warm gesture before setting her down on the natural hardwood floor. "Go on. Do as your mama says." The child's face flashed with fright and he quickly added, "I promise," he shot a hard look to the other adults in the room before redirecting to the little girl, "I'll still be here when you come back down."

Her relieved smiled kicked him right in the gut.

She nodded, then ran to Amir and tugged at Neena's hand, causing Amir to put her down. They scrambled up the stairs, and soon steps overhead signaled they were in a bedroom.

Delvin closed his eyes, trying to calm his raw emotions. He lifted his lids to Tailan. "Devi?"

Tailan nodded. "It means *goddess of power*."

He lifted his head in the direction of the pitter patter of footfall above them. While taking in the beautiful sound, Tailan blurted, "You made your choice." Delvin snapped his head in her direction as she continued. "I wasn't going to complicate your life. That's not who I am. You already had a deal with the devil, and she destroyed us with that pregnancy card she played." She lowered her gaze to the hardwood floor. "I'm not her, never will be. I did what I thought was best for me and my child."

"Did you think having Devi grow up without her father was best?" Delvin snapped back and charged forward.

"Better than having a father who could be taken away on a whim. You know that wench had you on lock," Tailan tossed back.

Delvin came up short at the mention of those bitter but true words.

"I want to take her to see my mother," he insisted.

Amir waved off the idea. "Absolutely not!"

"Mama's not well, Tai," Delvin said. "She needs to see her grandchild. Can you at least give me that opportunity?"

"You cannot take our daughter anywhere." Amir pushed between the two of them.

"*My* daughter," Delvin corrected with a pointed look at Tailan.

Tailan shot a look to Delvin, then her husband. She eased out of their reach. "Amir, she needs this, especially with the way your family treats her lately. I have to allow them time together."

"But why now?" Amir asked. "He does not live here. He might take her away."

Tailan's eyebrow shot up. "Delvin is a lot of things. But the one thing he is not is stupid. I'll be with her."

Delvin nearly smiled, recognizing that hubby was treading on choppy waters.

"Are you crazy?" Amir asked, gripping her shoulders and turning her to face him.

Delvin readied to yank the guy back when Tailan lifted her hand in warning. "I'm doing what's best for my daughter," she emphasized.

Amir's hands tightened. "Best would mean doing as your husband asks."

Tailan pushed his hands off, saying, "Anna Germaine is my family too. We're going." She turned from him and called to the girls.

Devi hurried down the stairs and into Delvin's waiting arms. Lightning quick, he picked her up.

"Come on, baby." Tailan extended her hand to Neena.

"She cannot go with you," Amir commanded, blocking his daughter's way.

Delvin knew enough about feuding parents to know this was about to get ugly. He stretched out his hand to Neena, and she scrambled out from behind her father and came to him. He picked her up in his other arm, then he stepped back to give the adults a bit of space as Tailan faced off with Amir.

"Don't you *ever* tell me what I can or cannot do with my children," she snarled. "I'm not separating my daughters."

"She's not—"

"Stop right there!" Tailan jabbed him in the chest with her finger. Her tone sent chills down Delvin's spine. Dear Lord, Tailan was a whirlwind of fierce protective instincts, and he wanted to fall to his knees and worship her.

Tailan crowded Amir and whispered through gritted teeth, "If you were about to fix your mouth to say Neena's not mine, I swear, I'll walk out that door and never look back."

She flipped him a look filled with rage. "I've raised that child since she was one month old. She. Is. *My*. Daughter! *Mine!*"

"Well, I could say the same about Devi."

Tailan lowered her voice to steady herself. "I will not treat your daughter in the same callous manner your family treats me and Devi. If you can't understand that, then there's more wrong with our marriage than either one of us can fix."

Amir withered under her hard glare but managed to say, "You come home tonight. With my daughters. That is fair to ask, is it not?"

She turned from him, then picked up her purse before saying, "I'll be in this house," she opened the door. "In your bed, since that's what concerns you the most." She took Neena from Delvin's arms and made tracks to the front door.

Amir caught up to them and said to Delvin. "I've had to fight you in her memories for the past seven years. I don't relish having to fight your physical presence."

"There won't be a fight," Delvin replied, halting in his efforts to follow Tailan. "Tai's a grown woman who can make her own choices." He gave Amir a suggestive smile as he watched her approach the limo, and the driver opened the door. "You just might not like what she chooses."

"True," Amir said, giving him a sly smile in return. "But since she is my wife, neither will you."

Chapter 21

During the ride over to the southwest area of Chicago, the girls bounced from one side of the limo to the other, counting the cars that were painted with their favorite colors. Their excitement eased some of the rising tension between Tailan and Delvin.

However, as the newness of the scenery out the window wore off and the girls settled down, Tailan noticed the vein throbbing at Delvin's temple. He was champing at the bit for a showdown. But she had to give him credit. The man had handled learning about his daughter better than she ever dreamed.

When Devi had realized one day that Amir's family treated her differently than they treated Neena, Tailan had told Devi who her biological father was. Showed her pictures and videos that had been stashed away. She did this in spite of Amir's wishes. She also told her daughter that Delvin loved her, and that he was traveling the country and the world. At the time, that was enough for Devi, but Tailan always knew there would come a time when she would demand to see Delvin.

Then, Tailan would be forced to deal with choices that were made in what she thought was in the best interest of peace.

Neena crawled into Tailan's lap, and Devi squirmed into Delvin's, and before they reached the next exit ramp, both of them were out cold. As their even breathing filled the enclosed space, Delvin said, "She's so beautiful." He looked lovingly at Neena. "They both are."

"Thank you," she said, keeping her eyes on anything but him.

Delvin rubbed his hand along Devi's sleeping back, and she nestled deeper into his chest.

"So much is running through my mind right now," he admitted, keeping his tone low. "I have a daughter, two in fact. The woman I have loved since I was a kid, blessed me with one of them. And to know that I've ached for her all these years; only to discover that she's married to a man she does not love."

Tailan turned her gaze directly to him. "That's not true."

"I know what I heard, Tai," he countered.

The limo slowed as it maneuvered to exit the expressway.

"I love Amir," Tailan stated and turned away.

"And you want me," Delvin shot back.

No argument there.

"That might be true, but I'm not free to entertain that want," Tailan confessed as she eased Neena higher up on her chest and caressed her sleeping face.

"Why's that?" he asked, reaching out to take her hand. "He's had how many women? Four? Where does that put you?"

Tailan pulled away from him and looked out the window.

"There are only four burners on a stove. Evidently, he likes keeping you in the oven."

Tailan elbowed him in the side. "Delvin, don't say something that will make me hate you. Despite what you heard or what you might think, I love my husband … in my own way. And he loves me."

Delvin leaned over and brushed his lips near her ear. "But you love me more."

Her head whipped to him. "I didn't say that."

Their lips were so close. Their breath mingled between them.

Delvin dared to brush his mouth across hers. "You will," he said and sat back.

She shrugged and stroked a hand on Neena's back. "It doesn't matter."

"It matters to me," he said. "It will matter to our daughter."

"I'm not leaving him."

Delvin tossed her a cold, determined glaze. "Then we have a problem."

"No, *you* have a problem," she gritted. "Amir was there for me when I wasn't even a speck on your radar. He didn't demand I give him a thing, which was quite a change for me after being with you for so long."

Delvin's face flushed stinging red. "I handled our relationship poorly. I'll own that."

The limo exited the expressway and headed west. As the traffic thickened, Tailan breathed deeply, trying to control her emotions.

Suddenly his finger slid knowingly down her arm.

She flinched as he said, "I love you. I never stopped loving you. And I want you back. All of you. I have no interest in sharing you with another man."

"I've heard enough," Tailan said, waving him off. "Your child deserves to have you in her life, but let's get something very clear— there's no room for *you* in *my* life. Except as my lover."

Delvin pulled his sleeping daughter closer. Instinctively she wrapped her little arms about his neck. The action chipped away at Tailan's straining resolve. She sighed once, twice, and said, "I apologize for not telling you about Devi. I'm saying it once, and I mean it, but there's no way that I'm giving up Amir just because your head is finally in the right place."

For the rest of the trip, silence expanded between them, each of them lost in their own thoughts.

* * *

They arrived at the Germaine's home on a tree-lined block in Beverly. The two-level brick home extended the full length of a half block. The garden that surrounded the premises, which popped with an array of colors and textures that were perfect for summer, had Anna Germaine's touch all over it.

"They still have those bowling lanes in the basement?" Tailan asked, keeping her focus on the yellow brick building.

"Yep. And I can still whip your butt by several pins."

"See, why did you have to go there?" she said, offering him the first authentic smile he'd seen from her in a long while.

Delvin opened the front door and ushered Tailan and the girls inside a marbled foyer.

"Mommy?" a little one piped up.

Tailan knew from her own warped childhood and the horrors that she had witnessed, that small children were keenly perceptive. Her little girls instantly sensed the heaviness of the visit.

"It's all right, Neena," she soothed.

Delvin must have sensed the wariness of the girls too. He took them gently by the hand. "Hey, I have a surprise for the two of you." He stooped to their level. "How would you two like to see the play room?"

"Yes!" the girls chorused, nodding emphatically.

He led them to the den and situated them among his old toys, games, and books. A few minutes later he stiffly escorted Tailan to his mother.

The moment Tailan stood at the threshold, Anna sat up in bed and stared openly at her. Soon her hand went out as though reaching across time and distance to bring Tailan closer.

Delvin lifted Tailan's limp hand to his lips, whispering, "I'll give you two some time alone."

Tailan nodded and was across the room in the time it took to breathe. She had loved this woman, and when she could no longer see her, she had grieved for her like the mother she had lost too soon. Tears flooded her eyes to the point she could barely see. Anna Germaine had helped bring Tailan back to a place where she could trust people. Delvin brought her to a place where she could love people.

"Hello," Tailan whispered.

Anna grasped her hands, and in that moment, Tailan was punched with the impact of just how fragile the woman's hold on life really was.

"I've missed you so, so much," Anna said softly.

Tailan's tears blocked her speech. This nurturing maternal soul was still helping her. Those six words meant something she never imagined she needed. They said, *I forgive you.*

"Just because you were no longer with my son, that didn't mean that *we* stopped being your family. I think that hurt the most. You didn't come to me—me and Delvin Senior—to talk about things." She placed a hand on the side of Tailan's tear-soaked face. "Things might've turned out a lot differently if you had, my sweet baby."

Tailan absorbed the emotional blow those words brought on. "I'm sorry. I ... I don't have any excuse," Tailan cried. "I was heartbroken. I couldn't think straight. I stopped trusting." She shook her head, hating the answer she offered. "I have no excuse," she repeated. "I'm so, so sorry."

Anna pulled her closer, and at the moment, Tailan wanted nothing more than to be wrapped in the woman's comforting embrace. She crawled into bed with Anna and let the woman's presence, her ever-ready arms, ease away the tension, pain, and frustration. Her tears soaked Anna's pajamas as she settled her head over the woman's chest and listened to her faint but steady heartbeat.

Tailan didn't know how much time had ticked by. Being with Anna again, it felt as if the whole world had paused. Anna smelled the same—a hint of floral and citrus. They spoke a few times, but mostly they spent their cocooned closeness in understanding silence.

A knock on the door forced Tailan from the bed. She kissed Anna's forehead and held her hand as she said, "Come in."

Delvin entered the room with her daughters. She felt a smile bloom across her face as she watched Anna's reaction when Delvin said, "Mom, I have someone I want you to meet."

Neena ran to Tailan, but Devi remained with Delvin, holding his hand.

"Daddy says you're our grandmother," Devi announced proudly.

Anna gasped, sat up in the bed, and covered her chest with a trembling hand. She looked to Tailan, to Delvin and then to Devi and cried, "Oh my Lord! She looks just like you—both of you. What a blessing this is."

Her smile was so bright, Tailan had to brush back more tears.

* * *

Neena and Devi were sitting on each side of *Grandma,* giving an up to the minute breakdown of their day, their lives, what they learned in school, what their names meant in their native languages.

Anna's head was tennis-matching between the two, nodding happily as she clapped. Delvin saw the interaction as the perfect distraction to get Tailan alone. He quietly slipped her from the room and down the hall.

She flattened her hand on his chest. "Why didn't you tell me? You could've found me." Tailan hugged herself as though trying to stave off the ache. "I should never have let my pain ... I shouldn't have cut myself off. Your mother and father treated me better than my own family."

"It's all right," Delvin said, caging her against the wall, comforting her as best he could.

"It's not all right," Tailan groaned. "I can never get that time back."

Delvin totally agreed but for entirely different reasons. He could definitely say the same about his daughter. Time was of the essence. Soon the girls would tire his mother, and they would need to collect them.

He shifted through scenarios, but none of them worked as efficiently as straight to the point. "I want to be with my child and the woman who should've been my wife."

She shoved him. "Delvin, I'm married."

"Married to a placeholder until your real man—me—stepped up. I want to spend time with Devi."

"Fine. We'll work out some type of arrangement."

Delvin crossed his arms over his chest and added, "And since your husband's still trolling for companionship, I want to provide you with some. I want my woman too."

Tailan just stared at him.

"You can't be in love with him, Tai. Tell me I'm lying about that." She was silent a few spells too long, and he smiled. "Then it's settled. When we get back, you'll inform him that I'm now part of this bizarre marriage of yours."

He crowded her against the wall again, forcing her to look directly into his eyes. "If he's willing to share you with another man, that man will be *me*. I will take *every* opportunity to have you until you trust me enough to make a clean break from him."

Delvin watched her like a hawk. Her gaze darted to the angel figurines in the curio cabinet, then to the diamond patterns on the floor, then down the hall. She was thinking too much. That was the last thing he needed her doing. He surged over to her and crushed his mouth over hers. The kiss took him to places his body had not been in years. Oh, how he had missed her lips.

"I can't just leave him," she gasped as she broke the kiss. "I took vows with that man."

"I heard you," Delvin countered. "You said *he* was the one who introduced this poly-whatever madness into your marriage," he growled. "He's supposed to make you his number one. He's supposed to make you happy. Instead he presents a loophole that allows him to exploit your vows. If he wants to play this game, then so can I."

She glared at him, and he gave it right back. "Marriage is about family. I married him because I love him, and I wanted a safe and stable place for our child. What we have chosen to do outside of that doesn't take away from that."

"Bullshit!" he shot back. "Marriage is about two people who love each other—make each other happy. And from *that*, they *build* a *family*. It's what you and I could've had if I'd known *my* seed was growing inside of you."

Tailan tried to worm away from him, but he pressed her tighter to the wall. "You're not happy, Tai, and don't you dare deny it. You won't be happy until we make things right." He planted another raw, penetrating kiss on her. "I'm not letting this farce of a marriage keep me from bringing my family together. I will reclaim my rightful position." He leaned in and whispered, "And just so we're clear, I won't be sharing you with any damn body."

Chapter 22

"Neena, Devi, it's been a long day. It's time for bed," Tailan said as they entered the house in North Pullman and shut the door.

"But, Mama," Devi whined with a longing look at her "new" father.

"Do not make her say it again," Amir said, pointing toward the stairs as he switched off the television and rose from the sofa.

"Goodnight, Daddy," she said to Delvin.

"Goodnight, sweetheart," Delvin replied, before he picked her up, gave her a hug, then planted a kiss on her cheek. "I'll see you tomorrow, okay?"

"Okay," she answered, her smile growing wider.

Devi then ran to Amir and said, "Goodnight, Papa."

He leaned in, planted a kiss on her temple, and said, "Sweet dreams, little princess."

Neena gave a wary glance to Amir before she inched toward Delvin, who obliged her with a goodnight embrace that matched the one he had given his daughter.

The two girls trudged up the staircase with a few curious looks back down the stairs at the adults. It was as though they could feel the tension and were reluctant to leave the grown-ups alone to handle things.

Personally, Tailan wished she could go with them. The predatory vibe between the two men was causing too much friction in her life.

The moment they heard the door close above them, Amir whirled to face Tailan. "What is really going on here? Why is *he* back here?"

Amir glared across the room at Delvin, and Tailan could swear their stone faces would crack any second.

Delvin shifted his gaze to Tailan and announced, "I'm here to establish that I'll be spending time with my daughter every day that I'm here in Chicago." He flickered a gaze between her and Amir. "And to establish some type of visitation for the times I'm in L.A."

"He can do this?" Amir's voice raised an octave. "Just demand time like this?"

Tailan would not insult Amir's intelligence with a lie. "It's only fair. She's his daughter too. But it doesn't change anything."

"It changes everything!" Amir growled.

Tailan went to him and tried to place a calming hand on his chest, which he did not allow. "You've been her father—the only father our girls have ever known."

"But that's because I didn't know!" Delvin interjected.

Tailan tuned Delvin completely out and focused on Amir with a softer tone. "That won't change because you're still a part of my life and hers."

He gave her a small, bitter smile. "For how long?"

She blinked, confused. "What do you mean?"

"How long do you think you'll hold out before leaving me for him?" Amir clarified.

Tailan winced at that suggestion because leaving him for another man was not on her agenda. She had married him and was in it for the long haul. And she definitely did not want to separate her daughters. The only thing that had given her pause was his blindness when it came to his family.

"I love you, Amir. I just need you to wake up and see that your family is tearing us apart. Leaving you has only entered my mind because of how you've allowed your family to treat me and Devi. I wouldn't leave you because of another man—"

"You think I did not know the times you missed him, longed for him?" He snarled at her. "Every time you saw him on television or in a magazine you ..." he shook his head as though unable to voice the rest.

"I'm sor—"

"No, no. Do not apologize," he said, holding up his hand. "I never lied to myself about who truly had your heart. I had hoped you would get over him. Seven years I have waited." He inspected Delvin with keen interest, then said, "Just as I could not get you out of my system, you cannot get him out of yours."

The words, brutal in their simplicity, held a ring of truth that Tailan never wanted to hear out loud.

"Amir, please listen to me," she whispered, moving so that they were almost nose-to-nose. "Delvin and I did not have sex."

"But he touched you in some way," Amir countered, and the pain in his voice was almost too much to bear.

"I want to take him as my lover, yes. Nothing more. That's all he can ever be to me."

Out of the corner of her eye, she noticed Delvin stiffen at those words. But at the moment, saving her marriage outweighed Delvin's bruised feelings. If Delvin was going to be in the picture, she needed her daughters' home life to be stable. She needed to weigh their well-being against her personal desires. The children always came first. Always.

The challenge behind Delvin's dark brown eyes was not a good sign. He was competitive to a fault when it came to getting what he wanted. She would be no exception.

"I know the boundaries we set," she continued. "I promise you that we didn't do anything." She shifted toward Delvin and said, "Tell him."

Delvin's stance screamed his defiance. There was no way in hell he would admit the truth. When Tailan turned again to Amir, her stomach dropped. He didn't believe her words but he did believe Delvin's body language.

"Amir—" Tai warned, moving to stand between both of the men.

"My presence is not needed in your life," Amir said in a resigned tone as he shifted his gaze between her and Delvin. "It is obvious what will happen. No need to prolong things. We will leave in the morning."

Tailan stared at Delvin's easy smile and fumed. There would be an avalanche in hell before she would just let him waltz in and dismantle her entire life!

"Don't go, Amir," she whispered, and he stopped on the bottom stair. "I love you."

"Maybe," he said. "But is it enough?"

"It has been for all this time," Tailan reminded.

Amir glanced over his shoulder with a smile that did not quite reach his eyes. "No love, it has been—how do you say—the consolation prize. I have been the runner up."

Tailan shifted to pure fighter mode. "I'm not letting you go. Not like this."

"You must, sweetness."

"I don't have to do a damn thing," she shot back, her voice holding that edge that signaled she had slipped from swaying to declaring. "I'm yours—have been since the first time we made love. I don't ever think of him when you touch me, hold me, love me."

Delvin cleared his throat and said, "Seriously? You could've fooled me."

She tossed him a frosty glare and a warning, "Delvin, stay out of this!"

"A part of me believes this," Amir reasoned. "But another part knows this as well: I cannot hold ground in your mind twenty-four hours a day. And you think of him at least some of that time. Yes?"

Tailan's entire face flushed crimson.

He gave her a half smile and started toward the stairs again. "I will gather my things, then Neena's."

"No!" she cried, pulling him back with a grip on his arm, holding him in place.

Amir's gaze at Delvin was intense, and Tailan trembled with what she witnessed in those black eyes. He turned that gaze on her, and it softened after a moment. "There are some things that need to be worked out here. I do not want to interfere."

"Don't leave us," Tailan pleaded.

"Don't remember you making that kind of statement when it counted for us," Delvin interjected, trying to reach out for her.

She shrugged him off and said to her husband, "Don't leave me, Amir."

He placed a gentle hand over hers. "I am giving you the space you need to settle your heart."

"This family needs you," she whispered. "You want me to make a choice, and I have. I choose you. I love you."

"I have no reason to doubt that," he said, stroking a hand through her curls before turning to make his way to the second floor landing.

"If you walk out tonight," she warned, "I will come for you every day until you come home. Don't make me do that. Don't make me into that woman."

Amir looked down at her but said nothing. Tailan took it as a sign that his resolve was cracking. She inched closer to him, stroking his sturdy arms and his too beautiful for words face, whispering, "You've given up so much for me ..."

Tailan could feel the resentment Delvin was feeling from hearing those words. Whether her ex believed it or not, she did love her husband. The love wasn't nearly as strong as she felt for Delvin, but it was love all the same.

She continued brazenly, "I don't take that kind of love for granted. Don't. Leave. Me."

Tailan followed Amir's gaze over to Delvin, who was two shades darker with smoldering rage. She looked up and saw Amir favor the man with a smile that was somewhere between acceptance and victory.

"I will be in our bedroom," Amir finally relented.

"You won't leave?" she gasped.

"And have you show up at my parents' restaurant wearing some seductive garment that will start a riot again?"

He had once made the mistake of leaving the house after an argument, thinking he'd won and intending to give her the brush-off. She put on a sheer, form-fitting dress and showed up at India House, knowing that's where he would be. The men in his family learned exactly why he was so taken with her. The couple barely made it into Amir's office before he ravished her.

Amir shook his head vigorously. "No my love, I do not think so."

She gave him that mischievous smile that he could always pull out of her.

"I learned my lesson the first time," he added.

Tailan edged closer to him, her voice husky with promise as she said, "So did I. I married you for better or for worse. I only hope you've done the same. Your family has been your worse. My feelings for Delvin are my worse. We can get through this somehow."

Delvin cleared his throat and barked, "I'll be back in the morning to see my daughter."

She curled into her husband's arms and watched Delvin storm out of their home.

Chapter 23

The weeks that followed Delvin's first encounter with Tailan's *other* life were confusing, frustrating, and annoying as hell. Tailan loved her husband. That right there was enough to make him roar. The way Tailan fought for Amir was eye-opening to say the least. Amir had the most diabolical hold on Tailan. But why?

Yes, Delvin recognized it as love. He wouldn't pretend that love was not a main component. But there was another element as well. It ran along the vein of manipulation by way of twisted logic. Much as he hated it, even he had to admit that Amir had made all kinds of sense when he laid his arguments on Tailan.

So where did that leave Delvin Germaine? For the moment, out in the cold without his woman. He was the outsider battling for dominance, and he was coming up short. And worse, he was in a never-ending holding pattern over which he had no control.

Then there was the added issue of his children—all of them. His ailing mother and her battle to live to enjoy her grandbabies. The long-distance career that demanded his attention.

All this meant that changes were coming at him faster than he could put on a baseball mitt and catch them. He had to get his life back in order before it broke through the fences and ran buck-naked down the street and never came back. Delvin was not new to multi-tasking. In the last ten years, it had become his middle name. Taking that skill by the reins, he moved with brisk intent to accomplish his goals.

As his driver took him down Tailan's block one afternoon, Delvin noticed a FOR SALE sign on a house just down the street from Tailan. He picked up his phone. "Quentin Daniels, please."

"This is Quentin," the realtor answered.

"My name's Delvin Germaine. I'm calling about a property I saw in the Pullman area. Is it still available?"

"Yes, we have several."

"Had a few questions about it if you don't mind."

"Of course," Quentin replied. "I can meet you at the property if that would be better."

"That was going to be my first question. I'm already here."

He gave the listing address and Quentin said, "Excellent, I'm on my way."

Delvin asked the driver to circle back around and park. Once he was stationed in front of the house, he put in another call. The second his party picked up, he launched with, "Katie, no more movie roles that'll take me out of the country for a while."

"What?!" she shrieked so loudly he had to pull the phone from his ear for a moment. "But that script I sent you is set to film on location in Spain, Belize, and Switzerland. That one might land you another Oscar."

"I can't do it. Got waaaay too much going on right now in my personal life."

"Sounds serious," she whispered, and he could imagine her playing with tendrils of dark brown hair as she always did when shifting gears. "What's going on?"

Delvin turned to the scenery outside his limo's window. "My mother. Health issues."

"Whoa!" Katie exclaimed. "I'm sorry to hear that. I'll keep her in my prayers."

"Thanks, lady," he said and ended the call with, "I'll be in touch."

Delvin flipped through the speed dial settings on his phone and called home.

"Hello," squeaked an adorable voice that always melted his heart.

"Hey, angel, it's me," Delvin announced.

"Daddy!" the child cried. Then Delvin heard her shout, "Jason come quick, it's Daddy."

There was a shuffling on the other end. Delvin could imagine they were each trying to get an ear close to the house phone receiver.

"Hey, Dad," Jason said, the pitch of his voice even deeper than it was the last time Delvin had seen him. His teen was growing up faster than he was prepared to accept. "When you coming home?"

"Yeah, we miss you," Ariel whined.

Suddenly, hearing their voices brought a stark realization to light. He missed his children—both of them—and he wanted them with him here in Chicago. Since he already had the court's approval to have the children in the first place, and the only reason Gabrielle was trying to back pedal was because Paulo was no longer in the picture, Delvin would proceed with doing the very thing that would bring everyone together—in one place.

"That's why I'm calling, guys. Grandma needs me to be closer to home for a while. And she misses you guys so much, so ... instead of me coming home, I'm bringing you two to me."

"Wow, Dad!" Jason exclaimed. "We're coming to see Grandma? We're going to Chicago?"

Delvin noticed a car pulling up to the side of the limo. The person inside said something to his driver. They both nodded, and the car parked in front of his.

"Need you two to do me a favor." When they got silent, he added, "Jason, I want you to help your sister with her packing. It'll be faster that way. Ariel, I want you to go get Ms. Bridgette and put her on the line for me."

"Okay," they chorused. As they ran from the phone, their *yaaaay's* echoed through the line.

Delvin was still grinning a few moments later when Bridgette said, "Sir?" He could practically hear the smile in her voice. "Ariel's skipping out of the room. Jason just moon-walked right by me. What did you tell them?"

"Oh nothing much. Just that you all will be making tracks to Chicago within the next few hours."

She gave a whelp of joy that almost mirrored the children's. "I'll get them prepared." Then she paused and said, "I have one request though."

"Sure."

"Can we get some Italian Fiesta Pizza while I'm there? My family swears by it."

Delvin couldn't help but laugh as he left the limo and said, "Consider it done, darling."

* * *

An hour later, Delvin and Quentin were leaving the house viewing. The house was an exact replica of Tailan's quaint dwelling. There was only one problem.

"It's entirely too small," Delvin admitted. When Quentin's face sagged, Delvin quickly redirected, "That doesn't mean I'm not interested."

"Would you like to look elsewhere? I'm sure we can find something that suits your needs, Mr. Germaine."

"No. This is where I want to be. I have no doubt you can make *this* place suit me, considering it'll be a cash deal."

Delvin could practically see the man's hard-on from where he stood several feet away. In this real estate market, those three words were purple squirrels—they did not exist. Delvin's finances were always in perfect order, and for that he gave Tailan all the credit. Early in their relationship, she always cautioned him to spend soft and invest hard, to make his money work for him and multiply it with the effort of others. He never forgot that lesson, and it had paid off with multiple zeroes in his bank accounts.

"Before I called you," Delvin continued. "I took the liberty of doing some research on the neighborhood and the city's plans for it. This entire area in every direction has been deemed a historical district."

Quentin nodded, leaning his muscular frame on the wrought iron fence. "The Pullman area has a long-standing history in the city, and the country for that matter, due to the Pullman Train Car Company. That owner wanted all of his employees residing close to the main factory. Thus," he stretched out his hand, "blocks and blocks of *row houses*."

"Which brings me to my next observation." Delvin started to walk down the block, and Quentin followed. "I can see the city's influence in the efforts to revitalize this area." He pointed in the direction of the expressway. "The Walmart just up the street." He pointed to two separate corners. "Those fruit and vegetable gardens being tended by gardeners. I noticed them right away because every garden sits on a vacant lot. They're beautifying the ugly patches of the neighborhood." Delvin turned to Quentin. "Lastly, the people."

Quentin blinked several times, then quickly admitted, "The developer of this area, along with the city, is striving to create a mixed community, shifting from the lower classes to a more upwardly mobile group of citizens."

Delvin and Quentin walked back toward the house of interest. Once they were standing near it again Delvin said, "And this is where you're about to earn your commission."

Quentin gave Delvin his complete attention.

"I had my people check into the developer," Delvin said, narrowing his gaze on the man. "He purchased the majority of these homes for *less* than pennies on the dollar to get the contract from the city. I don't fault him in that regard. But I do have an issue with the substandard work that he's doing to rehab these homes. So this is what you're going to do for me to earn my money."

Delvin faced the row house he wanted and pointed to the one on the left of it and the one on the right. "I want all three of these homes immediately, like today. And I want them combined into one house."

"What?!" Quentin gasped. "This is a historical district. We can't change the structure of the dwellings from their original design."

"Yes, you can." Delvin opened up his portfolio, pulled out several documents and a list of names and numbers, including that of his financial planner. "Like I said, I did some research." He handed Quentin all the paperwork. "The developer can't change the design, however the new owner can do whatever they want to beautify their property."

Quentin looked up at him with his mouth open. "Mr.—Mr. Germaine," Quentin stuttered. "This is a major undertaking. I'll need more time."

"Not really." Delvin walked over to his car, where his driver quickly opened the door. Before he stepped in he said, "Mr. Daniels, you have exactly forty-eight hours to put this in motion. Those documents you're holding are the contractors I've already commissioned to start work in six hours, and my financial planner is waiting for your call. I suggest you get started because in seventy-two hours, my family and I are moving in."

Just before the car door closed behind Delvin, he heard Quentin screeching into his cell phone, "Glasetta, drop everything you're doing and get into the office *ASAP!*"

Chapter 24

Tailan's headaches were her constant sidekick. They became more frequent with each passing week. Work was stressful, and she was busier than ever. Tailan was shocked at the daunting amount of work that David had actually been doing behind the scenes. Now that she had replaced him, she was expected to add his responsibilities to her own. The pressure was intense, especially now that she was expected to repeat the success of the Soul Express tour.

Every single member of The Vets, all eleven members of M-LAS, most of them virtually unknown authors, Lutishia, and Malcolm, all hit the *New York Times* bestseller's list within seven weeks of each other. Now the publishers—the ones who swore up and down she would fail—were ringing her phone off the hook to accomplish the same feat for their debut and mid-list authors. The publishers couldn't fathom that the reason those authors single-handedly achieved more than The Divas was because they supported each other on the tour and after.

Tailan was humbled by the success, and she should've been squealing for joy, but at the moment she couldn't do anything but reach for some pain meds.

Work was not the only cause of her elevated stress. Home was bringing up the rear and dumping tension in her lap too. Neena and Devi were sensing the strain. The thick cloud of unease was hard to miss.

Delvin was the only ray of light in her girls' day. When he came to collect them every day to spend time with Jason and Ariel at their grandmother's house, Neena and Devi would sail out of the house so fast, they often forgot to say goodbye to their parents.

Work and the girls would've been bad enough, but those issues were only the edge of the moon crater. The deep pit of tension resided squarely within the intimacy Tailan shared with Amir—the sexual intimacy. She was in trouble, and she knew it. Not even Delvin knew her body like Amir did. And her body could never lie to him. Amir was certain their bed play was a well-orchestrated act on her part. He was every shade of miserable.

Something had to be done. Her family situation, her love life couldn't continue this way. Yes, without question she *loved* her husband. During the past four weeks what really made her nervous was the alarming idea that she could actually still be *in love* with Delvin—a fact Amir had pointed out. Now her decision to work on her marriage was making both her and her husband miserable.

Tailan needed to wash away all of the nagging thoughts. She stepped into the shower. At least there, she could find some relief from the tension knotting every muscle in her body. Twenty minutes later, Tailan reached for a towel, wrapped it around herself, and stepped out.

Amir stood right in the doorway. She almost screamed from his abrupt presence. "Since the girls are not here, I wish to speak about the incident with my family."

Tailan felt her cheeks burst with heat. Amir's family had invited Neena to a family event and excluded Devi. When word got back to Delvin, he snapped. She had prayed this on-going issue with Amir's family would pass. This time, Amir saw things through a different lens and she hoped that the fact that he did see would force him to act.

"Delvin threatened to go over there and deal with it himself since you obviously haven't," Tailan warned, moving past him and into their bedroom. "I've told you for years that they treated Devi differently. Now Delvin wants the nanny to accompany her every time they go to see your people." She turned to him. "If things keep going like this, he'll probably go for full custody. I won't lose my daughter because of your family."

"It took his outrage and the look of pain in Devi's eyes to see the truth for myself. I understand. It's been real subtle before, but now ..." He stepped closer to her and kissed her damp shoulder. "For my part in our daughter's pain, I am sorry, and I vow that my family will honor and treat Devi the same as Neena. And if they cannot, then I will have no other choice but to break off from them."

Her heart softened. Amir was again making a great sacrifice for her and the children they loved. Going against the traditions of his people was not an easy road for him to take. And ever since that televised kiss, his people had been strangely silent on issues related to the marriage they deemed "inappropriate."

"I cannot control what they do," he said. "But I can control how we respond to it."

Tailan caressed his flawless golden face. "It's all I've ever asked for, Amir."

He continued to rub her bare shoulders. "There is one more thing I wish to discuss."

She moved closer, letting the warmth of his body seep through the cloth of the towel.

"Yes?" Tailan whispered.

Amir looked directly into her eyes and said, "I will permit you— with no consequences—to be with him. One. Time."

She flinched and jumped back as though she'd been punched. "What?!"

"Go to him," he said calmly. Only his eyes revealed the depth of his anger. "Do what you need to do so we can return to normal."

She dropped to the bed and shook her head. "That's not what I want."

Amir stood over her, looking down, his eyes determined and steadfast. "You have never accepted any of the men in the poly community. You have had plenty of choices. What is it about him? How can someone so selfish, so self-centered, still hold a place in your heart?"

"You don't understand him," she replied, holding her anger in check. "He's not selfish, just … single-minded."

"Selfish," he confirmed. "His needs before yours. I bet his lovemaking reflects this too."

Did it?

She had always had vicious orgasms with Delvin. She never gauged whether hers came before his—it never mattered. Because what Delvin brought to the table was more than what was between his legs.

Amir continued, his grin a perfect display of white teeth. "I have a proposition for you … go to him. Let him"—he grimaced—"make love to you. I want you to know the difference between what he can do for you and what a man who worships your temple can do. Does he worship you, my love?"

Tailan could only blink up at him as she struggled to find the words.

Her slow attempt to come up with something prompted Amir to add, "There will be no consequences to our marriage—"

She gasped and parted her lips to speak, but he held up a hand to halt anything she could say.

"But I do have one stipulation."

Tailan sighed.

"I would like to watch."

She was on her feet before she could blink. The action was so swift, the towel stayed on the bed. Naked, Tailan faced her husband and gasped, "You have lost what's left of your mind!"

"Have I?" he shot back, gripping her shoulders and pulling her into his hard chest. "Or are you afraid I might be right? That he is selfish. His needs before your own."

"He would never go for another man watching him that way."

Amir's eyebrow winged up his forehead. "You only say this because you are not a man. A man secure with his sexuality and his love-making skills will rarely shy away from a challenge aimed at both."

He slid his hands down Tailan's exposed back, kneading the tight knots he found there. Tailan wanted to kick her own behind as a whisper of a moan escaped.

"His ego will not let him refuse," Amir added. "Especially if he thinks it is how he can have you and how he can show me he is the better man."

Amir's mouth massaged her lips as his strong, knowing hands slid easily over her hips.

"But ... what ..." Tailan stammered as the kiss ended. "What are you trying to prove?"

He nipped at her chin and glided his tongue down her neck. "That once you have sated your lust, your need for love will be even greater."

"How can you be sure?" Tailan moaned. She was almost too distracted by his hands and by what his mouth was doing to her upper body to finish this conversation.

Amir fisted her curly hair and leveled his sultry eyes to hers. "Because when I am with you, inside you, it's always love—never lust. Always about me loving the physical part of you, when I already adore and love the rest of who you are."

Amir never lied to her—not with his words or his body.

"You could lose me," she gasped, holding his stare.

He abruptly released her, leaving her body aching for more. Amir walked to the window. "I can never lose what did not belong to me in the first place," he replied. "But until you know this, we cannot move forward, whether Delvin is in our lives or not."

Tailan padded over to him and spooned his back with her naked breasts. "You couldn't love me and send me—"

"That is where you are wrong," he said in a soft tone. "I love you more than you will ever know or understand. I am setting you free to see the real Delvin Germaine."

He turned to her and cradled her face in his hands.

"You have been fantasizing about him for years. The Great Love who got away."

Tailan's lids dipped, concealing the ugly truth those words revealed.

"So go to him," he whispered. "He will send you back to me—this time, for keeps."

She shook her head. "I can't do this."

Amir kissed her again, only this time it was soured by his pain.

"You can, and you will." He moved away from her to leave their bedroom. "Those fantasies come between us more than you realize. If I was not in the picture ..."

She whirled to face him. "Doesn't mean I would go back to him."

Amir opened the door and stepped through it. Before he closed it and the topic, he confirmed, "I am the only thing standing between your true forgiveness of him and your complete submission to him. So I am removing myself from the equation." He wagged his finger. "But just for one night. Then we will discuss returning our marriage to monogamy."

Tailan ran to the door just before it closed and yanked it back open.

Boldly she declared, "You're playing games, using me as a pawn. All because you don't like him."

"This is not about if I like or dislike him," he countered, coming back to her so he could stroke a hand across her face. "This is about how easily you can forget that *his* love was only balanced by how he could command your womb."

Well, he does have a valid point there.

"Then how can you ask to watch him with me?"

"I want to know that you finally understand the man who has been in your head is not the man in your bed. Not the man you have dreamed about for seven years. I do not want you to assimilate, justify it, and brush it off." Amir reached for the door again, preparing to close it. "If I witness it, you have no choice but to own up to who he is right now. You have never lied to me, and I do not expect you to start now. If you feel it, I will know it. If I lose you in the process ... well, then at least I did not lose you to a memory."

"No woman is worth what you're putting yourself through, Amir," she confessed.

"You are wrong," he said, planting a soft kiss on her lips. "You are worth that and more. He forgot that. I will not."

"I think you're underestimating him."

Amir's lips lifted at the corners. "For your sake, I hope so. For mine, I hope not." He kissed her again and pulled the door to close it. Just before it clicked, he added, "Bring him to our home, and I will lay down the terms by which your liaison will take place."

Chapter 25

Tailan's hand was trembling when she entered Delvin's house down the street. She closed the door with a soft click and took in the extensive work that had been done on the place. Delvin had provided her with an insane amount of money to furnish and style the home exactly as she wanted.

But he made a small request that the house reflect the family who lived there. So Tailan had decorated the home with loving care, respecting the diverse cultures that represented his family. She smiled as she moved to the den, taking in the African-American artwork alongside the East Indian influences of Neena's people. Although Tailan had no love for her Asian ancestry because of how her father's people viewed her, she wanted her daughter's Asian heritage to be honored.

The colors were warm and cozy. The furniture, inviting and sturdy. The massive kitchen was filled with stainless steel appliances and all the modern conveniences. The den was the social hub of the house and most likely where she would find Delvin. If he wasn't visiting his mother with the kids, on the days his schedule permitted, he was often with them in the den playing a game or reading to them.

Today was no exception.

Delvin was stretched out on an area rug playing *Sorry!* with Devi, Neena, and Ariel. She lowered to the floor to watch them, but mostly took in how wonderful Delvin was with the three of them—how patient, loving, kind, and most of all, fair. It was refreshing to see both of her daughters being treated well after dealing with Amir's family.

He shifted on the rug, looked up at her, and frowned. "Is everything all right?"

"Just wanted to have a word with you in private, please," Tailan replied.

"Okay." He turned back to the girls and smiled. "Just let me finish beating Neena real quick."

"I don't think so," Neena piped in and knocked his piece off the board and back to start.

Delvin's eyes bulged, too shocked to believe it. "What—" He retraced Neena's strategy. "Ah, that was just wrong, little girl."

All three girls giggled at Delvin's incredulous expression. They were the sounds she wished would echo in her own home.

"I won, Mama," Neena exclaimed, grinning as she wrapped her arms around Tailan's midriff.

"Yes, you did," she replied, smiling down at her daughter. "And he doesn't seem too happy about it."

"I want a rematch," Delvin grumbled playfully as he stood.

Ariel joined them, but timidly hung back as always, reaching out for her father's hand instead. She looked exactly like Gabrielle. She had her bone structure, almond brown eyes, willowy frame, skin tone, and lips. The other two ran to Bridgette, the nanny, who was putting the finishing touches on lunch.

Delvin turned to her and said, "Bridgette's got lunch ready. You head on over. Tai and I need a moment."

"Uh oh. It's time for the adults to talk adult stuff again," Ariel mused, causing Tailan to smile.

"Something like that," she confirmed. "But it won't take long. I promise."

Bridgette collected the rambunctious band and took them to the dining room. As squeals of oooh's and ahhh's echoed back to the den, Tailan announced, "My husband has given me permission to spend time with you."

Delvin's left eyebrow shot up. A second later he was closing the door. He turned and said, "How generous of him to finally be fair about things."

"No, he wants to make sure you're out of my system. For good."

Delvin pushed himself off the door and stood mere inches from her. "I'll never be out of your system," he said, his tone defiant. Tailan gasped. His finger stroked across her chin, eliciting an all too common response. "You belong to me."

She stepped back. "I belong with him."

Delvin's lips lifted at the corners. "Then why are you here?"

"Good question." She swerved around him and headed for the door.

"Come back here," he commanded, the words sliding through his teeth.

Tailan snatched open the door.

Delvin slammed it closed again. He pulled her away and warned, "Woman, if I have to chase you, it will not be nice."

She whirled to face him. "I shouldn't have come."

"But you want to—" he said, bringing her into a embrace. "Come, right?" He pressed closer, letting her feel the massive erection growing in his jeans.

Tailan tried to wiggle free but only succeeded in creating the most shivering friction down below. "Delvin, don't make this so difficult for me."

Delvin's tongue swiped across her lips. Tailan nearly pulled it into her mouth, she was so turned on.

"He will always come second," he bragged.

"See, that's where you're wrong," she answered and finally freed herself from his grasp. Tailan called upon all her will to level her breathing. She lowered onto the leather sectional and said, "He was hurting over the recent death of his wife, but found a small corner of his heart for me. Amir stepped in and handled *his* business and *yours*." She crossed her legs, reclined deeper into the sofa, and relished the annoyed expression on Delvin's face. "So, contrary to popular belief, it's you who's runner up in this camp."

A vein throbbed at Delvin's temple. Several spans of time passed before he said softly, "He says that you can be with me?"

"Yes."

Delvin stood in front of her, his eyes assessing her practiced breathing, her false bravado. "He's going to regret it."

The more she thought about it, the more she was forced to admit, "Somehow, I think I'll be the one with regrets."

His breathing hitched, and his hands fisted at his sides as he growled, "Oh, I don't think so."

Too quickly, Delvin had Tailan up off the sofa and was pulling her to the door.

* * *

Delvin needed a place to pounce. Moving down the hall, his mind fired up with several scenarios. His skin was ready to scream, his erection was on the verge of busting the zipper of his jeans. Just as he cleared the dining room, Delvin saw a way to get what his body was dying for. He tightened his grip on Tailan's wrist to ensure she would not make a scene as he said to the kids, "Hey guys, mom and me will be right in the basement. I want to show her the new additions since the last time she was here." He pulled her quickly. "We'll be right back."

Bridgette zeroed in on both of them, and her gaze locked right in his crotch area. She yelled out to the kids, "Who wants more pizza?!"

"Me," they chorused.

Bridgette moved with lightning speed to distract them, and Delvin crept down into the basement with a fidgeting Tailan at his side.

The second the door was locked behind them, Delvin dropped to his knees and pressed his lips to her thigh, cupping her buttocks within his massive hands. Tailan let out a low, breathy moan, all while trying to put some distance between them. He kept her locked in place as he parted her thighs …

"No. Stop!" Tailan panted.

He froze. "Did you say no?"

She nodded, and he released her instantly.

"What kind of games are you playing, Tai?" he said through his teeth.

"There's a condition," she said.

"Condition?" Delvin repeated. "A condition for what?"

"For having sex with you."

"Let me guess," he crossed his arms and he continued through his teeth. "He wants to see my medical history first," Delvin huffed, "This guy is something else! He gets to make love to you *plus* four other women and—"

"Amir wants to watch." Tailan crossed her arms this time.

Delvin's erection did a complete nose dive. He peered at her, taking in the solemn expression. "What. Did. You. Say?"

"Amir's one stipulation is he gets to watch us having sex."

"Oh, so I did hear it right," he snapped, glaring at her. "What kind of sick, twisted—"

"Not sick. He's seeking to prove a point."

"And what point is that?" he snapped.

"I can't tell you," she answered, her golden skin flushed an angry red. "All I can say is that if he's right, one time is all it'll be between us."

"And if he's wrong?"

She shrugged.

"Suppose I don't want to play his foolish game?"

"Your loss," she said in a matter-of-fact tone that caused him to bristle. "Because unlike you, I have a marriage that provides everything I need—including the option to take a lover."

Delvin was against her in a hot second. "Suppose I take you right here and to hell with what he wants?"

"We both know you won't," Tailan answered. "I know you know that *no* means *no*."

She was right. Taking a woman against her will was something he would never do. What had happened to Tailan growing up was one of the main reasons he didn't do rape scenes in his movies or even scenes where the lines could be blurred. That had limited some roles for him, but he was adamant.

Delvin backed away from her and said, "So when is this tryst supposed to take place?"

"The when and where is your choice," Tailan stated. "Actually, everything's on you."

He grinned, rubbing his jaw. "We might as well have a central location ... something close by. The best place for this to happen is— your bedroom."

"He'd never allow it," she gasped. "That's our Sanctuary. Our place. Don't be an ass, Delvin!"

"You said it was my choice," he protested, feigning an innocence he didn't feel. "I choose *his* bed."

"Then I refuse!" she said. "I won't have that memory with me for the rest of my married life."

"Who says you're going to be married to him for the rest of your life?!" Delvin waited several moments before he conceded with a mild, "All right. But I have a request of my own."

Tailan stepped away from him, circling around to the other side of the overstuffed sofa.

"What's good for him, is even better for me," Delvin said as he tracked her every feline move. "If he wants to watch me with you, then I want to watch *him* with you."

"Now *that* will never happen."

"Yes, it will," he said. "You fight for him in ways you never fought for us."

Tailan made fast tracks for the door. "I won't dignify that comment with a reply."

Before her hand touched the lock, Delvin had her pinned to the wall. Their breaths mingled as he pressed a hand between her thighs and stroked softly, teasing her to the point of distraction.

"Then let me rephrase it," he groaned. "Tai, you're missing *his* point. He demands to watch you with me. That shows how much he loves you," he spat. "How much he *cherishes* you. I'd *never* allow another man to have access to my most prized possession."

She stared up at him and gritted through her teeth, "And therein lies the problem—possession." Her hand squeezed his wrist, and Delvin stroked her with a touch so light, she trembled with the onset of an orgasm.

Tailan struggled to get out of his reach, "I belong to him because I want to, not because I have to."

Delvin felt his cheeks heat up.

"Yes," Tailan forged on when he said nothing. "There's a pointed difference between you two—he is sacrificing his queen for a night to ensure the balance of his kingdom. You, on the other hand, would wage war and destroy all you've built to be the winner of *nothing*."

Delvin did everything in his power to rein in his anger. He eased his play between her thighs and whispered, "I know all about sacrifice. I've lived with it for seven years."

"Your choice, not mine. I never had to wonder who loved me more—the man who put me first, or the man … who threw me away," she said, leveling an icy gaze at him.

He abruptly released her and was filled with so much tension he could taste it. Delvin leveled her with a resentful gaze.

Tailan gave it right back with a haughty side order of, "I'm still wet. Excuse me while I go home and make love to my *husband*."

Delvin's tethered control snapped its bonds. He pressed her again to the brick wall and spread her creamy thighs. Tailan's eyes had an ugly gleam behind them as she flashed a bitter smile and said, "Check."

"Really?" Delvin growled.

Tailan shivered as he slid her lace panties to the side. His long fingers teased her sweet spot.

Her lids dipped. As he played, his mouth pressed hot sultry words against her ear. "Let him watch." He circled her tiny knob of nerves. "I look forward to his look of defeat when you scream my name."

He sank two long fingers inside her and stroked. "And a word of caution to you as well, my dear." He pulled out his fingers, which were slippery from her nectar and focused solely on her pearl. "It's been months since I've indulged my *needs*."

Delvin looked at her. Her eyes were glassy with arousal, her face flush with passion.

He inserted his fingers again and treated her to a series of caresses against her pearl with his palm. Her panting gasps were like music to his spiraling hunger.

"I intend to unleash all my pent up passion with every thrust into your body," he warned. "Your cries of pleasure and screams of ecstasy will fuel me until you beg me to stop."

His fingers were lighting quick as he took her over the edge. She cried out, but it was never heard. He swallowed her scream as she climaxed in shivering ripples.

Delvin ended the kiss as Tailan's legs turned to rubber and she sagged against the wall. "Making up for lost time will be the most intensely satisfying experience of your entire life."

Delvin waited while she mechanically straightened her clothes. When she appeared somewhat composed he teased, "Check *mate*."

With that, he released her, and she practically staggered out of the basement.

"Send your husband my regards," he called after her.

Chapter 26

Tailan took a seat at the dining room table. Amir was on her left, and Delvin sat to her right. Her husband's face was nearly unreadable. Delvin's expression was calculating and shielded. The encounter with him yesterday had unsettled her to a point that it had her twitchy. Delvin's touch, his lips were like fire and ice fighting for dominance. She never felt that way with her husband. Amir brought a different kind of pleasure.

"He understands what is required?" Amir asked.

Tailan took a sip of coffee, studying both men intently.

Delvin drawled a simple, "Yes," in a deeper voice than she had ever heard, then gave Amir a lopsided grin.

Amir was not pleased with that answer or Delvin's stance. "Understand that I am only doing this because it is necessary."

"Yes, but we both know that this is all about Tailan," Delvin admitted. "Maybe that's what you're afraid of."

"I am not so naïve that I am blind to what holds her in marriage to me," Amir confessed. "I only know that you broke her heart once, and it almost killed her and the daughter she carried. *Your* daughter."

Tailan choked on her coffee and coughed into her napkin.

Delvin's smile disappeared as he looked to Tailan for an explanation.

Amir slid a glance in Tailan's direction and said, "I did not take her for one who would wish to endure that kind of disappointment again."

"Oh, I won't disappoint on any level." Delvin eased back in his chair. "Your daughter, Neena, is accepted into my family with no issues. Can you say the same about my daughter?"

Tailan's coffee cup clattered on to its saucer. "You two keep this pissing contest up, and I'll send you both packing."

Both men dialed it back a notch.

Delvin caressed her arm. "You said I should choose the time and place as well as what happens between us."

Tailan looked over to Amir. His stare was deadly. She eased out of Delvin's reach. "That's not allowed."

"What are you talking about?" Delvin asked, frowning.

"Open displays of affection," she said softly. "It's forbidden in front of him."

Tailan jumped, and Amir flinched as Delvin burst out laughing. He was gasping, trying to pull it together. Tailan shot him a look of pure irritation.

Delvin came to his senses and said, "That right there, is one for the books. He can't watch me touch you, but he'll be all eyes when it comes to me making love to you?"

"We aren't making love right now," she countered and edged a little closer to Amir.

"This is foreplay," Delvin teased with a smile Lucifer would envy.

"You're going to push him too far, Delvin." She locked a steely gaze on him. "And you'll be the one with regrets."

Delvin gathered up his glass of water and took a swallow. "You're forgetting one thing," he said, with a pointed look to Amir. "I have nothing to lose. Neither of you have considered or taken into account that *this* man"—he thumbed his chest—"can grow, learn, and ... change."

Tailan focused on Delvin. Her eyes narrowed as though seeing him for the first time. This arrogant side of him, the competitive side of him, were two of the things she least liked about him when they were growing up. His relentless determination was exhausting, but his delusion that he was entitled to things was the main reason their relationship fell apart.

"Have you changed?" Tailan asked in a solemn tone. "Have you really?

"You shall see." Delvin stood and swept a look to both of them. "I choose this Saturday. I'll start with breakfast, a walk on the lake like we used to, dinner, maybe theatre..." He cast his eyes directly to Amir. "Feel free to join us for the grand finale."

"I said *one night*," Amir shot back.

"Oh, but making love starts long before one hits the sheets," Delvin countered, reaching into his blazer pocket for his keys. Delvin tossed eye contact between Tailan and Amir and explained, "It starts in the mind. Tailan is not the same woman that I knew back then. Surely you won't have an issue with me finding out more about the woman who will share my bed for *one night*. She deserves at least that."

Tailan's heart was pounding. She had to take her hand off of the cup to keep it from clanking on the saucer.

Amir glared at Delvin, his hands gripping the edge of the table.

"Goodnight, wife," Delvin said.

When Amir didn't react to the jaunt, Tailan had the urge to kick Delvin as he moved to the door. He looked over his shoulder at Amir and added, "Goodnight ... *husband*."

Chapter 27

Delvin had pulled out all the stops for his evening with Tailan. She was still reeling from the whirlwind day they had spent together. She could tell that he had put a lot of thought into the preparation of their outing. A light breakfast early in the morning. A leisurely walk on the lakefront and then over to Michigan Avenue for a mini shopping spree. Lunchtime was just plain old-school fun as they indulged in a ride on Navy Pier's Ferris wheel, a few slices of Italian heaven at Flo & Santo's, then capped it off with some naughty but very tasty Garrett's Cheese and Carmel popcorn.

Tailan had to admit, the outing was relaxing and enjoyable. In those carefree hours she spent with him it was as if she was a kid again—a young girl traipsing down the path of love and friendship. Delvin had wanted her to remember their good times. And at the moment, she was hard-pressed to ignore the feelings.

The day was lazy, but the evening crept closer. Somehow a part of her was delighted that the time to share their passion had arrived.

Delvin didn't skimp on the location for their one night. On the contrary, the minute she, Delvin, and Amir entered the Mermaid Towers II on Magnificent Mile in downtown Chicago, she realized that Delvin was playing for keeps. This suite was a hot commodity, with a waiting list six to nine months long at any given time.

Delvin had to have purposely selected the suite to annoy Amir. The space shouted success, luxury, and glamour—all the things Tailan deserved, yet Amir was not in a position to provide.

As they toured the suite, Amir said, "I see you spared no expense for tonight, Delvin."

Delvin led them to one of the massive bedrooms and turned on the lights. "I have your wife for one night." He turned, giving Amir an arrogant look. "I need to make every minute count."

He showed them to the master bath. "I'll give you two a moment to prepare." His eyes delivered heated sparks to Tailan. "When I return, the three of us will begin."

Tailan blinked in Amir's direction and again to Delvin. "I don't understand. Tonight will be just us."

Delvin shook his head. "No," he looked to Amir. "This game you're playing starts tonight—ends tonight." He looked directly to Tailan. "You both agreed I get to choose the when and the where."

"But we never said that you could direct how the whole thing goes down."

Delvin gave her a patient smile. "You left that … open to interpretation." He stroked a hand in her hair. "I don't want to prolong this madness any longer than we have to. You'll be with me tonight so he can watch. He'll be with you tonight, and I'll watch. There'll be no illusions for any of us once this night is over."

"This isn't what we agreed upon," Tailan squeaked, suddenly feeling morbidly excited.

"You cannot change the rules mid-way, Delvin," Amir growled.

Delvin left the bath and said over his shoulder, "I never changed the rules … *husband*. I simply didn't reveal all of them. I believe I mentioned to Tailan that this would be the most intensely electrifying experience of her life. I definitely plan to do my part." His voice trailed behind him as he departed the bedroom. "Time is of the essence, people. I suggest you two get prepared."

Tailan almost fell into the oversized whirlpool bathtub as Amir turned on her. "This is an outrage," he growled. "Delvin is already proving my point. He is deceitful. I am not prepared to take you before him tonight."

She gasped, at a complete loss for words. Her gaze inched up, seeking Amir's. "We agreed to let him choose," Tailan reminded. "It's our error that we were not more specific." She kicked off her shoes and undressed.

"You are actually excited," Amir accused.

Her silence prompted Amir to march around her and turn on the double showers. He started to undress as he gritted through his teeth, "You could put an end to this right now."

"But I don't want to," she confessed.

"I hope you will remember you said that."

Tailan whipped around, and the look on Amir's face was pure sensual *sin*.

* * *

Delvin beat quick feet to the second full bath on the other side of the suite. He stripped and jumped into the shower. Everything was riding on tonight. His heart, his love, and his manhood. There was no way he was going to let a little voyeurism on Amir's part deter him from seizing the ultimate prize—Tailan and everything she represented.

He dried off, threw on a robe, brushed his teeth and gargled. He took a long look at his reflection and opened his robe. Years as an athlete had served him well. He was in his physical prime—from rippling shoulders to washboard abs to oak tree hard thighs. He was eye candy for any healthy red-blooded woman, and Tailan was about to get a full blast of his insatiable hunger.

Delvin doused the bathroom light and returned to the master bedroom. He entered, and for a split second he thought the two of them broke camp while he was away. But no, they had dimmed the lights. Delvin went to the night stand and increased the illumination. The bathroom door opened, and they walked out together, dressed in matching robes.

Tailan came to him and whispered, "I turned the lights down."

He collected her hand and planted a soft kiss. "No hiding." He looked over to Amir. "For any of us." He escorted her over to the bed as he said over to Amir, "I would invite you too, but I'm the kind of guy who likes to indulge the entire space."

"This will serve my needs, thank you," Amir responded stiffly as he moved over to the chaise lounge.

Delvin closed his mind to everything but the moment. No thoughts of how Tailan might be nervous, no second guessing whether once they started, Amir would interrupt. No ideas of dialing back his passion. Delvin was focused on one thing only—her pleasure.

He untied the knot in his robe and let it fall open. Tailan's gaze tracked straight to his erection. Her barely noticeable shiver did not escape him. He opened her robe and gloried in her perfection. Her full breasts called to be kissed, her flat, smooth stomach begged for the touch of his tongue. Oh, and the neatly trimmed curls nestled between her luscious thighs made his mouth water.

Delvin pushed the robe from her shoulders and kissed one of them. He collected her hands and placed them on his shoulders. She pushed his robe off, and he drew her closer. They were at last skin to skin. At first, he treated her body to the kind of welcomed touches that were all about reacquainting himself with her feel, her scent, her taste. She moaned as those touches became bolder and ignited a part of her that only Delvin could reach. He cherished the sounds of her pleasure, the softening of her body to receive him. The first kiss was light, exploratory, but the tremors that he felt whip through her body told him that toying with her any longer was not an option.

Delvin fisted her hair and pulled her into a raw, thirsty kiss. Her hands were caressing his back, squeezing his shoulders. And with every moan he pulled out of her, the dam to his need crumbled. Then she committed the ultimate act of desire—her thighs willingly opened to his prodding shaft, and Delvin lost it!

Tailan was pinned to the edge of the bed in a heartbeat. Delvin toppled her over and was quickly between her thighs with his mouth teasing her center. Her body convulsed and shivered; her breathing came in short pants as she cried. She had always liked to be stretched to the point of breaking. He kept her on the edge for long delicious minutes. The increase in her volume signaled she was toppling over. Delvin's fingers joined the fray and sank deep inside her core and tripped her into oblivion.

He didn't wait for her to come down. Instead he took her legs and pulled them over his forearms. He threw her arms around his neck and sprang up from the floor.

Tailan screamed, "Delvin!"

She was wet; the feel of her need rivering down to his body was all the invitation he needed.

He was so attuned to her that every nuance of her movements fueled his desire to please her even more. Delvin braced his thighs and surged hard, straight into her clenching muscles.

"I've missed you!" he cried. "I've missed this." He swallowed her gasp with his mouth, letting her taste her own tangy pleasure. He pounded quick drum beats that touched her womb. Her juicy muscles were locking down every time he slammed home. "You're mine," he whispered into her ear. "Don't you ever forget it!"

Delvin gave it all to her. He perched her against the wall and thrust into her as those screams of pleasure intensified. He had her legs propped on his shoulders, leaving her fully vulnerable to his pace, his passion, his purpose.

Her cries only escalated until he felt those creamy walls tighten around him even more.

"That's right, baby," he groaned. "Come for me." He emphasized every thrust with, "Come. For. Me."

Her body followed his command with shattering results.

"Oh, God!" she cried as her climax ripped her apart.

The woman was nearly in tears. He moved the session back to the bed. Delvin had her on her back with her legs over his thighs as he treated her pearl to feather soft teases and kept right on stroking. Tailan tensed and panted, yet she never cried for him to stop. From Delvin's vantage point, she looked as if she was beyond rational thought. And that was just the way he wanted her.

He switched their positions and put her on top. This move forced Delvin to call upon all the control he could muster. Tailan went wild on top of him; she rode him like the hounds of hell were chasing her and he was her stallion to freedom.

Tailan leaned over him and pressed her tongue into his mouth, holding onto him as though her connection to life depended on it. Dear God, she had to be as starved for this joining as he was. He surged his hips up into her rapid downward thrusts. Her grip around his shaft was taking him dangerously close to the edge. He could only pray Tailan crossed the finish line again before he did.

"Right, there!" Tailan screamed. "Yes, right there. Just like that!"

Combining their efforts was just what was needed to send Tailan into a screaming orgasm. She collapsed on top of him, weak as a newborn.

Delvin peppered her damp face with soothing kisses as she idled down. He let her see the intent in his eyes, and she gave a faint smile.

He eased from under Tailan and left the bed, then he brought her to the edge and pulled her on all fours. She was still gasping but never objected. Delvin positioned behind her and poised the head of his shaft at her core.

Delvin's hands tightened on her hips. "Scream for me again, baby."

He slammed home and drilled into her to sounds of her excited sighs, gasping pants, and blissful cries.

* * *

Two hours after they had begun, Tailan was nothing more than pretzeled exhaustion. Delvin was still basking in the afterglow of his orgasm, and she could feel the involuntary twitching of his limbs. Only then did she notice Amir. Only then did she remember what this night was about; take into account what else lay ahead. Her mind had shut down in the last hour and a half. She had been pure insatiable instinct, but now she had to face her husband, who rose quietly from the chaise. Delvin sat up in the bed as Amir opened and dropped his robe.

Amir reached into the bed and plucked her out. "You might want to join us so you won't miss anything," he taunted Delvin, while selecting a few items from Tailan's overnight bag.

Carefully he carried her to the bath and cleansed her with slow pleasing strokes that caused her to rest her back against his chest and close her eyes. He massaged every inch of her. He even went so far as to wash her hair with an apricot fragrance she loved. While these pampering baths were the norm at home, this one was mostly an attempt to wash away any memory that Delvin had freshly implanted. She surrendered to her husband in the same way that she had when he had first come to her. Although her surrender back then had taken nearly a year, he was persistent, using every method at his disposal to heal her body and mind. He had hoped his loving care would touch her on a soul level. And it did, to some degree.

He had introduced her to the arts of Tantric sex, Kama Sutra, and several types of Energetic Sex practices, all of which were designed to stimulate and heal, tease, and awaken. Over time, she had become multi-orgasmic and so responsive to her husband's touch that he could elicit pleasure with just a look, a scent, a taste—simple, but powerful. Sometimes their lovemaking extended the course of hours, with only small rests in between—and that was for her sake. Amir was insatiable, and he had made her that way as well. She loved every single pleasurable minute of it.

Amir had given her the kind of love that encouraged her to explore, to become. His ever-present and unwavering desire to keep them from falling into despair over what each had lost, slowly brought Tailan to the point that she could love again. And for that, she would be forever grateful and she would forever love him.

When they returned to the master bedroom, Delvin had also freshly showered and had now taken up residence on the lounge.

He eased deeper into the cushions as Amir said, "My love," and pulled away Tailan's towel. "The night is young. Now I will worship you as you truly deserve."

Amir's mouth touched hers and made a slow, sensual decent down between her breasts, over her quivering belly. He held her to him as if his very life depended on it.

"Oh. My. God," was the last thing she remembered saying as Amir took her to nirvana.

Chapter 28

Eight hours later, Tailan glanced over to the clock on the nightstand and then out the window. The master bedroom was quiet. Still. From the look of the sun creeping into the sky and the time on the clock, she'd only slept for about an hour.

Lord, she ached everywhere. She turned her head again and noticed that she was alone. Calling on the last reserves of her strength, Tailan found the command button in her brain to instruct her depleted, exhausted, flimsy limbs to move.

She hissed as she placed her feet to the floor and slipped on a robe. Carefully, very carefully, Tailan inched her way to the door and found Amir standing near the massive picture window, watching the night give way to the day.

"Amir, what's wrong?" she asked softly, moving to stand beside him.

The look Amir tossed her way was almost deadly. "It is best I do not speak my mind right now."

"I'm a big girl," she replied, edging over to the sofa. "I can handle it."

Amir turned, watched the way she moved, and grimaced. "Do not be too sure."

"And what's that supposed to mean?" she asked, reclining into the cushions.

Silence expanded between them for several minutes. Tailan almost fell off to sleep again she was so relaxed. Her eyes blinked opened as Amir said, "There is much I have to say. None of it is particularly pleasant."

"You asked for this," she said through her teeth. "You wanted an open marriage."

"That is what I keep telling myself."

Amir stormed over to the bar and yanked out a bottle of vodka. He didn't bother to pour himself a glass. Instead, he took a strong swig and slammed the bottle on the counter.

Tailan flinched. She had never seen him so angry or take in any form of strong drink. Amir's emotions were always controlled, calm, peaceful.

"When you're ready to talk, you know where to find me," she said. "I'm not going to beg you." She pulled herself from the sofa and started for the bedroom.

He shot over from the bar, grabbed her wrist, and whipped her around to face him. Her robe fell open.

"He damn near raped you," he roared. "He … he … he tore into you like you were some … some whore. Like your body didn't matter. Like *you* didn't matter."

Tailan blinked and attempted to replay her lovemaking with Delvin in her mind. It was intense, vigorous—the lovemaking of two thirsty people who had finally found that tall glass of water and knew they only had so much time to drink. She had loved every single moment of it.

She followed Amir's stark inspection of her naked body, looking down to take in what he saw. There were passion marks peppered across her breasts. Her inner thighs were slightly discolored. Her hips had visible handprints from Delvin's vice-like grip.

She could see how, from Amir's point of view, it may have been …

rough, feral. But it was only a slight bit more intense than the way they had always made love.

"He's an animal," he snarled, stepping away from her. "He doesn't deserve you."

Tailan closed her eyes against the pain caused by those words and fastened her robe.

"Just because his lovemaking style is different, doesn't mean he's barbaric."

"And you enjoyed it," he spat, giving her a look of shock as he paced before her. "So all this time that I have been making love to you, adoring you, treasuring your body for the beautiful temple that it is, all along you just wanted to be *fucked*?" He tossed her an enraged glare. "What were you doing? Humoring me?"

Tailan pulled in a deep breath. His ego was talking nonsense. He knew he was a great lover—just different. "Amir, you're getting dangerously close to pissing me off." She leaned her hip against the back of the sofa and added, "I won't ever lie to you." She waited for his eyes to meet hers. "Yes, I enjoyed it. It was raw and untamed and hedonistic, and I experienced a great deal of pleasure."

He turned from her, but Tailan would not allow him to hide any more than he would allow her to. "But what you did to me was no less climatic or enjoyable or mind-blowing." She bravely approached him. "Both of you made my body your temples of pleasure."

He looked at her and clasped her hand. "I was wrong about him. He actually put you first."

She knew that going in. Delvin always made sure she was pleased. But now her men had suffered a blow to their respective egos. How could she help them overcome that? Tailan should've never agreed to this. She had been greedy—the temptation too great to pass up. And now she would pay for it—emotionally and with every muscle in her body.

"So what do we do now?" she asked in a voice just above a whisper.

"I do not know, Tailan," he said before leaving her side to reclaim his place at the window.

Chapter 29

Delvin was overwhelmed. After what he had witnessed Amir do to Tailan, he was beyond dazed. Never in his life had he seen such a feat. Delvin was by no means a lightweight in the bedroom arts—but *damn!* Amir had introduced him to a whole new level of sensual pleasure. And Delvin was—by his own bright idea—forced to take in every single minute of it.

The final humiliation surfaced when Amir peered over his shoulder and saw Delvin's stark interest. It must have been written all over his face, not to mention the king size erection tenting his robe. Amir smirked at him and said, "Was it good for you too?"

Delvin couldn't get the sultry images out of his head. Tailan's cries of ecstasy, her delicate hands straining and fisting in Amir's hair. Her body bowing up and collapsing over and over and over as Amir pleasured Tailan, loved Tailan, devoured Tailan again and again and again!

A gentle touch on his shoulder pulled him viciously from his internal musings. He looked up. Tailan was standing beside him, holding a cup of coffee. He accepted it as she joined him on the stone bench facing Navy Pier across from the hotel.

"What are you doing up this early?" Delvin asked before taking a sip. "Better yet, how can you even move a muscle after last night?"

He glanced over to her and noticed she kept a stoic profile straight ahead but couldn't conceal the blush that fanned her features. She didn't rush to reply. They both sat in somber silence, each taking in the sunrise over the lake. Tailan reached out to touch him. He shrugged her hand off.

"Talk to me."

Her voice was strained, hoarse. No doubt from the never-ending cries and screams of passion from last night and into this morning.

"What is there to talk about?" he grumbled and sipped on his coffee. Several emotions warred within him that fit together like wrong puzzle pieces.

"Six hours and twenty-three minutes," he sighed, setting the coffee down next to him.

"What?"

"The man made love to you for six hours and twenty minutes. I thought I counted nine orgasms. And he never even penetrated you! Then I lost count of how many times he made you ..." he said, casting her a sideways glance.

Those few I gave you must have felt like an appetizer before his main course.

The first time Delvin thought they were finished making love, Amir released a throaty chuckle as he said, "Oh, I am not nearly done. I normally allow her small breaks in between orgasms so that I do not overpower her. I will be sure to let you know when we are truly finished. Get comfortable, this is going to take a minute. Or two."

"Is it like that every time?" Delvin asked, his morbid curiosity taking over.

His searching gaze bore into her, ready to detect a lie. "Sometimes it's only five hours," she squeaked.

Delvin snatched up his coffee and took a big swallow. "Riiiight," he taunted. "I guess his little East Indian ass showed me a thing or two."

Tailan moved closer to him and stroked his hand. He recognized the gesture. It was something she often did when he was agitated. The strategy was not doing the trick this time. He tried to pull away, but Tailan held firm. "Every man makes love differently," she whispered. "He's incorporated things from his culture." When Delvin frowned, she explained, "Tantric sex, the Kama Sutra, Energetic Sex practices, things like that. It's more about connecting with your partner on a soul level, spiritual level, and physical too. I won't lie to you any more than I would lie to him. I experienced pleasure with you both. No one was greater than the other."

Delvin focused on the teal waters of Lake Michigan for a moment, nodding as though he had just come to some understanding. "Now I see why you won't leave him."

Tailan released his hand and stared at the water.

He turned to her as she replied, "That's where you're wrong." She rubbed her forehead, as though attempting to form her words carefully. "I won't leave him because he loves me. I won't leave him because we have a family—that's intact. I don't want to destroy that. It wouldn't be fair to the children."

"What's not fair is that I'll never love any other woman but you," he countered. "I'm still paying for my mistake. I'll always pay for it. Losing you will haunt me to the grave."

Tailan placed her arm on his shoulder. Her touch, though gentle, hurt. He couldn't look into her beautiful face and accept the harsh reality buried in her soft eyes. He lifted his cup to his lips and redirected, "I'll have my lawyer contact you regarding visitation. And whenever Devi comes, Neena is always welcome to come. That won't change."

Her body flinched beside his. Warily she removed her arm and said, "All right."

Delvin was not sure how much more of her attentiveness he could handle. Between fits of disbelief and shock, her presence had introduced another emotion into the mix.

Embarrassment.

Yes, he knew that had been the feeling that swamped him in those final minutes of watching Amir with Tailan. She was in the throes of a toe-curling climax when Amir turned those light brown eyes to him. The look the men shared was as humiliating to Delvin as it was provocative.

Delvin had been *aroused* seeing another man pleasure *his* woman. He had gotten off on it. It mortified him and compelled him to rush from the bedroom and leave the suite.

He reached out, cupped her face in his hands. It took everything he had—every ounce of control to make this about them and not him. To make this about truth and not excuses.

Delvin brushed his lips to hers and asked, "I can't change the past, so how long are you going to make me pay for my mistake?" He pressed his forehead to hers, listening to her unsteady breathing. "I've gone all these years without you."

Tailan shook free of his hold. "That wasn't my fault. You had the child you wanted by a woman you chose. You had your career, you had everything—"

"But I didn't have you," Delvin reminded.

Tears filled Tailan's eyes. "You made me feel less than a woman because I wouldn't give you what you wanted," she cried. "You had no regard for my body—for what I wanted."

"And all of it was for nothing," he countered, reaching up to wipe away her single tear. "Because in the end you did have my child."

"I had no choice but to have her," she said. Her look was pure sadness. "I was scared every single day! I had complications with the pregnancy that robbed my body of strength. I was horribly ill. Every day I lived in fear that my body would give out, my child would be born sickly or worse—an orphan because I died giving it life." She glared at him. "So don't you dare trivialize my experience as an 'I told you so.' I'm not a violent woman, Delvin. But say something like that again and I'll slap you so hard—"

Delvin reached for her again, and she struggled for a moment, then finally gave in and cried in his arms.

After a long while he said, "Answer one question for me ..."

Tailan nodded. She lifted her head from his chest and waited.

"Do you love me?"

Tailan eased out of his arms and confessed, "I can't answer."

"Can't or won't?" Delvin persisted.

Tailan took in a deep breath and looked back at him. "Same difference."

"Then I have my answer," he said and stood then faced her. As she remained sitting, looking up at him, he announced, "I'm going to fight for us, Tai. In my own way. I won't touch you again while you're still married to him, but—"

"Delvin, please don't," she beseeched.

"Let me finish." He paced in front of her. "I'm not going to wage an all-out war, but I'm going to put old boy on notice." Delvin turned intense eyes to Tailan. "He can never, *ever* mess up. He can never give me a sliver of an opening because I will take it all—*everything*."

Tailan gasped, and he bent down and kissed her lips. "I'm man enough to admit when I have real competition. As much as it pains me to say this … Amir does love you. But so do I. More in fact, because I loved you first. So when he touches you, know that I'm not far from you. When he makes love to you, remember I'm just as capable of pleasing you. When you long for me, remember you're the only one who stands in the way of us being together."

Delvin straightened to his full height and offered his hand to Tailan to help her stand. As they walked back to the hotel, he added, "So that we're clear, one wrong move and I'm storming the castle and taking back what belongs to me. This is his only warning. Yours too." He brought her hand to his lips. "You feel me?"

She nodded, suddenly timid and silent.

They walked into the lobby, and he pulled her to the side. Delvin cradled her stunned face in his hands and said, "Don't play this game with me again, Tai. I won't be a party to some poly-whatever the hell you guys are doing." He breathed hot words into her ear as she trembled in his arms. "If you come to me again, if you open yourself to me again in this way, I promise you'll *never* go back to him."

She tensed.

"Do you understand me?" he growled.

"Yes!" Tailan panted.

He could practically smell her aroused fever for him. He gave a quiet chuckle and sealed his words with a steamy kiss. When he released her, she looked drunk.

Delvin pushed her to arm's length and finished, "Now get out of here before I forget my promise and make you my breakfast."

Without a moment's hesitation, she scrambled out of his reach and maneuvered through the lobby to the elevator.

His laughter followed her the entire way.

Chapter 30

Seventy stories up, Amir had witnessed the exchange between Delvin and his wife. They sat like old friends watching the sunrise. A sinking feeling lodged in the pit of his stomach.

Amir loved his wife, but at this very moment, a part of him resented her. She had shown a side of herself to him *and* Delvin that demonstrated to him just how wrong introducing a polyamorous element into their marriage had been.

Tailan needed him, loved him. Of that he had no doubt. But she craved the kind of intimacy that Delvin had offered her. It was something Amir hadn't factored into the equation. He had endured Delvin in Tailan's heart for years. He'd had no problem with that. But now to have the flesh and blood man in their lives was something he wasn't sure he could abide.

Delvin was a possessive predator in Amir's eyes. Yet each man had a hold on Tailan because of their daughters.

The real unknown factor to this entire situation was Tailan. Amir was at a loss to gauge her next move. His wife wouldn't leave him, of that he was certain. Only because Tailan would never allow her daughters to be separated. The very idea went against every instinct in her body. This was an advantage for Amir but a very precarious one.

It was no secret that his very traditional, *very* affluent family held no respect or love for Tailan and Devi. His family could become a major problem if Tailan's tolerance reached a breaking point. With Delvin Germaine in the picture, she suddenly had options she never had before. That made Amir very uneasy.

The honorable thing to do would be to let her go, but the selfish side of him rallied against it. Amir reminded himself that this shouldn't be about his heart, Tailan's heart, or Delvin's wants. This—was about their daughters.

Neena loved Tailan—called her mother. His adorable little princess had blossomed under Tailan's care just as he had. Tailan had healed his bleeding, woeful heart and filled it with so much joy, laughter, and serenity.

Amir experienced being *alive* again with Tailan. She always seemed more sparkling than other women. The way that Tailan put her everything into all that concerned her—the people around her, the children she raised, the dreams she pursued—made her vibrant and beautiful in his eyes. He felt it the first time he saw her, even with the shadows of pain that were evident in her eyes. He wanted her then, and knew he would never have enough of her. Amir only wanted to wash away that pain and love her until she thought of nothing but him and their children. It had worked well enough—until now, until Delvin reappeared after all these years.

Amir still couldn't understand how she could love both of them. They were so very different. Delvin saw Tailan as a possession—his woman. Amir would never forget how he mounted Tailan and plunged into her like a depraved stallion.

Amir had prepared himself mentally for any number of visuals that might present themselves, but none of his imaginings even came close to the graphic depiction of lust playing out in front of him. Not from

Delvin—but Tailan! She was just as insatiable in the act as he was.

Now, they were at a crossroad and the right direction was unclear. Amir had assumed that by allowing Delvin to show his true nature, his real side, it would wake Tailan to the fact that Delvin was not worth living in the past. Her concession to experience him *and* Delvin shocked him beyond comprehension.

Last night and this morning had confirmed the ugliest truth of all for Amir. As the door opened behind him and Tailan entered, he turned and saw it plainly. Tailan would miss Delvin now more than ever.

And there wasn't one thing Amir could do about it.

Chapter 31

Tailan was in a world of confusion. In the three weeks since her "date" with Delvin, work, family drama, and the ravaging dreams of being with her two men were ever-present.

The tension between her and Amir had simmered down. He was preoccupied with dealing with his family's increased demands. Something was brewing on that front, but she couldn't give his family too much energy at the moment. Delvin, as promised, had dialed back his heavy pursuit of her, approaching her only when it was a matter concerning the children. She was saddened that their easy banter and suggestive conversations had morphed into sickeningly polite and formal communications.

All four of the children had picked up on the vibe around them but were flourishing in spite of it. Neena and Devi were helping one another do well in school, the same way that she and Delvin once had. Jason had instinctively become overly protective of all three of his sisters. If they went out to play, he always tagged along as their guard. Nothing and no one ever got too close to his family. And Jason had reconnected with Tailan, sometimes coming down the street to her home to spend time with her, to talk over things and ask for her advice. But the biggest leap in all of it was that he called her Mom again. *That* touched her heart more deeply than she could have imagined.

Ariel had bloomed under Tailan's attention and care. The nanny was great with all of the children, but Ariel seemed to relax better when Delvin or Tailan were near. And Devi was the ringleader of the whole gang. There was no mistaking her natural leadership abilities. Tailan knew she inherited that trait from both of her parents. Devi didn't have a jealous bone in her body. The little girl took to Jason and Ariel like they had grown up together their entire lives.

It was odd but no less wonderful.

Tailan felt her goals of keeping her family together and making it strong and healthy had become a reality. There was only one hiccup.

Her body craved the touch of a man she could not have. She ached for the intimate connection she had with Delvin. To make matters infinitely worse, this longing in no way lessened her appetite for Amir.

"Good Lord," she whispered to herself. "Somehow, I'm addicted to both of them."

She needed to table these thoughts because Valarie would be arriving in her office any minute. Pam had sent her to discuss what was next for M-LAS.

Tailan rose from her desk and turned to the window overlooking the Chicago skyline. The image was serene and she tried to use it to rein in her ravenous thoughts. If she approached Delvin for any issue that was not related to the children, he would consume her. Plus, he had already vowed that if she did that, or if Amir or his family slipped up one more time, he would break the delicate truce and do everything in his power to reclaim her.

The problem was that Delvin had her heart, but Amir and her children had her soul.

How does a woman choose between water to survive and oxygen to breathe?

She paced before her office window, trying to devise a solution.

Valarie interrupted her by saying, "What the hell are you thinking?"

Startled, Tailan turned around. "What?"

Valarie's smoothed a caramel hand over her hips, sauntered over to her desk and took a seat. "The look on your face just now was so weird."

"Oh," Tailan said as she returned to her desk. "I have a lot on my mind."

"The new promotion that bad?" Valarie asked.

"Nothing I can't handle." She slid a weary glance to Valarie. "My love life is all over the place. And I think I'm about to make it worse."

"Oooh," Valarie sighed. "Now you know I'm always looking for new source material for my next novel. Spill it." She rubbed her hands in excited anticipation, though Tailan already knew the woman was only teasing. Valarie would never break a confidence.

Tailan propped her elbows on the desk and dropped her head into her hands. Selectively, she explained the developing love triangle playing out in her life. "I don't know what to do," she finished.

"Good God, girl," Valarie exclaimed. "I couldn't even make this one up. Talk about playing it close to the vest. Hell, I didn't even know you were married." She ran her hand through her shoulder-length bob. "When Delvin Germaine entered the picture, I just knew you two would be sailing off into happily ever after. Especially since the rumors about his pending and very public divorce are true." Valarie shook her head. "Now you're saying that not only does Delvin want you back, you refuse to leave your husband, and it's possible that you just might want both men?" Valarie let out a low whistle of appreciation. "Lord have mercy, if that isn't a love triangle, then I don't know what the hell is."

"Exactly," Tailan confirmed.

"I will say this …"

Tailan looked over shoulder to Valarie.

"Baby doll, it's not a bad problem to have."

"Please," Tailan groaned, massaging her temples in an attempt at some relief. "This is awful! I feel guilty all the time. Thoughts of Delvin make me feel like I'm betraying my marriage vows. My love for my husband cause me no small amount of stress when I'm near Delvin." She closed her eyes; images of her husband's solemn expression transformed into Delvin looking at her with those piercing brown eyes.

"Delvin watches me all the time, looking for signs of whether I'm happy or not. And I'm not. And he knows it. And he's waiting … he's just biding his time to pounce."

"Hold up," Valarie said, frowning as she slid to the edge of her seat. "Why do you have any dealings with Delvin Germaine outside of doing publicity for his book? I don't understand."

Tailan hesitated for a moment, trying to decide whether to share this nugget of information. "We have a child together—a daughter."

Valarie's generous mouth sagged to the floor. "That's got to be the best kept secret on the freaking planet. No wonder your panties are in an uproar."

Tailan nodded.

"It still doesn't change my first assessment."

Tailan glanced over to her.

"Not a bad problem to have."

"Val, this is a problem any way you look at it."

"See, that right there *is* the problem." Valarie pointed a finger to Tailan. "You're a woman who has fought tooth and nail for others, for your career, for your success. No matter how people swore up and down it couldn't be done, you proved them wrong. And you want to know why?"

"Because I never take no for an answer?" Tailan chirped.

"That's part of it, yes. The other part is that you play to win. There has to be a way for you and your eager men to find a happy medium." Valarie crossed her arms and arched her penciled eyebrow. "From where I'm standing, I only see one option for you."

Tailan took a long, slow breath, giving Valarie her undivided attention. "What?"

"Put yourself first for once." She slid the Soul Express DVD from the desk and flipped it over in her hands. "Take charge of the situation and lay out a brand new set of rules."

Tailan tried to imagine how that would work and came up empty.

"Both men have made demands on you, asked you to yield to *their* wishes, *their* desires, *their* choices, *their* needs." Valarie twirled the disk on her finger, looping it as she offered, "I think it's time you gave them both a dose of their own medicine. Now, how you do that is the real magic trick."

Tailan was silent a long while, bouncing one scenario through her mind after another. Finally, the corners of her lips turned up.

Valarie stood and stepped back. "Whoa, I don't like that look in your eyes." She propped her hands on her curvy hips, and when Tailan didn't answer, she said, "I think I've created a monster."

"No, you didn't create the monster. You simply woke her up from a long sleep."

Tailan switched on her computer and searched for a number. She reached for the phone and quickly dialed.

* * *

Tailan held her meeting in an intimate and very public location—the Chicago Stock Exchange Restaurant. The place boasted of elegance, money, and privacy. Getting a reservation took skill, finesse, a ton of ingenuity, and the mention of Delvin Germaine.

When her guests arrived promptly at eight o'clock, Tailan was properly suited for battle. She had chosen her armor with infinite care—a flattering clingy number that ended near her ankles. The color was a seductive red—a shade both of her guests adored on her. The top of the dress left her shoulders bare and inviting to the touch.

Tailan didn't waste time with her hair and make-up. Instead she hired a stylist and make-up artist to complete the task. She was going for a certain look, and that look was—*I'm worth the effort, gentlemen.*

As Amir and Delvin joined her at the secluded table, the waiter appeared out of nowhere. The lanky young buck had showered attention on Tailan since she arrived.

"We'll start with water and coffee," Tailan said. Then she turned to her men, "Gentlemen, would you care for something else?"

They stared at her, their eyes raking over her sensual curves, her naughty smile, and her bold eye contact.

"Well, actually," Delvin replied, "I'm good."

"No," Amir answered. "I do not require anything at the moment."

Tailan turned to the waiter. "That will be all for now, sir."

Once he departed, Tailan turned to her guests. She sized them up, practically reading their thoughts. They wanted her. They wanted *all* of her. Unfortunately for them, all of her would now come at a price—their egos.

"I extended you both an invitation tonight," Tailan said, with a flicker of a gaze at both of them. "It occurred to me that none of us can continue on this way. So I've decided to bare it all."

Tailan leaned back in the chair and crossed her long legs, taking in how Amir and Delvin watched her every move.

"I've been living a lie and trying to make it the truth," she confessed. "I'm going to be very honest, and I'm almost positive you won't like it …"

Delvin's eyebrow shot up to his hairline.

Amir's expression didn't change, but a sliver of curiosity lit in his eyes.

"I want you both."

The silence that fell after her declaration was heart-pounding.

"Have you lost your mind?" Delvin gritted between his teeth.

Tailan sat up and turned her full attention to them. "Both of you have chosen others over me and expected *me* to just get over it or deal with it." She crossed her arms, causing her generous bosom to rise, then stared directly at Delvin. "Those days are over. Going forward, *I'm* the one who'll be making the demands."

"I will not share you with another man," Amir protested.

Delvin shot back to Amir, "You started this mess," he growled. "You're the one who opened Pandora's Box, and *now* you're trying to force that heifer back in? Typical!"

Amir gave him the evil eye.

Tailan whipped her attention to her husband. "He's right."

His expression was pure shock.

She flipped a glance over to Delvin's arrogant, smiling face. "I love you, Delvin, and I always will, but I love Amir just as much. The fact that he's been forced to sever all ties with his family to keep peace in our household is something I won't dismiss or ignore. You are both important to me. For totally different reasons."

The waiter timidly inched closer to the table with their order. She glanced up at him, detecting that he sensed the conversation was intense and heated.

"Please," Tailan gestured to him to come forward. "Winston, I think my guests are ready for refreshments right about now."

Both men ordered a shot of heavy liquor, a surprise because neither one normally drank anything that strong.

The silence was unnerving, but she could tell from the rapid eye movements and shared glances that they were pondering what she had said.

Winston set out the beverages and hightailed it out of there.

Amir and Delvin swallowed down their respective liquids, each buying more time to think. Tailan watched the flickering movements of their eyes and knew that wheels were still turning in their heads.

"Amir, you said you won't share me with another man," she continued. "We both know the solution is to divorce, and that's something I won't allow. So the way I see it, you will share me, as I've shared you with four other women."

Amir tossed her a thunderous look. "You're my wife!"

"A wife who will keep her lover just like you've kept yours." Tailan sipped her wine.

"We said that we would go into a traditional marriage after that night."

"You said that we would discuss it," she countered. "You can't toss monogamy back on the table because it suits you."

"I never had sex with any one of them," Amir confessed in a low tone.

Delvin choked on his drink and quickly grabbed his napkin. He shot Amir a look of complete disbelief.

Tailan placed her wineglass on the table as that admission doused her with cold water shock. She searched his eyes for signs of duplicity and found none.

"I … I could not … And they recognized my limitation for what it was," Amir admitted. "I did not even indulge in our kind of foreplay where I would be intimate with them." His gaze was nothing short of intense. "I always saved that for my wife."

She lifted her glass again, took a sip as she mulled over his words. "So basically what you're was saying is that you've only had platonic relationships with the women you've chosen."

Amir's gaze locked with hers. "That is why there had been so many. They wanted more than I was able to give."

Delvin took a sip of his wine and said, "Even if you're telling the truth--."

"He's telling the truth," Tailan admitted. "It would be too easy to contact the women and verify it, but one thing Amir does not do is lie."

"But that is of no consequence," Delvin countered, glaring at Amir. "Because for all this time you've allowed her to *believe* there was more between you and those women. And that was for a purpose too. Unfortunately, it's come back to bite you—and me—in the ass."

Tailan reached for her menu, and while scanning the dishes, she re-affirmed her stance. "Gentlemen, it's all or nothing. Whoever wants to walk away has my blessing. Other than our children—whom I'll never allow to be separated—there's nothing binding either of you to me."

She peered over the menu and stared directly at her men. "Remember, you two put this into motion. Face it, fellas. Women share men all the time."

Tailan glanced at her menu again as the men tried to blame one another for their current predicament and exchanged accusatory glances.

She hid a wicked smile behind her menu as she said, "I'll simply know about it, and so will the two of you. The ball is definitely in your court."

Chapter 32

Amir hated how easily he had adjusted to the idea of sharing Tailan. The night that she had laid down the gauntlet on him and Delvin, he was outraged. But as the days stretched into weeks, and the harmony of his home improved dramatically, his resentment of the situation slowly dissipated.

Tailan was in complete control of their sensuality. She had established strict rules regarding how each man would be involved in her life. Amir had believed that the compulsive selfish streak that coursed through Delvin's veins would take him immediately out of the running. The stubborn worm actually conceded, but only on certain levels—as long as Tailan was married, Delvin would not make love to her. They could share surface intimacies, but it would not cross the line of penetration. Amir was so thrown it took everything in him not to show it. To Delvin's declaration, Tailan only smiled. Amir knew that smile. She believed she could wear him down. Evidently, she didn't know Delvin Germaine as much as she thought.

Tailan had his heart and Delvin's, and the woman had used that alone
to make both men yield to a certain degree. Amir wanted to feel more
angered by the entire situation, but the results were more astonishing
than he could ignore. The tables had definitely turned—now Tailan was
doing the very thing with Delvin that Amir had done with the women he
had developed loving relationships with.

Truthfully, she and Amir were closer than ever. Their love life had
flourished in ways that nearly brought *him* to tears some nights. She had
completely changed. The tension that always seemed to follow her was
gone. She now took the challenges created by her job in stride. The time
she spent with the girls was full-on and engaging. She glowed with an
inner light that made him breathless.

Under the shadow of her happiness was the doubt in his own mind
that he was not enough for her. Though they never spoke of her private
time with Delvin, the jealousy surfaced more often than Amir cared to
admit, as well as the fear that at some point, she would leave him for
her first love. Sometimes he wondered how Delvin fared in this regard.
And there were times that when she came home from being with Delvin,
she was sullen, almost unhappy. Probably because she hadn't been
successful at getting Delvin to bed her. All this sacrifice on both men's
parts to make sure that Tailan's desires were met. But was it worth it?

In some regards, Amir felt blessed to witness such a transformation
in the woman he loved. He assumed that eventually, he would understand
the reason why she needed Delvin so much. And then, maybe he would
be able to fill the void, and she wouldn't need Delvin at all. Right now,
that was the only thing brewing in his mind.

So when his parents made an impromptu visit, he feared that the
very foundation of his happiness was about to crumble.

* * *

Uma, Amir's mother, swept into the house, giving a cursory glance
to the furnishings that she always said were far beneath her son. After
all, he was used to the elaborate decor of the family's Skokie compound.
Adesh, Amir's father, marched in right on her heels and stood beside
her.

Uma inspected the sofa, practically weighing whether she would catch anything if she sat on it. Amir nearly gave her a menacing look. She didn't move right away, but finally edged over to the corner and perched on the end.

"The family has made a new arrangement for you," she announced in her thickly accented English.

"What *kind* of arrangement, mother?"

"You are to marry Roshni, your deceased wife's sister. The union is the wish of Esha and Roshni's parents, and you will do it to keep our ties with the Sengupta family and to restore your honor."

"I have honor. And I am already married," he countered smoothly.

"To a woman who has no morals. A woman your family will never recognize as your equal," his father said, scowling. "And she is a negative influence on the daughter of the Sengupta family."

He should have known Tailan's public episode with Delvin would not go unanswered. "That is unfortunate," Amir said, glaring at the man whose thunderous expression was commonplace these days. "Mother," he continued, "I cannot do what the family is asking."

"Listen to me," Uma implored. "Because she is not a suitable wife, the family wishes you to take on a second wife—an East Indian wife— to raise your daughter."

"You mean a third wife," he corrected. "Why is this so important to you? Why is it so important to father?"

She lowered her hands to her side. "You have been disgraced before all of the family because of her public displays of affection with another man. And the family wants to make sure the wealth stays where it should."

"You mean you do not want my inheritance going to a woman who is not of our culture."

"Amir," she whispered then rose to stand before him. She placed a hand to his cheek. "Son, if you do not fulfill this obligation for the family, I will lose you. I will lose my son. I have already had a daughter taken away."

"What are you talking about?" he asked, his gaze flicking between his parents.

"Dhara's death was not an accident." She shook her head. "She had defiled her purity. The men of Roshni's family insisted that her disgrace be paid for with ..." Uma's lids dipped.

Amir gasped and turned from his parents, trembling with an anger he had every right to feel. The implication of his mother's words was agonizing to hear. All this time, he had believed that his sister's death was a result of an unfortunate accident. To know that it was a misguided honor-killing filled him with more rage than grief. They had kept this information from him; they only told him now to manipulate him.

He had always treaded a thin line between his culture and his heart's desire. Being an American raised in an extremely traditional East Indian family had always been a struggle for him. He had done everything they had asked of him, even forgoing his dream of becoming a doctor to go into the family's business of introducing East Indian cuisine to the very Americans they held in such low esteem. Couldn't they allow him this one small slice of joy that being with Tailan brought him?

Amir turned to face his parents, his eyes brimming with unshed tears. "Yet, I'm expected to take another bride from the same family that killed my sister? Though I have already fulfilled my obligation with my marriage to Esha?"

Uma gripped his hands. "If you do not marry Roshni and satisfy this family's new obligation, then the Sengupta family will take great insult."

Amir stepped away from his parents and turned to see Tailan descending the stairs. Her expression was blank. He was certain she had heard everything. Their bedroom had no television or radio, and there were no other noises in the house because the children were visiting with Delvin.

Tailan grimaced before saying, "Do what you have to do. I can't very well love you if you're not alive."

"They won't harm me," he said to Tailan.

"That might be true," Adesh said, almost relishing his coming announcement. His tone put Amir on full alert. "But if you do not comply, and the Sengupta family feels it is because you have an unnatural attachment to Tailan, then ..."

Amir whipped around to Tailan. Her normally golden skin was practically white. "Well, that solves that doesn't it?" She leveled an icy gaze at Adesh that revealed how she felt about him.

"Mother, give us a moment to discuss this," Amir offered.

"No need to discuss anything," Tailan said, perching on the bottom stair. "I like breathing; you like breathing. It's as simple as that."

Adesh's lips slanted in a sly smile. "Good. She is more sensible than I gave her credit for." He hurried to the door before Tailan could let loose with something that dismantled his manhood—a regular occurrence when those two went head to head. "I will wait in the car."

Amir looked at Tailan before focusing on his mother. "I will only consider your unreasonable request if you help me find Dhara's children."

"That is impossible!" his mother said, her raven eyes widening to the size of saucers.

"The family sent them away as though they were lepers!" he barked. "I want to find them, care for them. They are *my* bloodline. I will share my inheritance with her children." He looked at Tailan. "With all of my children."

Tailan nodded, and he took that to be significant.

"And another thing," Amir began. "I will not live in Skokie. My life is with the woman I love."

"He will marry Roshni but live here," Uma said to Tailan. Then she turned to Amir and offered, "Move Roshni here away from the family so it is less likely someone will find out that you are still with Tailan."

"Mother that—"

"I know how you feel, and I am trying to find a way to a suitable solution," Uma said.

Amir studied his mother with keen eyes. This was so unlike her. She sided with his father in most things. She had really only rallied against Adesh twice. Once, when she convinced him to allow Amir to finish his education at the university. The second was when Amir insisted that he would marry Tailan—a woman who was not of their culture, or he would break from the family completely. Under his stark gaze Uma eased back over to the sofa and sat down, her head low.

He lowered to his knees in front of her. "Mama, you can be censured, even punished for suggesting something like this."

She lifted her face, unveiling a bitter smile. "When they killed Dhara, a part of me died with her. If they kill you ..." Uma shivered from the internal thought.

Amir slipped into the seat right next to her. "So you will help me find them?" he asked.

She lowered her gaze to their clasped hands. "I know where they are."

"Why did you keep it from me?" he asked.

"I did not want to prolong your pain. There is nothing you can do to help them."

"You cannot believe that!" he said, pulling his hand away. "You know what it is like for children who do not have family to claim them."

She avoided his gaze for several moments. "They are in an orphanage in Mumbai. How will you bring them to America?"

"We could adopt them," Tailan offered.

Amir looked to his wife. "You would do that?"

"You loved your sister, and they are a part of her and you," she said, rising from the bottom stair and joining them on the sofa. "And it's the least that I can do for you, with everything you've done for me."

Amir's heart felt a stab of dread that he might lose the most precious thing he had, mostly because of how he had mishandled their relationship. If he had never brought that element into their marriage, if he had been more steadfast in his efforts to bridge the gap between his family and Tailan, she would have held steadfast to their vows, and she would not have been an easy target for Delvin. He was certain of it. "I love you."

"So it is settled," Uma said smoothly. "You will marry Roshni—before the families."

Amir blinked at his mother, astonished at how easily she could enter his home and demolish his entire happiness. "Mother I cannot just—"

"Amir, please do not look so defeated," she interjected. "I am not the monster you think I am. I understand what love is. You will still spend your time with Tailan, the woman you love."

"Why are you defying father this way?" The question jumped from his lips before Amir realized it.

Uma's dark pools turned glacial. "Your father," she spat. Her eyes became vacant as she quickly reined in her emotions. "I believe it is the way to keep you alive and for you to have the woman you want." Uma treated him to a rare smile full of more joy and contentment than any other he had ever seen from her. "Arranged marriages worked well in my day. Not so good now since children are so willful, so headstrong. Like my Dhara." She looked back at her son. "Like my Amir."

The slow, rhythmic circles Uma made along his palm had always soothed him in his youth. This time, it made him hone in on her beautiful face, which was lined with the strain of having to act as an intermediary for her son and her husband for years.

"You have never seemed happy," Amir admitted.

"Happiness had nothing to do with it," she replied, the sadness reaching her eyes. "Arranged marriages kept families together, and wealth and prosperity in our communities. Marriages endured because they came with absolute certainties—the same caste, religion, and goals. It was built that way into our culture to support these things. There was no walking away."

"But what about love?" he asked with a look in Tailan's direction.

"We learned to love as best we could," Uma confessed. She fidgeted with the scarf draped around her neck before getting to her feet. "Once, I shared happiness with someone—true, real love with someone."

Tailan stroked a hand over his.

Amir clasped it, then peered at his mother, waiting.

"Your father," she whispered, tears pooling in her eyes. "Your sister's father."

Amir glanced over to Tailan. Her look mirrored his—they were both stunned. Obviously she didn't mean Adesh.

Uma lowered to her knees before her son. She took his hand, then

Tailan's hand and shared, "Kamal, my husband's brother. You are his child. Adesh, the man who raised you, never forgave me." She patted the tears from her cheeks and whispered, "I wanted to marry Kamal. But Adesh was so angry that we had fallen in love, he refused to allow our parents to make the exception."

Amir squeezed his mother's hand tightly, giving her his strength to go on. So much about his mother was surfacing into the light.

"I never stopped loving Kamal," Uma rushed on to say. "Days after you were born, I ran away. But I was forced to return to Adesh because I had no place to go, no money to speak of. No way to care for you." Now her tears ran freely. "The second time I ran away, Kamal and I were together, but we were found."

This time it was Tailan who gently eased to the floor and offered comfort to a woman who had made her entire married life to Amir a living nightmare. She pulled Uma into a comforting embrace as Amir held onto her hand.

Uma took the comfort and choked out, "They killed him—right before my eyes." Her bloodshot eyes sought out Amir's. "They killed Kamal in such an inhumane way. I still have nightmares." Uma shivered. "Adesh let me live. Told them that living with Kamal's death on my head would be punishment enough. And he was right. There is not a day that passes that I do not think of him."

She nodded over to Tailan, whose eyes were glazed with tears.

"But I was pregnant again," Uma said with a wan smile. "I knew who had fathered my child. I would have two living reminders of my love, and Adesh could not kill them—as much as he wanted to. He had no heirs—no children. He could not kill you or Dhara because telling everyone that his brother had fathered my children would have been an admission that he was—" she looked over to Tailan, searching for the phrase. Then she blinked as a light bulb lit over her head. "Ah, yes. How do you Americans say—*shooting blanks.*"

Amir nearly laughed. His mother never struck him as a humorous person. She must really resent Adesh.

"But when Dhara went to be with the man she loved, instead of staying with the man she had married, it was all Adesh needed to agree with the Sengupta family that my baby needed to be killed." She pressed a hand to his shoulder. "He has been angry with you ever since you told him you would break from us. Now he has found a way to make you pay. I will not let him have you!" She looked at Tailan, but said toAmir, "Fulfill the obligation and keep your lady love. I have suffered all these years to keep you safe—alive. I will not fail now. You are all I have left of my beloved Kamal." She cupped his face in her hands. "Please humor an old woman."

She turned to Tailan and gathered her hands. "I have shared my secrets with you. And I know you both will keep them." She caressed Tailan's face. "I wanted you to know that I understand. I know what love is, but I do not wish that love to destroy him or you."

Tailan reached out a hand to wipe away the woman's tears. Uma's smile was faltering, but it was there nonetheless. The first kindness and understanding between the two women Amir loved most.

"All right," Amir said. "I need to talk things over with Tailan first."

"But I thought it was settled," Uma said, frowning at him as she stroked a nervous hand over the silk scarf.

"Mama, it is settled in your mind. But this affects her more than anyone, and she has not said much. I need to hear from my wife."

He extended his hand for her to take, then ushered her toward the kitchen where they would have a moderate amount of privacy.

"Do you truly understand what this means?"

Tailan pressed a hand to his face. "It means you must divorce me to legally become Roshni's husband and fulfill your family's obligation." She gave him a smile that didn't quite reach her eyes. "You have my blessing,"

Amir was instantly suspicious. "Are you just saying that because—"

"This has nothing to do with him," Tailan emphasized, her gaze narrowing on him.

"This has *everything* to do with him," he countered. "It has taken so long for you to heal from what he did. It has taken my own mistakes to completely appreciate you and strengthen what we have. I love you. I will not see you hurt by Delvin because my family is forcing my hand. I would rather die first."

She looked away.

"Your agreement has come too swift. You are not fighting for us as much as you have fought for everything else." He leaned in to whisper. "Is your concession just about my safety? Your safety?" Amir queried. "As much as you love me, you cannot deny that Delvin still sits right here." He placed his hand over her heart. "The only reason you still feel anything for me is because we are connected through marriage."

Tailan stepped back. "That's not true! I love you so much I ache with it." She pressed her back against the stainless steel fridge. "But, I will not be the reason your mother loses another child. I will not be the reason Neena loses another parent. I will not let you stand here and tell me how *I* feel about you. That my love for you isn't enough. If you ever say something like that again, I will—"

Amir blanched at the thought that she would probably slap him.

"Are you trying to convince me or yourself?" Amir pressed his forehead to hers. "If Delvin walked through the door, and you were free of all attachments—*of me*—would you deny him?"

Tailan's lips pressed into a strained thin line.

Amir only smiled.

"But the most important thing is, I would never leave you for him," Tailan stated. "I love you. I love him—but I'd never choose him over you."

"So you say." Amir kissed her forehead. "Thank you."

"For what?" she sniffled as her tears started to fall.

"For giving me the happiest seven years of my life. For honoring me with the privilege of loving you and being loved by you."

"Amir—"

He silenced her with a full kiss on the lips. "I will not put you second again. Taking a wife—legally—means that you are seen as second—I will not allow that. I am not so selfish that I cannot set you free." He extended his hand to her. "Come, let us tell my mother the news."

When his mother left their home to tell Adesh the outcome, Amir extended his hand to Tailan. "Let us say our final goodbye," he whispered.

Tailan nodded, and he led her into their bedroom. She unbuttoned his shirt as he removed her blouse.

Their caresses, exploration, and kisses were memorable. The love they made this night would be all they had.

For this one night, they were all that the other would ever need.

Chapter 33

Delvin was snatched from a sound sleep with a call from Amir.

"Is Tailan with you at the moment?"

"No," he replied, with a quick glance at the clock on his night stand. "I would think that at this time of night your wife would be with you."

"She has not told you?"

Delvin sighed, turning over in his bed. "Amir, it's three in the morning. I don't have time for this."

"I had thought that she had come to you with the news. We are divorcing."

Delvin shot up in the bed. "When did this happen?"

"Yesterday."

"And you have no idea where she is?" Delvin swung his legs over the side of the bed and was at the closet in seconds, pulling out a pair of jeans and a t-shirt.

"There is only one place I could think for her to go. I have been with my family, and when I returned, I had a feeling that something was wrong," he confessed. "I only called because that feeling has become so strong that I could not sleep. I apologize for disturbing you."

"She's not here, and what's worrying me is that there's an anxiousness in your voice that's putting me on edge."

"Perceptive," Amir countered. "I have reason to worry for her safety."

Amir went on to fill Delvin in on what had transpired with his family and ended with, "We should call the police."

"Give me a minute," Delvin replied, snatching his wallet and keys from the night stand. "I have a feeling I know where she might be."

"I will wait to hear from you."

Delvin disconnected the call and first drove to his parents' place, but he didn't find her there. He called her numerous times as he drove, but went to voicemail each time. He checked the Nelson Entertainment Group offices but found she wasn't there either.

When American Express alerted him that a strange charge had hit his card, he knew that she was safe. He sent a text to Amir letting him know.

Delvin peeled out, tore up Lake Shore Drive, and was downtown in half the time it would normally take. She had checked into the same hotel, the same suite the three of them had shared that fateful night.

Since the room was charged to his name, the manager gave him a key. He entered to find Tailan's broken frame curled up in a sofa in the suite's elegant living room. Just by looking at her and remembering the concern in Amir's voice, Delvin could tell that Amir and Tailan's separation was not of their own accord.

Delvin had kept his word to Tailan—he had not and would not touch her sexually while she was still married to her husband. The most he would do when she came to him was cuddle or hold her, but sex was off limits. He would not cross that line again, no matter how much he or she wanted.

And if she was available to him now, regardless of what Amir had introduced into their love lives—the polyamory—Delvin would not make that same concession for Tailan. Children learned from what they watched. And he wouldn't be one that would set an example for his daughters that might lead them to believe they would not be enough for the men they choose. He had learned that lesson the hard way. He couldn't set the example for his son that one woman could not be enough.

Polyamorous marriages may have worked to some degree for some people, but in Delvin Germaine's household, he would establish that relationships were one man, one woman. This man, and Tailan as his woman. If she could not embrace that concept, then they would not make it a second time.

He was stunned with a sickening truth—something that Amir had warned him about the first day they had met. As Amir's wife, Delvin would not like the choices she would make. He gasped at the stark realization of how true that became. Delvin literally felt those words and the ugly numbness that slithered through his entire body. Her choice? To love both of them the best way she knew how. Her choice? Not to say that either one of them was greater than the other. She felt a deep love for Delvin, but stayed in marriage to Amir because she loved him too.

He stepped forward into the room, startling her as he gathered her into his arms.

* * *

Tears overwhelmed Tailan, and they soaked Delvin's shirt as they fell. She was an emotional mess. Her life was spiraling out of control once again.

It was horribly unfair to lean on Delvin in this way, but she loved Amir as deeply as she was in love with Delvin. Thinking she should and could have both men was one of the worst mistakes she'd made in her life. Her actions had brought Amir's family down on them. If she had been honest with Delvin on the first day of the tour—he would never have kissed her the way he did. His family would not have had the ammunition to separate them. Then the decisions she had made since had put a wedge between Delvin and herself that she couldn't seem to bridge.

To her heart it didn't matter. She couldn't go to Delvin as Amir had encouraged her to do. It would not be fair to him. These two men where her Alpha and Omega—her beginning and end. How could she possibly go on without one or the other?

"Tailan," Delvin whispered, brushing a wayward strand of hair from her face. "I have no love for Amir, but the way you're falling apart is freaking me out," he admitted. His lips caressed her forehead. He kneaded her lower back, trying to soothe her.

"How could they do this?" she sniffled, wiping away tears with the back of a trembling hand. "It's my pain. Let me feel it; let me work through it. We were a family. I can't just turn that off."

She pulled from his sheltering arms and said, "This isn't fair to you. That's why I'm here, trying to sort everything out on my own. I didn't run to you, even though I knew you wouldn't turn me away. I created this mess, and I have to deal with it."

"You don't have to deal with it alone," he offered.

Tailan placed a hand on his cheek. "Yes. I do."

She retreated to the master bedroom.

He scrubbed his face in frustration. The roles had reversed. The ramifications of that were humiliating. For so long, Delvin only saw what he wanted—Tailan. Now he had to face that having her meant that going forward, *he* would be the one fighting the ghost of Amir in her heart.

* * *

Delvin allowed her a few hours of peace. Then he drew her a bath before going to her, carrying her from the bed, undressing her, then placing her in the warm water, hoping it, and he, could soothe her soul.

He slid her a cup of chai tea, and she settled it on the edge of the tub.

"I chose him because I longed for you. I will not make that mistake again," she said, taking a sip of the dark liquid. "When I come to you, I want it to be because my heart and mind are clear." She locked gazes with him, asking, "Is that fair?"

Delvin took her from the water, dried and oiled her body, then settled her among the pillows, praying that she would come to her senses soon. She slept pitifully, tossing and turning, calling the names of the children she had abandoned so long ago. The ones she had left in that horrible situation all so she could save herself.

Delvin left the pallet he'd placed on the floor. He slipped into the bed to comfort her, to hold her until those nightmares had passed.

* * *

Morning came, and he was still with her, his arms wrapped around her in a safety net she did not feel she deserved.

"If you won't trust me," he whispered, stroking a hand down her back. "ask God to help you through this."

She stiffened, and a fragment of unease slithered up her spine. "God?" Tailan pulled away to look down on him. "God? Seriously? You want me to ask God for help sorting out my life?" She shook her head. "God forgot about me. Where was God when those men killed my family? Where was God when my uncle raped my mother? Where was God when my uncle raped his children and their children?" She slammed her hand against his chest. "When Amir's sister and father were killed? When my cousins were killed? Where was God when all of these horrible things happened?" Tears blurred her vision as she asked, "What kind of God would allow people to hurt others this way?"

Delvin closed his eyes against the vehemence in her voice, against the deep-seated anger and pain that he had always felt from her when it came to these matters. He had always skirted around this issue, but today, he realized it spoke to the heart of things when it came to her ability to trust him or anyone, to love him completely or to let him go. He had to meet her where she was.

"I'll tell you where God was," he said in a soft tone as he lifted her chin so they were eye to eye. "God was whispering in your parents' ears to get you to safety. God was whispering in your mother's ear to give her the strength to tell the world what your uncle had done. God whispered in your ear, urging you to leave the west side that night." His eyes searched her tear-filled ones for a moment. "God whispered in my ear and said I should go into that classroom instead of going home. God whispered in my ear that I should take you home with me and keep you safe—even if I would get in trouble with my parents."

Tears fell from her eyes at a rapid pace.

"God whispered in my ear that I should love you and show you the side of God's love that is spoken of in words and song. God whispered in my mother's ears to make you the daughter she always wanted." On these words, Delvin's voice wavered a little, the emotions coming too fast to keep them at bay. "God whispered in my ear to get my behind on that tour bus and ask your forgiveness for what I did to hurt you. God whispered in Amir's ear and said to make you his wife for that period of time it took for you to heal from the pain I'd caused. God whispered into your womb and planted a child that is the best parts of both of us, and who will bind us for the rest of our lives."

Delvin pulled her head against his chest. "God is right here with us, watching over us, keeping us safe. God is right here in my heart and yours, whether we ever act on that love or we remain apart. God is in the tears that are falling from your eyes, because God knows you need them because you hold in so much."

She was silent for so long, he thought she might have fallen asleep. Then her hand reached up and rested on his cheek.

Delvin kissed her forehead and said, "Those ugly things that you've experienced, that's a man thing, a human thing—the kind that devours, hurts, and harms, the kind that is selfish and evil. That's not of God. God is love. God is everything that is good. The tests and challenges that come from people who don't embrace those parts of God are all about strengthening us, forcing us to draw on The Source, that Higher Power." Delvin held her even tighter. "God put us here to have an abundant life, to live our dreams. We live off the prayers of our ancestors who didn't have nearly as much as we do. But it doesn't mean that we're going to sail through life without some kind of challenges along the way."

Delvin looked down at her. "My challenge right now? To love you, even when you don't feel you deserve that love. To love you in spite of the pain you cause me, every time I'm forced to accept and respect that I am not the leading man in your life." He cupped her face in his hands. "God gives me the strength to get through because it is not easy to love a woman who I feel is rightfully mine and keep enough distance that I'm respecting her marriage vows. I ask God for strength every single day because I need it now more than I ever did." He locked a gaze with her. "That's the kind of God I believe in, Tai … and in time, I hope you will too. Then you'll stop searching elsewhere for the very thing that you already have."

Delvin gathered her into his arms, holding her while she cried out for her loss, for her pain, her anger at the being that created them and every living thing on earth.

"It's all right to be angry at God, Tai," Delvin said in a breathy whisper. "God can take it. God's a pretty big God. Can handle anything. You'll see."

Her smile was fleeting, but it was there. And it was a sure sign that Delvin was reaching her on some level.

* * *

And on the third day, Tailan came to him displayed in every inch of her naked glory. Awaking him from a dream that had catapulted him back to the time when they first met and she trusted him to keep her safe, trusted him when nearly everyone in her life had shown her that a man cannot be trusted. He had failed her then, but with God's grace and mercy, he would not fail her ever again.

Delvin went to her then, accepted her, accepted everything she brought with her—memories that did not include him, pleasure, pain, love, joy, and a completion he had never felt with another living soul. She was his. He would make sure she was very much aware of this fact. And he would be damned if he'd lose her again.

The love they made that night was a pure rekindling of what they had lost, not a mechanism to wash away the memories of past loves, but of what both wished to share, wished to become—lovers and partners on an equal plane.

Yes, she had loved her husband. But the truth of the matter was that she loved Delvin all the way down to her soul.

And no other kind of love could ever surpass that.

Chapter 34

"Tailan," Amir said. "I need a huge favor please."

"Is everything all right?" She sounded nervous, when he was the one who actually needed to be.

"I am going to be at the Indian Consulate a lot longer than I expected. They are finishing the paperwork to bring my nieces to America. I need you to pick up Neena from Skokie."

There was dead silence on the other end, and for a moment, he thought she wouldn't answer.

"I can do that," she replied.

Amir released the breath he didn't realize he was holding. "Once you get her, then we will discuss a decision I've made regarding the children."

"I'll be there," she whispered.

He ended the call and faced his lawyer, giving him a nod to continue.

Amir was about to commit an act of extreme defiance. The life he wanted for himself might be over, but the life and happiness of his child would continue. What he intended to do would rattle the very foundation of his family to the core, but *nothing* was more important than his children and Tailan.

* * *

Tailan settled on a plush sofa in the parlor of the Kasturi family, unwilling to go any further into the mansion than necessary. The place was palatial with marbled floors and walls, elegant fountains, and colorful bursts of ornamental sculptures and artwork. She had arrived early to collect Neena in order to return in time to pick Jason up from basketball practice and shuttle him to his saxophone lessons. She was amazed that the teen was following so closely in Delvin's footsteps.

"I have never liked your kind." Adesh's harsh voice snapped her to the present. "Too wild, too uncivilized."

"Oh?" she replied, giving him an icy smile as she left the sofa and walked to the foyer. "I bet that woman who was raped by those seven men in India felt *your* kind were very civilized," Tailan countered, pressing her back against the glass doors.

"An isolated incident," he defended with a dismissive wave of his hand.

The bastard hid his inner monster well. Tailan had despised him the second they met. All of her instincts fired warning shots about him. The man was too much like her Uncle Lin—evil incarnate. Women and girls were not human to them; they were "things" to be used and toyed with. Evidently that extended to his son.

Now that Uma had shared the depths of his depravity with her, Tailan would not put any despicable act beyond Adesh's capabilities. She shivered at the thought of Neena being under his influence for any length of time.

She crossed her arms and defiantly reminded him, "Women and girls all around the world are beaten and abused every day. India is no exception. Women have a hard time feeling safe in *any* culture. Only now, the world is watching." She swept a gaze over the women crowded in an area off to the side, who were watching her intently. Some nodded slightly despite the fact that her view was not held by the men in the family. But Uma, who almost never made eye contact with Tailan, did so this time. "Women in India have had enough, and they're speaking out about injustices. The fact that they should have a choice to aim for peace, to control some parts of their lives. One day, that will hit closer to home."

Some of the men situated close to him frowned at what they perceived as insolence from Amir's wanton wife. But the women—they were listening, she was certain of it.

"You have been a horrible influence on my granddaughter," Adesh growled, tearing his gaze from Uma. He stood from the bed of silk cushions on the floor.

Tailan took a battle stance as he snaked closer. "How so?"

"Neena is willful—too inquisitive." He towered over her, assuming his powerful presence intimidated her. Adesh flashed a serpentine smile and added, "But not to worry. When she is fully under our care, we will remove all of your influence, all signs of you from her life."

"Oh, I'd like to see you try," Tailan shot right back, her hands curled into tight fists.

Uma stepped forward to speak, but Adesh turned to her sharply, giving her a look that silenced her, but not for long.

"Adesh, stop this madness," she said through her teeth. "You have cost us enough!"

"There are ways to tame a child of such a wild nature," Adesh announced, ignoring his wife by focusing on Tailan once again. "She is young. We have many years. By the time she reaches maturity, she will be elated to marry the man we choose for her."

This time Tailan got in his face, but she flickered a gaze to Uma as she said, "What about what *she* wants? *Her* happiness? Haven't the women in this family paid enough cost for their children to have a better life."

Adesh turned from her as though she wasn't even worth his breath. "A woman's happiness is not a man's concern," he said.

"No," Tailan agreed. "It is a *woman's* concern. She has the right to be happy. She might not have been given a choice in some aspects in her life, but she can control some parts of it. Happiness, peace, fairness should top the list."

Adesh maneuvered so that he blocked Tailan's view of Uma. "We are all unhappy in one way or another." He turned to his wife, then scowled at the woman's thoughtful expression. All of the women were focused on Tailan. He glanced at Tailan over his shoulder. "Now that you are out of the picture and back with a mate of your station—your own kind—the family will have full rein to train Neena *properly*."

Tailan moved so they were inches apart. "She deserves to have choices in her life just like anyone else. Just like you."

"No," Adesh gritted. "She will do as she is told. Choices are not an option for women. Look how your choices ruined the lives of so many. My son, my granddaughter. You chose to leave my son rather than stay with your family."

He flashed a deadly smile. If Tailan didn't know any better, she would've sworn he was actually getting off on what he was saying.

"That's a bald-faced lie," Tailan seethed, as she stalked him. "I would never leave my husband for another man, whether I loved another man or not. You—" she fanned her hand out for emphasis. "You and this family left us the only choice that will keep us alive. I won't have his blood on my hands because he loves me."

Shared glances between the women and then amongst some of the men, spoke to the confusion her words had created.

"You say I'm uncivilized.? Tailan jabbed him in the chest. "At least I don't secretly hate my own child so much that I wish him dead."

The shocked gasps that echoed in the room were a sure sign that she'd hit home.

Uma's hand flew up to her bosom. Adesh blanched, and Tailan

grinned. Murmurs of discontent echoed from several family members.

"We both know that you *wanted* Amir to refuse this arranged marriage so that you could be rid of him," Tailan accused, her gaze unwavering. "You want to take his child and make her the success that you feel he and Dhara failed to become."

The twisted fiend didn't even try to deny it. Instead, he glared at her with a hatred he never tried to conceal.

"You. Make. Me. Sick!" she snarled.

"Your actions put my granddaughter right where I want her—back where she belongs," he proclaimed with relish. "You defiled your marriage and dishonored my son, who made the grave mistake of marrying a woman who was not only beneath him, but a whore as well."

Tailan backed away from him, disgusted. She opened her mouth to respond, but out of the corner of her eye, she saw Neena timidly descending the stairs with a dour faced woman following. Neena's normally jubilant manner was subdued. Eerily so. The bruises on her olive skin shone like a spotlight on the horrors she had endured.

"What have you done to her?" Tailan gasped and ran over to her baby.

"What we have a right to do," he roared. "Discipline her so she knows her place."

Tailan charged over to Adesh and shoved him hard against the wall. She pressed her elbow into his throat, nearly cutting off his supply of oxygen. "You *ever* lay a hand on my child again … and so help me God, I will slit your throat!"

Those nearby blanched at the coarse language. She stormed over to Neena and the female escort. When the woman wouldn't release Neena, Tailan snatched the woman out of the way and collected her child in her arms.

Tailan shot a murderous look over to Adesh, whose eyes were wide with fright, but quickly morphed into anger.

She stepped toward the door, but with Adesh's signal to the men standing nearby, they blocked her exit.

"Move," she commanded. "Or this will not be a pleasant evening for any of us."

At that moment she was grateful, so very grateful, that Anna Germaine had made good on her promise to send her for Martial Arts classes. Tailan never had the opportunity to achieve higher than a brown belt, but at the moment, belts didn't matter—skill and the ability to throw a punch and take a punch did.

"You put your hands on me!!!" Adesh growled, shaking a fist in her direction.

She placed Neena behind her, ready to take up a fighting stance. "You put your hands on my daughter. So we're even. And you will never have any opportunity to hurt her again."

To this Adesh choked out a bitter laugh that cause of slither of unease to slither up her spine. "But my dear, thanks to your *mistake* you will have no say in the matter."

Chapter 35

"Calm down, Tailan," Amir pleaded as he paced after her.

"He beat her!" she cried and flung her hands towards the upstairs bedroom. "You saw the marks on her body!"

"Sweetheart, please calm down," Amir pleaded. His heart was breaking. The horrors for his little girl had already begun.

Tailan whirled on him with eyes streaming with tears.

"You know that's not right. *We* have never laid a hand to her," she reminded him. "And she knows how to behave. And you *know* that!"

Amir carefully eased closer to Tailan and let her get it out.

"She's a good girl," she whispered into the wall of his chest. "She's a good baby."

After a moment, he escorted her to the kitchen and sat her down. He prepared a cup of tea to settle her nerves. Amir helped her with the first sip because her hands were still shaking. "Adesh was angry and tried to hold us captive when I tried to leave with Neena," she said.

Amir stiffened with anger.

"For the first time, the women finally spoke up. They defied their husbands and moved them out of the way so we could go. Every single woman said something. I have never seen anything like it."

Amir's eyebrow shot up, he gripped her arms. "*The women*?! My *mother*?!!"

Tailan nodded, giving him a wan smile. "She had the strongest voice. She told Adesh to end this foolishness, end his bitterness, or she would leave with me and take every single one of the women with her."

His jaw dropped and when Tailan saw it, she tried to smile and finally succeeded.

"Ease your fears, my love," he whispered, placing a hand on her cheek. "This will be over soon."

Tailan set her cup down and stared up at him.

He pulled out a folder and placed it on the table.

"What's this?" she asked.

Amir fought for a calm that was hard to feel. His next words were agonizing to form.

He closed his hand over hers. "My family has sealed my fate," he started. "But I cannot allow what happened to Dhara and to my mother to ever happen to Neena or Dhara's children." Amir pushed the folder forward. "I have added a codicil to our pending divorce decree."

Tailan snatched up the folder and flipped it open.

"Amir … no," she said, raking a gaze over the words again and again. "You can't do this! You *can't*—I won't let you."

"All it requires is your signature."

"There has to be another way," Tailan continued.

Amir rose from the table and said, "The madness of my family's obsession with tradition and purity will end with me." He turned to her and explained, "I will not continue the line. My new wife will never have children sired by me. If I must sacrifice my happiness, then I will extract my pound of flesh for the arrogance of my family." He returned to the table and gathered her face in his hands. "I love you, Tailan. If you cannot be the mother of my children, then no one will be the mother of my children."

"Amir, please."

"I will see her. I will be there," he forged on. "But she will be where she is safe and nurtured and loved—she will be with you." He kissed her forehead and added, "Dhara's children will be delivered to me soon. But I ask that you allow them to be our children."

"Of course," she whispered. "Whatever you need."

"They will be my focus," he said, stroking a hand across her face. "We will help heal them like you healed me. And I will keep them safe from my family's influence. At least, I have that written promise from them in order to agree to marry Roshni. But this," he gestured to the document she held, "protects Neena from both my family and Esha's and puts her firmly in the care of the person I trust."

Tailan read the document again, practically hyperventilating as she did. Suddenly she pressed her forehead to his as their falling tears blended together.

"I love you so much, Amir," Tailan sobbed.

"I love you forever, Tailan," Amir added as he eased her around to face the codicil. He handed her a pen, and she trembled with hesitation. She clenched her fist and hurriedly added her signature.

Tailan shoved the pieces of paper across the table and embraced him with a fierceness that spoke of how much she meant those words.

Soothingly, he added, "It is done. Our divorce will be submitted as final when the adoption is finalized. You will have sole custody of Devi, Neena, and the twins."

Her tears broke his heart, but they also gave him hope.

"My mother actually threatened my father?"

"She most certainly did!"

Amir laughed as they walked upstairs to Neena's bedroom to comfort her and help her get ready for bed.

Epilogue

The next few months spun by. Once the divorce was finalized, Delvin was insistent Tailan marry him immediately. She couldn't do it. Not because she didn't want to, but because she was solely focused on smoothing the way for Amir's nieces to adjust to America. The children were leery of every adult except her when they arrived. With her, Lali and Bela relaxed and sometimes even smiled. Soon things changed so that when Neena and Devi were present, the twins morphed into rambunctious, playful little girls again.

Tailan had seen so much horror inflicted upon small children in the course of her life. Thoughts of how she was not able to protect her cousins drove her to be a fierce protector of the children she cared about. Amir's family learned that ugly lesson the hard way.

When word spread that Tailan had sole custody of both of her children and Amir's nieces, his family went berserk. However, there was nothing they could do. When Adesh tried to use the legal system to steal her child away, Amir's mother found the courage to drop a few words in his ear, "I will tell them *everything*."

Soon after, Amir received a sizable inheritance that Adesh had kept from him for all these years. All because it originated from Kamal. Amir immediately enrolled in medical school and set out to fulfill his dreams.

They never discussed the details of the conversation, but Tailan conceded *just* a bit. Lali, Bela, Neena, and Devi would visit Amir's family compound once a week and during special ceremonies related to their culture. But no one there was ever allowed to exclude any of the children from any event, speak harshly to them, mistreat or belittle them. No one could touch them in anger or as a form of discipline. It there was any infraction of this rule, the nanny and bodyguards who would be accompanying them *every time* would crack skulls first and ask questions later.

* * *

When the families settled into a routine that worked for both households, Tailan finally felt like she could breathe and give Delvin a date when they would get married. The girls were flourishing. Jason and Ariel were adapting well to their extended family. Anna, Delvin's mother, received joyful news that her body was responding much better to her cancer treatments. Delvin and his father had been right. Anna fought tooth and nail to have more time with all her grandchildren.

"You all really took that be fruitful and multiply thing seriously, eh?" Anna teased. But everyone knew they were her reason to live and get better.

Amir and his new bride were slowly adjusting to each other. Delvin was at least entertaining the thought of doing more films now that his mother was better and he was free of his diabolical wife.

Delvin and Amir had eventually found a respectful medium. They took a private meeting without her, and she nearly had a heart attack. She thought there would be bloodshed for sure, but they emerged from Delvin's office shaking hands.

"We cleared the air," Delvin said as she approached them. "We both agree that we love you, but nothing comes before our children."

"I see why he was hard to shake from your heart, Tailan," Amir said, with a seeming admiration for Delvin in his voice as he kissed her goodbye and collected Lali and Bela to take home.

Tailan looked after him in stunned silence. Then she shifted her gaze to Delvin, who smiled and pretended to button his lips.

One week after that milestone conference, Tailan had quite a scare. She almost fell back into the bath tub she got so dizzy. "Oh, no," she gasped as she tried to level herself down on the edge of the tub. She waited for the room to stop spinning. Ten minutes later, she rushed to her bedroom and grabbed her cell phone and clicked on the calendar app.

Damn!

* * *

The pregnancy test flashed positive like a neon sign three hours later. It told Tailan what her body already knew.

She cancelled all of her appointments at work and made a mad dash to the family practitioner since her OB-GYN couldn't fit in an emergency appointment.

"Those over-the-counter tests are spot on accurate in most cases," Dr. Taylor confirmed. "Our test says the same thing. I'll do a blood draw and a quick ultrasound too."

Tailan absorbed those words as she reflected on her first pregnancy. "I had major complications with my first time," she said.

"I'm reviewing your chart, and I see that. We'll start earlier monitoring due to your high-risk history." Dr. Taylor gestured to the spot behind them. "Lie back on the table."

She did, but she held her breath for a spell.

Dr. Taylor started the ultrasound and paused, frowning at something.

Frantic, Tailan blurted, "What is it? What's wrong with my baby?"

She turned to her. "Well, you're pregnant all right, but you're not *just* pregnant—you're *very* pregnant. This little guy has been camping out in your lower back. That's why you don't have a baby bump yet."

Well that explained why her lower back ached all the time. She thought it was the way Delvin had been handling his business—combining some of the techniques he had learned the night the three of them were together. She had been amazed, but mostly realized Delvin had upped his game because he didn't want her to miss Amir for that reason.

"Is the baby okay?" she asked.

"The baby looks real good from what I can see. Take a look."

Tailan craned her head toward the screen and saw a tiny fetus sucking its thumb. Seconds later, she burst into tears.

"Now, now Tailan," Dr. Taylor soothed. "The baby is doing well. From these images, this little guy is holding his own."

"His?" Her eyes snapped up. "It's a boy?"

The doctor nodded.

"I'm having a little boy," she sniffled. "Jason will be so pleased to have another man in the house." She chuckled then asked, "When am I due?"

"A lot sooner than you think," Dr. Taylor replied. "Tailan, these images reflect a fetus well into the second trimester. From the length of the baby, I'd guess you're at least five and a half months pregnant, closer to six."

"Oh my God," Tailan gasped.

That puts the time of conception around...

* * *

Tailan called a private meeting with Amir and Delvin. The mistakes of the past compelled her to take a different path this time.

"The last few months have been hard on all of us," she confessed. "And yet, we have managed to pull off a miracle and stay together as a family—albeit a very forward-thinking family. But through all the challenges, we, as the adults of this little tribe of ours, have weathered the storms, made peace, and put all of our children first."

Both men looked at her, and each nodded or smiled in their own way. She went over to each man and pulled them to stand. She took their hands and placed it on her womb.

"I'm pregnant," she admitted.

Their eyes dropped instantly to their hands covering her belly and her hand covering theirs.

Amir turned to Delvin.

Delvin turned to Amir.

She waited, holding her breath. Neither man spoke. She couldn't read their faces. Slowly they turned back to Tailan.

"I need the two of you to love this baby no matter which one of you fathered it," she said to Delvin, then looked to Amir. She dried her eyes and covered their hands again.

The men nodded.

"Now that that's out of the way," she said, giving them a megawatt smile, "I can give you the really good news."

Delvin's head tilted to the side, while Amir's right eyebrow shot up.

"We're having a boy!"

"Thank you, God!" Delvin exclaimed with a fist pump that signaled his elation. "More testosterone in the house. Jason's going to flip."

Amir chuckled at that statement and added, "A son is a blessing from God."

Tailan shared a speaking glance with Amir and gave him a small smile, which caused him to narrow his gaze at her and then nod. He understood her meaning without her having to voice it.

She brought the hands of the men she loved to her lips and said, "And you both have been a blessing to me."

Tailan floated into their combined embrace. And for the first time in a long time, the gray areas of her life were filled with sun and hope.

Naleighna Kai

Naleighna Kai is the national bestselling author of the provocative novels: Was it Good For You?, Open Door Marriage and Every Woman Needs a Wife. She started writing in December of 1999, independently publishing her first two novels before acquiring a book deal with an imprint of Simon & Schuster and most recently a book deal with an independent publisher. She is a contributing author to a New York Times Bestseller, an award-winning author, and The E. Lynn Harris Author of Distinction.

Naleighna works for a major international law firm and is the CEO of Macro Marketing & Promotions Group, the Director of Marketing & Promotions for Brown Girls Publishing, as well as the marketing consultant to several national bestselling and aspiring writers. She is also the brainchild behind the annual Cavalcade of Authors events which takes place in her hometown of Chicago. Naleighna pens romance, contemporary fiction, erotica, and speculative fiction and is currently working on her next novels: Rich Woman's Fetish and Slaves of Heaven. Find her on the web at www.naleighnakai.com, www.thecavalcadeofauthors.com and on Facebook under Naleighna Kai.

Naleighna Kai's post to C.V.S. Class of 1984 Alumni Page

Tribute to Derek V. Fields

Saturday, I did two things that I never do. One, I attended my first home-going celebration since early 2000. Personally, it had become my stance that I won't attend any funerals (not even my own :)). However, I came on Saturday to pay respects to Derek and learned more wonderful things about him through the eyes and the ears of the people who had more interaction with him than I ever have. No one is going to stand up at an event like this and say anything negative, but it speaks whole-heartedly to who he was that almost every single person had the same to say about him. His smile, his sense of humor, his love for his wife and children, his love of C.V.S. and especially the Class of 1984, his ability to resolve issues and help keep the peace, his love of House Music, (no one spoke on his love for sports--but we knew); his 35 year friendship with David Jones and Delvin Fuller that spanned the kind of moments that could land them in trouble and others that had "Pig" (Derek's nickname) covering for them (or at least ONE of them) avoid the wrath of their parents.

All of that says to me is that Derek had a game plan for his life. A game plan that included embracing everything and everyone that he loved. A game plan that didn't include letting a health challenge sidetrack his goals. A game plan that included spending as much time as he humanly could with those that he loved. A game plan that meant putting his pain aside an attending the class reunion cruise, and other events where he could reconnect with people who had been a part of his life since we all came together at Chicago Vocational School in 1980. A game plan that meant showing up at the all class alumni picnic, wheeling his chariot through the grass, maneuvering through those tents to position himself in a spot where people could come and say hello.

That brings me to the second thing that I sometimes fail to do--listen to that still small voice that encourages me to do something right then and there. As I sat under Q's tent at the picnic working on an upcoming project, I watched as so many people surrounded Derek, you could barely lay eyes on him. I kept saying, "I'll wait until the crowd thins out before I go speak." Well, after a few moments, something said, "Don't wait. Do it now." I got up immediately, and went over to embrace him. It was the last time I would be able to. I certainly didn't know it then, but the Creator knew. Saturday at the repast, I did something else inspired by what happened the last time I saw Derek. Before I left (I was actually on lifeline to complete Was it Good For You Too?), I made it my business to embrace every single classmate that I could. Why? I didn't need that still, small voice to encourage me this time—Ilearned that lesson. I don't want the next time to be prefaced by a statement, "Oh, I wish I had ..."

That being said, "I wish I had," is not something I want to ever say about my life. That's why I'm going to encourage each and every one of you, to stop putting off the things you want to do most in life. How many times have you heard people say, "When I retire I'm going to do X, Y and Z?" Then life takes them before they get to do any of those things? Don't let that be your life. Don't let that be your "I wish I had" moment. If it's a trip to Paris, Africa, India, or Italy--wherever--GO FOR IT. If it's going back to school to get that degree that had to be put on hold because family took a front seat--GO FOR IT. If it's writing a book that's been in your heart and mind all these years--GO FOR IT. If it's a new job, losing those extra pounds, learning a new skill, going out to dance, sky-diving, playing an instrument--GO FOR IT. And if that still small voice encourages you to do something--don't second guess--GO FOR IT.

And don't get upset when you see me out there doing my thing--writing, getting my books turned into movies, dancing, loving, living life to the fullest. Just come along for the ride--and we can both ... GO FOR IT!!!

Naleighna Kai,
September 15, 2014

Naleighna Kai's reflection on C.V.S.

Let me tell you how important CVS and my class was--and always will be to me. If it wasn't for you all, I would never have finished school. While enduring sexual and physical abuse at the hands of my father and mother during the school year, coming to that building on 87th Street, in the heart of the South Side of Chicago, sometimes provided the only peace that I would be afforded. Interacting with members of my class gave me the only laughter, the only growth that would mean so much to me. No one knew what I was going through. I couldn't voice my pain, pain was "normal", but I also knew there was one place that I was going to be every single day where no one hurt me, where there wasn't anyone there who didn't respect my right to say, "No, don't touch me."

There were times when I wasn't fed at home (not because we didn't have food, but because it was a punishment) and the meals at school or Malina's hoagie sandwiches that she brought in as a kindness were the only things I was able to eat. I didn't talk to anyone about that either. And truthfully, I've forgiven my mother—so I don't blame her, I just wish I understood why at that time. Some of you read my books or posts on my FB page and how I told how my mother gave me away at birth to my aunt, my aunt killed her husband and landed in prison, I ended up back with my biological mother anyway--who was forced to adopt me in order to care for me--and the abuse was monumental). My father, I've forgiven him, too—as for whatever reason, when I ran away from home to seek his protection after overhearing my aunt making arrangements for my uncle to have sex with me, my father didn't see me as his daughter, he, like my uncle, saw me as an extension of my mother--just another piece of ass.

Through all of that, some my classmates, individually impacted my life with acts of kindness--a spoken word, help with school work, dealing with teachers who sometimes showed their human failings, classmates who went to bat for me when I was teased or humiliated by someone else, classmates who allowed me to be connected with them in some small way. The immense feelings of gratitude for those times will forever be with me. We're adults now, and I'm sure our life experiences and choices have made us who we are today. Maybe, I'm the only one who feels like this, but I don't have any desire to have my view of my class tainted in any way. You all were my calm in the middle of the storms of my life. I'd like to always keep it that way.

Open Door Marriage

A chance encounter lands NBA star Dallas Avery back in the arms of the woman of his dreams. A woman he hasn't seen in years. A woman he soon discovers just so happens to be his fiancée's aunt! But Dallas' fiancee, Tori, isn't ready to give up all that she's worked for, so she makes him a shocking offer – go through with the wedding and she'll still allow him to be with the one woman he now can't seem to do without. Dallas will get a family, something her much older aunt, Alicia can't give him. Tori will get the lifestyle she clamors. And Alicia will get the love she's longed for all her life. Everyone will get a little of what they want. . . and maybe a whole lot of what they don't.

The details of the trio's love life play out in the tabloids and on talk shows, making Dallas the center of an NBA scandal. And eventually, the doors slam shut on this open marriage and Dallas is forced to make a choice to end the chaos. But moving on is easier than it looks and by the time all is said and done, secrets will be revealed, passions will be extinguished, and everyone's lives will be forever changed.

www.naleighnakai.com

Novels by M-LAS Members ...

WWW.MACROMPG.COM

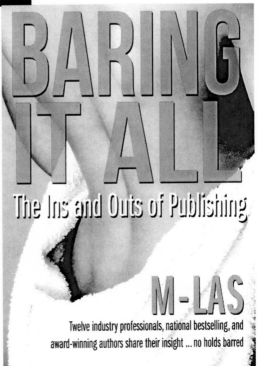

CPSIA information can be obtained at www.ICGtesting.com
Printed in the USA
LVOW09s2005051114

412188LV00004B/157/P